Crossroads in Time

Book Three in the *After Cilmeri* Series

CROSSROADS IN TIME

by

SARAH WOODBURY

To my Carew

A Brief Guide to Welsh Pronunciation

c   a hard 'c' sound (Cadfael)

ch a non-English sound as in Scottish "ch" in "loch" (Fychan)

dd a buzzy 'th' sound, as in "there" (Ddu; Gwynedd)

f   as in "of" (Cadfael)

ff as in "off" (Gruffydd)

g   a hard 'g' sound, as in "gas" (Goronwy)

l   as in "lamp" (Llywelyn)

ll a breathy "th" sound that does not occur in English (Llywelyn)

rh a breathy mix between 'r' and 'rh' that does not occur in English (Rhys)

th a softer sound than for 'dd,' as in "thick" (Arthur)

u   a short 'ih' sound (Gruffydd), or a long 'ee' sound (Cymru—pronounced "kumree")

w   as a consonant, it's an English 'w' (Llywelyn); as a vowel, an 'oo' sound (Bwlch)

y   the only letter in which Welsh is not phonetic. It can be an 'ih' sound, as in "Gwyn," is often an "uh" sound (Cymru), and at the end of the word is an "ee" sound (thus, both Cymru—the modern word for Wales—and Cymry—the word for Wales in the Dark Ages—are pronounced "kumree")

CAST OF CHARACTERS

The Welsh

David (Dafydd)—Prince of Wales
Anna—David's half-sister
Llywelyn—King of Wales, David's father
Meg (Marged)—Queen of Wales, mother to David and Anna
Math—Anna's husband; nephew to Llywelyn
Cadell–son of Anna and Math
Lili–Ieuan's sister
Ieuan—Welsh knight, one of David's men
Bronwen—American, married to Ieuan
Bevyn—Welsh knight, Captain of David's guard

The English

Edward I (deceased)—King of England
Humphrey de Bohun—Earl of Hereford
William de Bohun—Humphrey's son
Maud de Bohun—Humphrey's wife
Hugh de Bohun—Humphrey's son
Roger Mortimer—Lord of the March
Gilbert de Clare—Lord of the March
John Peckham—Archbishop of Canterbury

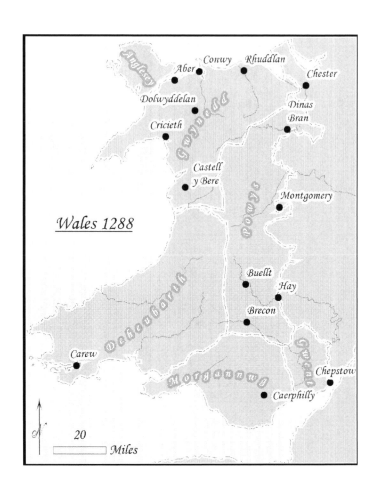

Wales 1288

1

Anna

"**Are** you really asking my brother to ally himself with you?" Anna glared across the nave of Valle Crucis Abbey at Humphrey de Bohun. He stood before her, looking as arrogant and self-satisfied as ever, with one hand on the hilt of his nonexistent sword. Like David and Math, he had removed it before entering the building out of respect for the Church.

If Bohun tipped his nose any higher he'd be gazing at the ceiling. "And you are?" He spoke in Welsh—and far better than Anna might have expected from a Marcher lord.

David held out his hand and gestured Anna forward. "This is my sister, Princess Anna. Her question is a legitimate one."

Bohun eyed her. "Yes. That is exactly what I'm suggesting. I offer him custody of my son as surety for our agreement."

Anna wasn't buying it—neither his words nor this agreement between England and Wales that Bohun claimed to want. Papa and David had already signed a treaty, three years ago at Shrewsbury, in the aftermath of an ill-conceived plot against Wales. Bohun and his fellow Norman barons had consented to trade their holdings in Wales for peace—and for Bohun himself, whom David had captured.

"All you've told us so far is that several of your fellow barons are plotting against us." Anna was being more outspoken than was normal for her in the company of a man such as Bohun, but his smirk annoyed her so much that she found it impossible to keep silent. "Surely, this isn't news? You've come a long way in secret to tell us something we already knew."

"They plot against you *and* against me."

"But why?" Anna said. "And even if what you say is true—and so far we have only your word for this—why should we care if some of your fellow barons threaten you?"

"You should care if it means war, young lady."

"But the Treaty—" David said.

"Kirby and Vere don't care about the Treaty!" Bohun threw out a hand in a gesture of exasperation and stabbed his finger to a point beyond the church wall. "Even as we speak,

2

troops are massing at Bristol Castle in preparation for an assault on your southern coast. The barons seek to cross the Severn Estuary and take back the lands you took from them."

Math, standing beside Anna, had stayed silent throughout their conversation, leaving Anna to express the indignation they all felt. Now he spoke: "Which barons? Kirby is a man of the church and Vere has been ill of late. Who strikes at us? You still haven't said."

And by the look on Bohun's face, he didn't want to. They waited, striving for patience. That Bohun wanted to speak to David in private, that he'd crossed the border into Wales under the cover of darkness with only a handful of men to protect him, meant that he thought the stakes were very high. At least for him.

"Bigod for one. He wants Chepstow Castle back. It was his pride and joy and he was loath to part with it three years ago, treaty or no treaty."

His face intent, David closed the distance between them in two strides. He and Bohun now stood a foot apart. "Bigod just married Vere's daughter, did he not?"

Bohun nodded. "Bigod is only one of a dozen whose eyes look covetously on Wales. Those southern lands are rich. They want them back."

"We will see about that," David said. "But even were Bigod to win back his lands in Wales, it shouldn't affect your

3

station as regent. It shouldn't bring you here, to Llangollen, in the middle of the night."

"Shouldn't it?" Bohun said. "I cannot win. If I turn a blind eye to Bigod's violation of the Treaty, it calls into question my ability to act as regent. If I actively refuse support for Bigod's endeavors, and yet he succeeds, it calls into question my station as regent. Two against one and I find myself in the topmost room in the Tower of London, all my lands forfeit, and no say in the matter."

"The Archbishop of Canterbury himself put his signature to our treaty," David said. "What does he say about this invasion?"

Bohun shrugged. "Peckham doesn't know."

"Why didn't you go to him instead of to us?" Anna said.

"I feared he wouldn't believe me," Bohun said, "that he wouldn't want to believe me."

Which was a remarkable admission, coming from Bohun. "And yet, you thought we would?" Anna said.

Math clasped Anna's hand in his and squeezed. It wasn't so much a warning, as a suggestion that she not press so hard. She subsided as David took up the argument. "So, these barons hope to take a piece out of Wales before anyone is aware of what they are doing, at which point Peckham will accept the dissolution of the Treaty and Bigod supplants you as regent."

Even as Bohun nodded again, David broke away from him, swinging around to gaze at Math and Anna. For this secret meeting with Bohun, he'd taken care to look nothing like the prince he was. His tousled brown hair and oft-patched breeches belonged to a man a dozen stages further down the social ladder. He wore unpolished boots and an unobtrusive brown cloak and shirt to hide his mail armor.

Even the sheen worn into the leather of his bracers, and the glint of finely worked metal in the handle of his belt knife, spoke of a once-trusted but now down-on-his-luck man-at-arms. Only the blue stone broach at his throat that secured his cloak and exactly matched his eyes—a gift from Ieuan's sister, Lili—belied the image he was affecting.

The role Lili played in his life was something Anna hadn't yet asked him. Anna hoped he might have mentioned her without a prompt. He'd had the chance. Before riding to meet Bohun at the Abbey, they'd eaten dinner at Dinas Bran *and* sparred together afterwards, which would sometimes get him talking.

Anna kept up with her *katas*, but didn't have anyone with whom to spar other than her brother. While David practiced nearly every day, and had incorporated his knowledge of karate into the medieval martial art of sword fighting, Anna, as a woman, had to work harder for the opportunity to maintain her skills. Frustratingly, none of Math's men would even consider fighting *her*.

"You do have a third choice." David's eyes flicked from Anna upward, to the rose window at the western peak of the church. Since it was after midnight, it lay in shadow. With the moon to the east, only stars shone through it to light their meeting. "You could counter their treachery merely by supporting their efforts. Or by informing the Archbishop. Yet you do not. You come to me." David turned back to Bohun. "Why?"

"I choose the greater risk for the greater reward," Bohun said.

Pause.

"I see," David said.

A coldness settled in Anna's belly as she saw too.

"If I defeat Bigod for you, exposing his machinations with Vere and Kirby for all to see, it will leave you as sole regent, with control of England to yourself." David allowed himself a bark of a laugh. "You have a fine mind for devious plotting, sir."

Bohun spread his hands wide. "The young Edward is ill with smallpox. The disease has swept like the plague it is through London. He is not expected to survive."

And then everyone in the church understood the real reason Bohun had come to Wales.

Abbot Peter, who'd been standing by as a neutral party without inserting himself into their discussion, was the first to blurt out what Anna was thinking. "You hope to place yourself on the throne?"

6

Bohun glanced at him, a smile twisting at the corner of his mouth. "Not me. My son. His name is Humphrey, after me, though we call him William." Bohun gestured to the boy he'd brought with him, as surety for their agreement, and William stepped into the light at his father's signal. He was a well set up lad, with dark blonde hair and brown eyes that gazed calmly out of his cherubic face.

"He has no royal blood," David said.

"As part of my agreement to take the regency three years ago," Bohun said, "we engaged him to Joan, King Edward's daughter. The wedding date is set for eight weeks from now, when he reaches the age of thirteen. It is through her that he will claim the throne."

Internally, Anna shook her head. No wonder David had left Papa frustrated these last two years. William stood before them, unquestioningly accepting that he had no say in his choice of wife, because marriage was about political alliance, not love. Papa couldn't get his head around the fact that David refused to accept such an alliance, no matter how high it raised him. Papa would have married *David* to Joan, and through her, have him gain the throne of England.

"Edward had other daughters." It was the Abbot again. "Eleanor takes precedence as the eldest."

"Eleanor is engaged to Alfonso of Aragon," Bohun said. "That is not a contract that is in our best interests to break."

"Besides which, England will never accept Alfonso as king, no matter what the Spanish might hope," Math said.

"My son is also a direct descendant of King David of Scotland," Bohun said.

David laughed genuinely now. "I'm sure the Scots will be very glad to hear it. When the time comes, William can claim the Scottish throne too, is that it?"

Bohun flashed a wicked grin, appreciating David's observation. "We need each other, my lord," Bohun said.

"And what is to prevent you from stabbing us in the back while our attention is elsewhere?" Math said. "Perhaps Bigod attacks from the south, distracting our attention and leaving you to regain your lands in Powys?"

Bohun nodded. "I predicted your concerns. And that is why I have brought you my son."

The more they listened to Humphrey, the more Anna became convinced he wasn't telling the whole truth. Again, she couldn't keep silent. "Is that really why you're giving him to us?"

Bohun's eyes narrowed. "Of course."

"He is your *son*," Anna said. "Have you heard whispers of a threat against his life? Do you fear that a powerful baron has gotten wind of your plans for England? Perhaps this meeting is not as secret as we all might hope."

David's lips quirked in a half-smile. "Tell us, my lord. We can't make a decision if you are not frank with us."

Bohun contemplated Anna, his gaze steady. "You are as beautiful and perceptive as Morgana must have been. Are you a healer as she was?"

Bleh. The legend again. Bohun's tone was mild, but his question was a serious one. He really wanted to know. This King Arthur thing had gotten way out of hand. The legend followed David everywhere. Anna understood the reason for it, but she hated it just the same. He was *David.* And she was no Morgana, especially if the label carried with it the stain of witchcraft. It was difficult enough for her, her mother, and Bronwen to function in the Middle Ages without having that fear hanging over their heads.

Anna glanced at David, who'd stilled his expression. They'd both watched with trepidation as the legend had grown. To the people of the thirteenth century, King Arthur was a real person, a war leader who led his people through many battles to victory against the Saxons and who would return in their hour of need. The Welsh *knew* he was real; their ancient stories and songs told them so, even if nobody had ever written them down and they hadn't survived to the twenty-first century.

"I am a healer, but ..." Anna stopped. For the first time, she found herself not wanting to admit to it. Up until now, she'd always been proud to be a healer, but would confessing it to Bohun confirm all his preconceptions?

Yes.

9

Bohun's face took on a look of satisfaction. His chin firmed, jutting forward at Anna. "It is to you, also, that I entrust my son."

"My son is three years old," Anna said, her thoughts flying to Cadell, asleep in their castle with a maidservant to watch over him, "and I lost a second son, just six months ago. I know what it is you are giving us."

"My life." Bohun bowed towards David. "My lord, Arthur."

"Others have chosen that name for me," David said. "My name is Dafydd, son of Llywelyn, the King of Wales."

Bohun waved his hand dismissively. "It matters not. If I leave my son with you, do you give me your word that you will keep him safe, as you keep yourself?"

"More so than I keep myself," David said. "As Arthur would have ... though I have not agreed to your plan."

Bohun smiled, confirmed in his opinion and assuming he'd already convinced them, despite David's denial. Yet he'd still neglected to say from whom he was hiding William. The baron must be powerful indeed for Bohun not to want to speak his name until he had to.

The door behind them swung open and banged against the wall. Owain, David's new captain, bounded into the church. "My lords! Someone comes!"

Math, David, and Anna spun around to look through the open doors which framed the road that led west from the church. A lone rider pounded towards them along it. At a nod from David, Math trotted to where Owain stood in the entrance.

The previous summer, Owain had replaced the former leader of David's *teulu*, Bevyn, who'd retired to lands on Anglesey, protesting loudly all the while that he wasn't old, not even forty. And yet, the median age of death for men in the thirteenth century was forty-eight. Anna didn't know if her mother had actually *told* Bevyn that, but when Anna had seen him four months ago, he had married a girl fifteen years younger than he, who doted on him and was pregnant with his first child. Bevyn had confessed that he hadn't imagined such happiness was possible for him.

The two men waited until the rider pulled up on the hard-packed earth in front of the steps to the church. He spoke urgently, and then Math ran back to David. He held a sheathed sword in each hand. As he handed one to David, Anna recognized the artwork on the scabbard. It was David's new sword, finer than any in all of Wales, which Papa had given him for Christmas the previous year.

"Soldiers are coming." Math unwound his sword belt and wrapped it around his waist. "No more than twenty, but riding hard. They must have crossed the Dyke less than a mile from here, to the northeast of the Abbey."

"Whose men?" David said.

Math shook his head. "The scout recognized their livery, but I can hardly credit it. Mortimers. Or at least their men."

David faced Bohun. "Which Mortimer knows that you are here?"

"Edmund," Bohun said.

"I'd forgotten he survived Lancaster," David said. "A good reason to eat sparingly at official meals."

Bohun was still struggling with this news. "But it can't be. His mother and mine were sisters and he's married to my wife's niece. They had their first child only last year. I've spoken to him of my plans, but ..." He broke off, shaking his head.

"You should have waited until you'd spoken with me before putting all of us in danger." David pointed at Owain. "You know what to do."

"Yes, my lord." Owain saluted and left the church.

Math closed the doors behind him. "Where's the bar?" Math swung around to look at the Abbot.

The Abbot shook his head. "Our Church is open to all. In all my years of service, we have never locked it."

Math didn't bother to shake his head at the innocence that statement revealed. "To think a Mortimer would plague us again." Leaving the doors, he strode back towards Anna.

"I need my sword," Bohun said.

"Where is it?" David said.

"On my horse. I didn't want to leave it with the monks."

That was a mistake.

David met Anna's eyes. Just for a second, she saw the mockery in them. If he'd been sixteen still, instead of almost twenty, he would have snorted in derision. "I will see you safe and then Math and I must return to our men," David said. "Can you help us, Abbot Peter?"

"This way." Abbot Peter grabbed a torch from a sconce on the wall and headed towards the choir and the south transept.

Bohun took long strides in an effort to keep up with David and Math, who held his arm around Anna's waist and swept her along with him. David had been just fourteen when they'd come to Wales. At the time, Math had topped him by more than half a foot. Now at nearly twenty, David was two inches taller than Math, although thankfully, not still growing. Even so, according Mom, you wouldn't know it by how much he ate.

The Abbot led them through a door at the back of the church, down a slender set of stairs and into a subterranean passage beneath the chapter house. Stone surrounded them on every side, including the two-foot wide flagstones under their feet. Anna put out a hand to the wall, feeling the dampness that even a dry summer couldn't cure. At least she smelled no mold, which would have made her head ache.

Several doors stood open on either side of the corridor, revealing storage rooms and a wine cellar. Abbot Peter by-passed them all before approaching another set of stairs that led upwards. When he reached the bottom step, he paused. "Would you prefer to stay inside, or exit through the graveyard?"

"If Mortimer's men get into the Church, we're not safe here. I'd rather have room to run," David said. "But we'll wait a moment to give Owain a chance to report back."

"How many men do you have?" Bohun said.

"Fifty." David looked at the Abbot. "Do I have your permission to draw my sword, Father?"

Abbott Peter nodded and David pulled his sword from its sheath. It glittered in the torchlight and William, who had followed closely behind his father, gasped. David heard the accolade and canted his head in acknowledgment. "Italian steel."

Those two words conveyed far more than their overt meaning. Papa's acceptance of Jewish émigrés had allowed the resources of the Jewish trading networks to benefit Wales. Although the Treaty allowed commerce between England and Wales, Wales didn't *need* England anymore. And Wales certainly appreciated having the greater part of its overall wealth flowing into Welsh hands rather than English ones.

Math pulled out his sword too. His other hand held a torch. He and David took the stairs two at a time to the landing above, that fronted a wooden door, fastened with bronze hinges and fittings. David pressed his ear to the crack between the door and the frame. He shook his head. "I hear men calling, but nobody is right outside the door. Mortimer's men haven't found it yet."

Math glanced down at Anna, and then back to David. "How do we want to do this?"

Now that they were closer to the exit, Anna could hear sounds from outside the abbey—men shouting orders mostly. She took courage from the relaxed demeanor of the men with her who appeared unmoved by the threat. When she'd kissed Cadell goodnight earlier in the evening, it hadn't occurred to her that she might face danger at the Abbey. And if Math or David had feared it, they would have been united in their refusal to let her come. Still, in the face of the quiet competence of her husband and brother, she felt calm too.

"So, is it Mortimer who threatens William?" David said to Bohun, still with his ear pressed to the door. "You never answered my sister's question."

Bohun shook his head. "You know what we in the March are like. These may be Mortimer's men, but they could just as easily belong to Bigod or Vere. Any one of them could have had word we were coming here."

"More likely, you have a traitor among your men," David said.

"It's Gilbert de Clare that's got my father most worried," William said, proving that his grasp of Welsh was excellent.

"*Tch.*" Bohun flung out a hand to his son. "Ah, Will, I wouldn't go that far—"

Anna and Math exchanged a look that said, *I would.*
While the flower of the nobility of England had died at
Lancaster, as well as Papa's brother, Dafydd, a few had
survived, whether because they'd eaten less of the poisoned
meal or from a naturally hearty constitution. Edmund
Mortimer, his brother, Roger, and Gilbert de Clare had been
among those who'd been made sick, but hadn't died, although
Gilbert had been in a coma for several weeks. He had almost
been buried alive by those who found him, overwhelmed as
they were by the number of dead.

"If it is Clare, he *is* someone to worry about," David said.
"His lands in Ireland and England are extensive, but he was one
of the richest of Marcher barons too and lost more than anyone
when you signed our treaty."

"He does have the resources, and the drive, to put
something like this into play," Bohun said.

Both Humphrey de Bohun and Gilbert de Clare had been
raised by Humphrey's grandfather. Both Humphrey and
Gilbert had fought with Simon de Montfort against the English
crown in the Baron's war, when Gilbert was only twenty-three
and Humphrey sixteen.

But after Gilbert had been named a rebel and
excommunicated by the Church, he had suddenly switched
sides, joining Edward and his father, King Henry, as a valuable
and powerful ally against the Bohuns. Humphrey's father had
died from his wounds at the battle of Evesham, the final battle

in the war, and since then, Humphrey and Gilbert had hated each other. It was no surprise that they'd ended up on opposite sides in yet another war.

Anna saw real concern come into David's eyes. "I've never been that impressed with Bigod, actually. To learn that it's Clare—"

"We don't have time to worry about *who* is responsible just now," Math said. "It's what, when, and where that most concern us."

Footsteps sounded along the passage, moving at a run. Owain came into view, along with four other of David's men. "They don't overmatch us and we plan to give them more than they bargained for," Owain said. "But we need to get you out of the Abbey before they discover this entrance. If Mortimer's men get past us on the west side, the Abbey won't provide you a safe haven."

"That was my thinking," David said.

With a glance at Math, who nodded, David pushed through the door.

They spilled into the graveyard, eerie in the moonlight and empty of enemies as of yet. Math pulled Anna to him and kissed her forehead. Anna clutched at his cloak. "Stay safe," she said.

"Protect Anna and the boy," David said to two of the men whom Owain had brought with him.

"Into the trees." Math pointed with one finger, indicating the direction they should go.

"For the rest …" David took a moment to clasp Anna's hand before vanishing into the shadows that cloaked the walls of the monastery, moving silently with Math and Owain, their steps muffled by the thick summer grass.

Anna allowed Bohun to pull her along, away from the church, William tight against his other side. The Abbot kept pace behind.

"*Sweet Mary,*" Bohun said. "To think my trust was so misplaced. Edmund has been my friend since we were boys. To think his men followed me here—to think Edmund would openly attack the Prince of Wales on his home ground."

"He doesn't think David should be the Prince of Wales," Anna said. "Or that Wales should exist at all. You Marcher lords have always viewed my country as your private play ground."

"You have a point, my dear." Bohun showed a glint of white teeth, amused despite the duress.

Bohun pulled her and William behind a rickety shed on the far side of the graveyard and pushed down on their shoulders. They crouched just below the level of the long grass that had grown up between some of the gravestones. Summer flowers in pink and yellow, closed now that it was night, showed among the green. Anna recognized pimpernel and speedwell, and the red-dotted leaves of St. John's wort.

Anna lifted her chin so she could see the Abbey. Nothing moved on their side of the church.

"Go, man," Bohun said to one of the men David had left with them. "You'll do more good over there than here. Now that we're out of the church, I can protect them." Both he and William held long knives down at their sides. Anna felt for her belt knife and pulled it out too. She would use it if she had to. She knew how.

"Neither of you wear a sword," the man said. "My lord would have my head if I abandoned you."

"How far did you ride today? Every one of you looks tired," Anna said.

"It is an honor to serve the Prince of Wales." The man's chin firmed. "He drives himself harder than any of us."

He looked away without answering her question, however. It was her experience that men often didn't know how to answer her. She was more outspoken than most women and was willing to ask the questions she was thinking.

Anna's ears strained for an indication of how the skirmish was going. Her heart constricted in fear for both of her men. She loved them and the thought of either of them not returning had her knees trembling. She'd learned to survive without hot showers or email. She would never *ever* get used to watching her men go off to battle.

"All will be well," Bohun said, reading her mind. "Your son will not be left fatherless this night."

Anna nodded and swallowed hard. Bohun sounded sure, but both of them knew that even the most valiant man could be felled by an errant blow.

A chorus of shouting sounded from the far side of the Abbey. The air was still enough that Anna could hear the swords clashing. It went on far too long. She wanted to straighten. It was painful not to know what was happening, but she didn't dare move until Math returned. She and Math didn't have a traditional thirteenth century marriage, but she knew better than to disobey him—or her brother—at a time like this.

Bohun was feeling it too. "By the Saints! I hate this waiting."

Their guard put out a hand. "Stay, my lord."

Bohun looked ready to spring to his feet, but before he could, Math appeared around the corner of the Abbey and signaled to them with a raised hand. One second, Anna was crouching behind the shed, and the next, she'd run forward and wrapped her arms around Math's waist. She was able to take a deep breath for the first time in twenty minutes.

"Success?" Bohun brushed at the knees of his breeches.

"Yes."

Anna pressed her face into Math's neck. She knew what his tone meant. That one word told her how he felt about the night's work.

"None of Mortimer's men can live to bring news to England of my presence here," Bohun said.

Anna twisted to look back at Bohun. His eyes glinted in the moonlight.

"That will be up to Prince Dafydd," Math said.

"None of them may see me," Bohun said. "If my fellow barons knew that I had entered Wales to speak to your Prince …"

Math hitched one shoulder, as if to say *you knew the risks when you came here.* He didn't say it, though.

Bohun closed the distance between them. "My men wear my colors. Mortimer's men will know that I was here. They will report it to him."

"I can only tell you to stay here until we leave with the prisoners and then head for England with your men, as quick as you can," Math said. "It's only a mile as the crow flies."

Bohun's jaw worked. David's men had worn brown and green homespun, though, upon close inspection, the mail under their shirts would indicate that they were something other than simple men of the woods. Bohun hadn't thought this through as clearly.

"Whether or not Edmund Mortimer acknowledged our treaty once, his men have broken it and are defeated," Math said. "They will not see England again this month. By the time they do, our fight with Bigod—or Clare—or whomever leagues against us—will be over, for good or ill, and then we will decide what to do with them. Neither I, nor my prince, will kill any man unless we have no other choice."

Bohun glared at him, but Math turned away, his arm still around Anna. His shoulders said, *Enough!* He stalked towards the Abbey. Anna clutched her cloak more tightly around her shoulders and then felt for Math's hand. After a moment's hesitation, he took it and squeezed.

"Are you okay?" Anna said.

Math didn't speak American English, but he knew the word, knew what it meant to Anna. In fact, it wasn't just Anna and David—or Mom and Bronwen—who used it these days. The word had spread in the thirteenth century, as it had in the modern world.

"Yes," he said. "Or as okay as I can be right now."

Anna glanced at William as he came up beside her. He'd left his father and Abbot Peter behind, standing together among the graves. William kept his head high, his eyes fixed on a point somewhere beyond the Abbey. He didn't look back at his father. Anna didn't remember her brother ever saying it, but it looked as if he and Bohun had an agreement. William was now in David's charge.

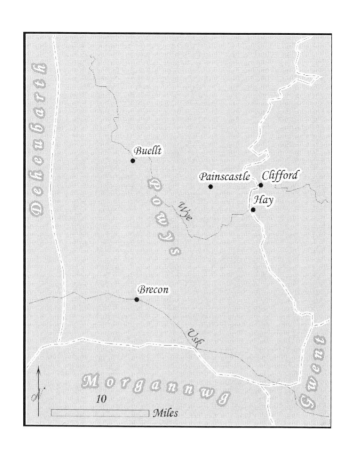

Buellt

Painscastle Clifford

Hay

Wye

Brecon

Usk

Dehenbarth

Powys

Morgannwg

Gwent

10
Miles

2

25 August 1288

Buellt Castle

Lili

"**W**ake up, Lili!"

Lili shot out of bed at the sound of her brother's voice. He banged on the door a second time and she ran to open it. "What's happening?"

Ieuan stood in the hall before her, booted and cloaked for a journey. A single candle lit the table in the corridor and flickered behind him, casting his face in shadow. Still, the set of his shoulders told her that all was not well.

"A messenger from Dinas Bran has arrived."

Lili's heart caught in her throat. "Are Anna and Cadell all right—"

Ieuan reached out a hand and touched her shoulder. "Everyone's fine. For now. May I come in? I don't want to talk about this in the corridor."

Lili nodded and her brother stepped into the room and closed the door behind him.

"Everything may be fine," she said, "but you *are* leaving Buellt Castle?" Lili sat down on the end of her bed. She'd left the curtains around her bed pulled back overnight because the room wasn't cold, and she liked to see out the window in the morning. For now, it remained dark beyond the shutters. The only light that reached her window came from the flickering torches in the bailey of the castle.

"The messenger was from Dafydd." Her brother eyed her carefully. She knew that he was wondering how she'd respond to the mention of Dafydd's name.

Lili kept her expression calm. "What does he say?"

"Dafydd met with Humphrey de Bohun, who has entrusted him with his son."

Lili's eyes widened. "Why would Bohun do that? And why would Dafydd accept?"

"The Normans have gathered an army at Bristol Castle." Ieuan gave Lili a quick summary of the news the messenger had brought regarding Dafydd's meeting with Bohun, which Lili listened to with a mixture of horror and incredulity. He concluded, "I must go south to counter them."

"And rouse the countryside on the way," Lili said.

"Yes." Ieuan had many tasks in this new order of Dafydd's, including command of the Welsh foot soldiers, were Wales to go to war. Lili had always been proud of her brother, but after he'd gone to Dafydd's world and returned with Bronwen, who'd become his wife, he'd grown to be something *more* than he had been before. More confident. Wiser. Dafydd trusted him more than any other man, barring his father or Math.

Ieuan bent his head to his sister. "Dafydd should arrive here by tonight."

Lili looked away. A bird chirped outside her window and she gazed into the darkness. The moon had set some time ago, and in the short span of time she had been talking with Ieuan, the sky had turned to gray murk. Dawn would come soon.

"You need to end this, Lili," Ieuan said.

Lili's chin came up. "I did end it!"

Ieuan looked down at her, his face filled with one of his more condescending expressions, which he saved especially for her. "I don't mean it that way and you know it. You love him. Why won't you admit it?"

"King Llywelyn—"

"King Llywelyn will come around. You have to give him time. Dafydd has made clear time and again that he will marry a woman of his own choosing, not some six year old from Scotland, France, or England, whom his father has picked out for him because she has royal blood. Sending Dafydd away isn't the answer, not if it means that you spend your days pining for him."

"I'm not pining—"

"You are." Ieuan's tone brooked no argument. "I don't know if he and his men will rest here tonight or push on, but regardless, you must ride with them. They'll head to Caerphilly. You need to go there too."

Lili knew her lower lip was sticking out, but she couldn't help it. "No."

"This isn't a request, Lili. No castle is safer. I need to know that you are within its walls before the Normans attack."

Lili ground her teeth. She'd intended to travel to Caerphilly weeks ago when Bronwen had ridden there to be with Meg. Both women were pregnant: Bronwen, at long last, with her first, and Meg, newly so and unexpectedly with her third, at the age of forty-one. Although Lili was delighted for both of them, births and babies unsettled her. And if she was honest with herself, Bronwen's happiness reminded her too much of what she didn't have with Dafydd.

King Llywelyn would be there, too, and she couldn't face him. It wasn't so much that he didn't believe she was good enough for his son. He believed, rather, that by selecting her to marry, Dafydd was wasting an opportunity to create or cement a relationship with another country. Wales *needed* alliances if it was to survive.

The King had refused permission for them to marry and suggested that Dafydd could resolve the matter by taking Lili as his mistress, which Dafydd refused to do. And Lili wasn't going to marry Dafydd in secret, as he wanted. She'd sent him away because she refused to be the wedge that drove Dafydd and his father apart.

"Yes, Ieuan."

"Good." Ieuan eyed Lili carefully, and then leaned forward to kiss her forehead. "Dafydd will have fifty men with him at least."

"I know how to manage a castle, Ieuan," Lili said.

Ieuan strode to the door, but turned back to look at her before he went through it. "I know you do. Be careful."

"You be careful," Lili said. "You're the one riding to war."

Ieuan shook his head. "I'd hoped the Treaty would gain us more than three years."

"We knew the peace couldn't last," Lili said. "The Normans were chained, not defeated. Be glad we had so much time to prepare."

Ieuan shrugged. "I'll be gone before the dawn. Obey me now."

After Ieuan left, Lili sat where he'd left her on the end of the bed, kicking her heels into the wooden frame as if she were a child instead of the eighteen year old woman she'd become. Shouts came from the courtyard. At least half the garrison would go with Ieuan. Those that were left behind would be the old, the young, and the discontented, unless Ieuan took the latter with him to keep them out of trouble. Either way, the garrison of Buellt Castle would be much diminished in Ieuan's absence.

The portcullis cranked up, screeching as it locked in place. With a thunder of hooves, the company rode from the bailey, pounded down the road from the gatehouse, and was gone. Gethin, the captain of the guard whom Ieuan would have ordered to remain behind, was a smarmy fellow who looked at Lili in a way she didn't like. Maybe she *would* go to Caerphilly. Maybe she would go *today*, before Dafydd arrived. It would be cowardly of her, but she couldn't face him, not after she'd turned down his proposal for a second time.

She had known when she'd sent him away that there wouldn't be a third. He'd told her as much. Shouted it, even. That was two months ago and she hadn't seen him since.

Lili kept her male garments in a trunk set against the far wall. She went to it and lifted the lid. To his credit, Ieuan had never confiscated her breeches, though he preferred not to see her robed as a boy past the dawn hour. Bronwen, for her part, laughed every time Lili wore her breeches and told her she wished she could wear them too. Not that any breeches fit Bronwen anymore, even if her belly still hardly showed despite being six months pregnant. Lili hadn't seen Bronwen clothed as a twenty-first century woman since the day she put on her first dress. She'd embraced this life with Ieuan. Lili was thankful for it, but often felt that Bronwen belonged in this time more than Lili did herself.

Maybe that was because Bronwen had chosen this life while Lili couldn't help but chafe at the restrictions put upon her.

Lili dressed in the dark, having done it so often she didn't need a candle, and left the room. Down the stairs, through the deserted kitchen where she grabbed a day-old biscuit (or two), and then into the kitchen garden. Once outside, she slowed and sniffed the air. No wind blew, as was often the case in the lull before the dawn.

The guard at the postern gate, a man long since accustomed to her routine, waved her past him. Lili gave him a nod and left the castle. She skipped down the hill and passed through the cut in the rampart, before heading southeast, away from the castle and the Wye River.

Some hundred yards from the last of the castle's earthworks, Lili opened a rickety wooden gate that led to the archery range. By the time she reached it, the darkness had turned to murk and she could see something of the field in front of her. How many times had she come here to think and to be alone? Especially recently, it had been her refuge whenever she didn't want Dafydd in her head.

Today, however, he wouldn't leave. Her first arrow went wide, and then her second. Then she shot over the target on purpose—out of frustration and guilt, and maybe even a bit of fear—losing the arrow in the trees beyond the range. Ieuan was riding into danger and she was loosing arrows at a target, safe at Buellt. She didn't want to be safe. She wanted to yell and fight and blow up a curtain wall like they had at Painscastle. Her life was so sedate, so set, and not what she wanted. She would have screamed in frustration if the air wasn't so still that someone on the castle ramparts might have heard her and come running to see what was the matter.

Lili bent her head and pressed the hard wood of her bow to her forehead. *This* was when it was most important to shoot straight, when her emotions were running high. If she could hit the target today, she could hit the target any day. Taking a deep breath, Lili set her feet in preparation, bent her bow, and steadied her arrow on the string. And then the earth rumbled beneath the turf.

At first she felt it more than heard it. Clutching the arrow and bow in her left hand, she knelt, put her right palm flat to the ground, and listened hard. The sound grew louder and unmistakable: many horses pounded down the road, coming from the east and heading towards Buellt. Trees screened the archery butts from the road so she couldn't see who it was.

Lili glanced towards the towers that loomed above her to the west, measuring the distance back to the postern gate verses how far she had to go to reach the road. She was equidistant from both. She decided not to retreat. Not today. Not even from Dafydd, who had arrived too soon for her to flee, though it was odd that he came from the east and so soon. Perhaps he'd had business that had taken him to the border of Wales, before bringing him here.

Lili ran to the far side of the field, some hundred yards away, and climbed the fence at the other side. Once into the thick woods beyond, she slowed, though still moving steadily, and came to rest in a stand of rowan trees ten yards from the road. The Romans had built this avenue, so it was raised slightly above the level at which she stood, with ditches running parallel to the road on either side.

The thudding of the horses' hooves came louder now. She grasped the trunk of a sapling, that was growing out of the wall of the ditch, to help her climb it. Her boot slipped and she fell to her knees, scrabbling in the dirt so she wouldn't slide back down. She snorted through her nose at what she'd look like to Dafydd, with mud on her breeches and hands, and her hair in disarray.

She glanced up as the company galloped towards her. Her fall had made her too late to intercept them without startling the lead horses. She crouched where she was, deciding that she'd accept the gift fate had given her and *not* confront Dafydd just yet. Bushes lined the road and blocked her vision of all but flashes of the red and white tunics of the riders. They swept by her: a company of two dozen men.

Their passing left Lili gasping, for the company wasn't Dafydd's. Everything about them, from their beards to their banners, was wrong.

They were from England.

When the last of the riders had passed her, she pushed up from her crouch—which possibly had just saved her life—and climbed onto the road. At the sight of the Mortimer red, instead of Dafydd's dragon banner, she bit her lip. The Mortimers had owned Buellt Castle before Dafydd's father had taken it from them. It seemed they wanted it back. But how? The lookout on the battlements would see them coming as Lili had. He'd see them more easily, in fact, since the sound of the horses' hooves would have carried high into the air, and those on the stone walkway would have had ample time to warn the rest of the garrison and close the gate.

Still looking west and standing in the center of the road, which was deserted except for her, Lili followed the path the company was taking with her eyes. Then she began to walk towards the castle. She didn't fear the riders: if a stray horseman looked back, he would see a peasant boy and think nothing of it. The riders disappeared around a bend, following the curve in the river. The sound of the horses' hooves faded. Lili mocked herself for fearing to see Dafydd more than foreign soldiers, and then she began to run.

She crested a rise in the road, from which point she had a good view of the path in front of her, along with Buellt's gate that fronted the Wye River. At the sight of it, she pulled up short. The last of the Englishmen was urging his horse under the portcullis and into the bailey.

Lili stared after them, aghast. A string of curses bubbled up in her throat, for she had spent enough time among the garrison to be able to curse as fluently as a man. But what came to her lips was something Bronwen would say, and for the first time Lili truly understood what it meant: *no freaking way!*

Stunned and disbelieving, Lili gazed at the rider's retreating back, knowing what had to have happened but not wanting to believe it. Gethin, the captain Ieuan had left in charge of Buellt Castle, was a traitor. The Normans had bought him—and then he'd invited them in.

As she glared at the castle and the hated foreigners inside it (whom she couldn't see, of course), Lili knew what she had to do. Fate, it seemed, had ensured that she would see Dafydd today whether she wanted to or not—though surely that was a petty complaint compared to what the English had just done. They'd walked in and taken over Buellt Castle right in front of her nose. Ieuan would never forgive her if she didn't do something about it. Nor would she ever forgive herself.

Right then and there, before she second-guessed her plan of action, Lili began to walk. Although the western ford was closer to her current location, she headed east, to a good ford of the Wye River downstream from the castle. It meant a delay, but to go east meant she wouldn't have to pass in front of the gatehouse. Peasant clothes or no peasant clothes, men of the garrison had seen her garb more times than she could count and would recognize her instantly.

She didn't have to walk to Dinas Bran to find Dafydd, of course. If Dafydd had pushed the horses on his ride south, which surely he would have, he'd have spent the night north of Caersws. His company would have rested only as long as the horses needed, sacrificing human sleep out of the urgency of the moment, and should have left with the dawn. Only one road led to Buellt from there. Somewhere between Caersws and here, she would meet him.

Him.

It took Lili half an hour to find the ford. With her bow in one hand and her boots in another, she waded across. The river widened here, with the water only knee deep this time of year, though it was still very cold, having come down from the mountains to the west of Buellt.

Lili laced up her boots again and set off, thankful she hadn't worn a dress, and even more thankful that Ieuan had woken her when he had. She strode along, mile after mile as the road climbed towards Caersws. The Romans had built this road too. After a while, she began counting the paces in her head, calculating distances like one of those mathematical problems Ieuan had enjoyed tasking her with when she was younger: If Dafydd rode fifty miles the first day, he'd have thirty left to reach Buellt, and if Lili walked four miles an hour, she should be meet him by noon—

In the same way that Lili had known the company of riders from England was approaching before she saw them, she heard Dafydd's *teulu* before she saw it. Resigned to whatever might come, and to whatever he might say or not say—recriminations or silence, she was prepared for either—Lili came to a halt in the center of the road, and simply waited.

3

David

David knew who was standing in the middle of the road from the moment he crested the rise and gazed into the valley in front of him. It was the way she stood and waited, the shape and stance of her, her hands on her hips, even from that distance and wearing boys' clothes. She was mad at him; he knew it. What exactly he'd done, he couldn't say, but given that she had walked miles from Buellt to meet him, likely she blamed him for the need.

Which brought him to the most important point—*why the hell* had she walked all the way here to meet him? If an imminent invasion from Bristol wasn't enough, if having to babysit Bohun's son (though William had behaved perfectly the entire journey from Dinas Bran) wasn't enough, he had to find his beloved standing in the middle of the road, in the middle of nowhere, with her bow in her hand, a quiver on her back, and a glare in her eyes.

The company slowed and then stopped, twenty paces from Lili. Utter, total silence descended on his *teulu* after the initial *hush, man!* from Math. David's men gave him space, as well they might. Most of them had ridden from Buellt with him after Lili had sent him away two months ago. They knew how he felt, not that he'd worked very hard to hide it.

It was impossible to keep secrets when men worked so closely with one another day in and day out. They were comrades in arms. He trusted these men to do their job. He trusted them with his life. It seemed purposeless to try to hide from them that Lili had broken his heart. They would have wondered why he no longer went to Buellt and then guessed the answer, even if he hadn't stormed out the castle with his color high and his tail between his legs.

Alone, David trotted his horse up to Lili and reined in. He gazed down at her and she up at him for a count of ten. And then—"What's happened?"

"English cavalry have taken Buellt," she said.

Crap. David looked back towards his company. "Take a break, Gentlemen." He dismounted along with them and then waved Owain and Math closer before turning back to Lili. "The horses are past due for a rest. We'll take it here while you tell us all about it. You've walked far."

"I would have walked to Dinas Bran if I had to, but your messenger arrived in Buellt in the early hours of the morning to say that you were coming. Ieuan has already left for Chepstow."

"If the English have taken Buellt Castle, how did you escape?" David took Lili's arm and walked with her to the edge of the road where his men had gathered.

Trees lined the road on either side. Beyond them to the east, a field of oats stood ready to harvest. Some of David's men settled themselves onto their helmets, while others crouched in the grass. David made sure he and Lili remained out of earshot.

"What is it, Dafydd?" Math came to a halt at David's side, Owain right behind him.

"Our Norman friends have taken Buellt." David gestured to Lili. "Tell us."

"Ieuan woke me to say that he was leaving. He told me about your meeting with Humphrey de Bohun," Lili said. "Instead of going back to sleep, I chose to rise and shoot. It wasn't yet dawn when I arrived at the archery range. I'd hardly unlatched the gate when I heard cavalry coming from the east, down the road from Offa's Dyke."

"How many?" David said.

"Two dozen?" Lili said. "I thought at first that it was your company, riding to Buellt from the wrong direction for some reason. When they passed by, I was still in the trees beside the road. Once I knew they weren't Welsh, I stayed hidden until I was sure I was safe."

"How did you know who they were?" Math said.

"They wore red and white, which is why I thought they were yours, my lord, but then I saw that the emblem on their tunics was that of the House of Mortimer. They rode right into Buellt ..."

"What do you mean, *rode right in?*" David said.

Lili shook her head. "Ieuan left one of his lesser captains, a man named Gethin, in charge of the garrison. I can only surmise that he opened the gates for them. Though it could have been whoever was on duty at the time."

"How many men did your brother leave?" David said.

"Ten," Lili said. "If I'd asked any to ride with me to Caerphilly, it would have left even fewer. Because of the shortage of men, Ieuan said that I should wait to go with you instead."

David schooled his expression before it could betray his surprise at her admission. *She had been going to go to Caerphilly. With him.* Maybe she was softening. The instant the thought crossed David's mind, he brutally shoved it away. Better not to think about it. Better to take her presence now for what it was.

"Even if every man in the garrison didn't have a part of Gethin's scheme, ten men would have had a hard time defending against two dozen, once they got inside," David said.

"And you walked all this way to tell us?" Math said.

Lili lifted one shoulder. "The English will know you are coming because Gethin knew."

"That must have cheered the English commander," Math said. "With a help of a traitor, he rides to Buellt and takes the castle without a fight, to find that an even bigger prize is on his way, riding innocently into his arms."

David gazed south towards Buellt. He'd never liked the place, not since the former owner, Edmund Mortimer, had set a trap for his father that had almost meant his death. David and Anna had saved Dad's life by driving their aunt's minivan into medieval Wales and eliminating his attackers.

David wondered sometimes—though he'd learned not to think too hard about it because the uncertainties could drive him insane—what was special about his family. His mother had done the same as he and Anna, driving her car into the swamp beside Cricieth Castle, with baby Anna strapped into her car seat in the back. Was it God at work? Or magic? A robot controlling the universe from a hidden moon? Or a random hole in the time-space continuum, linked somehow to his family's DNA? He didn't know, and mostly likely, he never would.

Owain folded his arms across his chest. "The English will try to trap you, my lord."

"They don't even need to trap us," David said. "All they have to do is keep flying the Welsh flag, post Gethin on the ramparts, and wave us in."

"We have more men than they do," Math said. "Many more. They'd be taking a chance that they could overpower us. Odds are, they could lose the castle on the very day they take it."

David studied the ground. *What I wouldn't give for a cell phone to call Dad.* But of course, that was needless wishing and he put the thought aside. It was up to him and Math—and their men.

"We could avoid them entirely," Owain said. "Why go to Buellt at all? We have a greater mission than the taking of one castle."

"You are correct—perhaps," David said. "But what if this is a bigger piece of the Normans' plan than we presently know? How many other English companies have entered into Wales today?" He met Math's eyes. "Is Dinas Bran safe? Or Dolforwyn? Or maybe they'll send a fleet to Anglesey or attack Aber itself."

Math nodded. "We cannot be in two places at once. Or three. You sent a messenger to Aber, to warn them of the Norman plans. We know of the action in the south—whether spearheaded by Clare, Bigod, or Mortimer—only because Bohun warned us. All we can address is what is before us. Guessing isn't a winning strategy."

"If not for the presence of William, I might think that Bohun's news was a ploy to get us to strip Gwynedd of its defenders so that the Normans *could* invade in the north." David glanced at William, who was feeding a carrot to his horse.

"But he gave you the boy," Math said.

"And thus, I must believe the rest," David said.

Lili's eyes flicked to William and then back to David. "That's William de Bohun?"

David gazed down at her. His arms itched to go around her. But he kept his hands at his sides. Those days were over. "Yes," he said.

"Wow. I scarcely believed it when Ieuan told me that Bohun had left him with you." And then Lili hastened to put a hand on David's arm in reassurance. "Not that he shouldn't trust you, my lord, but this is his *son*."

David smiled. He loved it when Lili spoke American. Even more, he loved it that she'd touched his arm, if only for a second. A girl didn't touch a man she didn't like.

He cleared his throat. "One threat at a time, then. The English at Buellt first. We'll take steps to counter this particular foray, and maybe we'll learn something about the bigger one."

"Agreed," Math said.

Owain nodded. He wasn't as sage a counselor as Bevyn had been—and certainly didn't grow his mustachios as large—but he was good with a sword and had a quick mind. He reminded David of Ieuan a bit. David made a note to himself not to take Owain to the modern world, find him an archaeologist like Bronwen to marry, as he'd done with Ieuan, and lose him as a captain immediately afterwards.

Owain and Math walked back to the men, leaving David with Lili. He thought for a few seconds about what to say to her and then decided, *screw it. We're friends, right? Friends! Always have been.* And if they weren't, they shouldn't be getting married anyway. "Would you like some food? Water?"

"Both, if it's easy," Lili said, and actually gave him half a smile. David went to his horse, untied a water skin from where it rested near his saddlebags, and handed it to her.

"So you were going to shoot this morning?" David said.

"I often do." Lili took two long swallows and then swapped the water for a piece of bread. "I have to go early because Ieuan doesn't like it if I look like this in the middle of the day." She smiled for real as she looked down at herself.

Progress.

Lili continued, "Ieuan is tolerant, urged on by Bronwen, of course, but I am a lord's sister. I do have to think about his feelings a little bit."

"Have you been working on your karate too?"

"More than a little," Lili said. "Last time I saw Anna, she said I was at least a purple belt."

"Congratulations." That gave Lili just enough knowledge to be dangerous—mostly to herself—but it was a good start.

Lili smiled back, and David gave an inward sigh. *Maybe they could get through this.* "Come on. You'd better ride with me." David mounted Cadfarch (meaning 'battle horse'—completely without irony) and pulled Lili up after him.

"He's new." Lili patted the horse's side. "Bigger than your last one."

"My father gave him to me."

What David didn't tell her was that his father felt guilty for rejecting Lili and was trying to make up for it. For David's part, he'd been not much more than civil to his father for so long it was threatening to harden into true dislike. His mother despaired of them both, but Dad was unbending, and thus, so was David. It made family gatherings—which were few and far between as it was, given the distances involved—unpleasant.

But David didn't know what else to do when the alternative was to pretend that he would accept a marriage for political reasons to a woman he'd never met and didn't love. His father had a vision of the crown of a united England and Wales on David's head. He thought that *David*, not William, should marry one of Edward's daughters and combine the rule of both countries under the Red Dragon of Wales. The kingdom was David's for the taking. All David had to do was reach out and grab it. His father couldn't understand David's obstinacy. *Why didn't he merely keep Lili as a mistress?*

To which David could only reply: *I don't think so.*

Lili tightened her arms around his waist and David's hand went to hers and squeezed once. It made his heart skip a beat to know that she was with him.

4

25 August 1288

North of Buellt

Lili

Just for a moment, Lili pressed her cheek into Dafydd's back, before she remembered that she was supposed to be keeping him at arm's length and loosened her grip. Being with him was almost worse than not being with him, because now she had to keep herself tightly contained all the time so he wouldn't know how she felt about him.

"I assume you have a plan," Lili said.

"Math and I will come up with something between here and Buellt," Dafydd said.

Lili gritted her teeth because he was keeping her out on purpose, where in the past he might have consulted her too. "Perhaps I can help?"

Dafydd tipped his chin toward a trail that led off the road just ahead of them. "I've a mind to split up. I don't want all of us to trip blithely down the road to Buellt and end up dead. We aren't going to walk innocently into whatever trap they've set for us." He paused. "What do you think they'll do? You know Gethin better than I."

"I don't like Gethin," Lili said, "so that colors my judgment, but I think they'll risk leaving the castle and choosing their ground, rather than waiting for you to come to them. If I were Gethin, I'd suggest to the English commander that he set an ambush for you. That way, they keep the castle no matter what happens, and if you have the greater numbers, they can even the odds by surprising you."

"You think they'll go for open war? Really?"

"Once you get inside the castle, were they to admit your *teulu*, they run a real risk of your force overcoming theirs. They have thirty-some men. If that many. You have fifty. It isn't great odds, especially if your men are even slightly wary."

"Why should we be wary?" Dafydd said. "Gethin surely will try hard to make everything look perfect for me."

"Except for one thing, Dafydd," Lili said. "Me. I won't be there to greet you. All things being equal, that has to worry Gethin. And given that I'm not in evidence, Gethin will wonder where I've gone. Even if he decides my absence isn't important, it will niggle at the back of his mind. He will wonder if I've done exactly has I *have* done, and brought you warning of the danger."

"I see the problem," Dafydd said. "He's making a mistake if he dismisses you because you're a woman."

Lili felt a warmth in her stomach at the pride in Dafydd's voice. She swallowed it away. "For them to come out after you doesn't even the odds, but as Math said, even if you escape their clutches, they can simply drop the portcullis and keep you out of Buellt. The English captain will accept the risk of losing men, if it means he keeps the castle."

Dafydd shook his head. "They're taking a risk, either way."

"I think you are too big a prize to forgo the chance," Lili said. "Edmund Mortimer would want them to chance it."

Dafydd stared straight ahead as he thought. "You are probably right." His men had formed up on the road behind them and now Dafydd waved Math forward. "Lili and I have talked further. She thinks the English will prepare an ambush."

Math eyed Lili and she gazed back at him, struggling to contain the flush of red that threatened to suffuse her face. He would know all about her refusal of Dafydd's entreaties. There was no question that Math blamed her for Dafydd's unhappiness, if he was unhappy.

Which, now that she thought about it, he showed no sign of being. In fact, he acted as if they'd never had a relationship at all beyond friendship. Lili suppressed a sigh as the realization hit her: Dafydd was no longer in love with her.

Here, she had pined for him (as Ieuan said), spent many a sleepless night wallowing in guilt, and he was nonchalant.

Lili gritted her teeth. She needed to behave the same as he, even if it meant swallowing down her feelings until she choked on them.

"Where would they set up?" Math said.

"Ieuan would know better than I," Lili said, "but I've just come that way. The English will assume, as I did, that you'd ride down this road, won't they?"

"How else?" Math said. "This is the quickest way and our company would be moving fast, unsuspecting of danger. Or so the English would hope."

"The road narrows between two hills about a mile and a half to the north of the Wye River," Lili said. "Both sides of the road are tree-covered as well."

"I know the place," Math said.

Dafydd grunted. "So do I. My father and I spent many days surveying the roads around Buellt Castle. He almost died here, you know. He has made a study of good ambush sites—here and everywhere he travels when he has the time—and has used them himself with great effectiveness."

"Your father is a brilliant tactician, my lord," Math said.

Lili caught the look Dafydd shot his brother-in-law, and despite her earlier assumptions about his state of mind, there was no mistaking what his expression said—something like, *I don't want to hear it.* At the same time, Math left unspoken

50

what was plain on his face, namely, *I'm not going to deny what is the truth* or maybe *when are you going to work things out with your father?*

"I know," was all Dafydd said.

And what did Dafydd and Llywelyn have to work out, but *her*? Lili hated that. She hated that she'd been the cause of discord between Dafydd and Llywelyn, which is why she'd sent Dafydd away in the first place. It didn't seem to have changed things, however. If anything, they appeared worse. Maybe Dafydd blamed his father for Lili's actions, rather than Lili herself.

"We should split up as you suggested," Math said. "But do it now."

"I will lead fifteen men down the main road to Buellt," Dafydd said, "which seems to me the smallest number of riders that the English might expect to accompany me. The rest of you take to the fields and woods on either side of the road. Don't get too far from me because I need to hear your horn if you come upon the English unexpectedly."

"It's putting you at unnecessary risk," Math said.

"Is it?" Dafydd said. "I don't think so. We have to sell them on the idea that we are unprepared and unwarned." A sheepish look crossed his face. "It *would* be better to find them before they attack us."

"And Lili?" Math said.

"I can fight," Lili said.

Dafydd pursed his lips and Lili thought that he was going to deny her request, but then he nodded. "We'll find you some high ground." And then he grinned. "You can shoot anyone who gets close to me."

"Yes, my lord," Lili said.

The company did as Dafydd suggested, moving within half a mile of the spot that Lili had indicated. Owain took one group into the fields to the east, circling around a great tumulus that rose up beside the road, and Math directed his men to the west, probing ever further forward.

Dafydd took the remaining men, with Lili still behind him, at a walk, straight down the road. He didn't speak and Lili didn't interrupt his concentration. What might be coming at them had all of his men on edge. One of the younger soldiers in his company, who looked no older than Lili, appeared close to puking.

William, Bohun's son, rode at Dafydd's right flank. Lili glanced at him and he caught her eye. Though Dafydd didn't look around and see their exchange, he seemed to have eyes in the back of his head. "If anything happens, William, you break for the trees," he said. "At the very least, ride back the way we came."

"I am not worried, my lord," William said.

"I am," Dafydd said. "None of this feels right."

They reached the possible ambush site with no sign of the English—or Math and Owain, for that matter. Then a scout galloped up the road towards them and reined his horse in front of Dafydd. "Nothing, my lord," the man said. "We've been all through the area, almost to the ford of the Wye."

Dafydd pulled up too and waited. They were only a mile from Buellt Castle now. Finally, the rest of his company returned. Math shook his head, agreeing with the scout's initial report. "Nothing."

"I guess I was wrong," Lili said. "I've wasted most of the day for you. You could have been halfway to Brecon by now."

Dafydd's face had fallen into grim lines. "We'll see. I don't like that you were wrong because what you said felt right to me." He jerked his chin at Math. "Something still isn't okay about this."

"We saw no one, Dafydd," Math said.

"Not where we thought they might set up, but what about at the ford? It's close to the castle. They can't see us yet, but once we crest that rise"—Dafydd gestured to a spot a quarter of a mile ahead of them—"we'll be within sight of Buellt's towers. Take your men off the road, back the way you came, but ride all the way to the river this time. A path parallels it. Take it east. We'll meet on the north bank, just before we cross the ford. I'll give you a short head start."

Math bowed, not questioning Dafydd's decision, gathered his men, and departed. Dafydd pulled out his water skin and drank long from it, before passing it to Lili. "Drink the rest. If it comes to a fight, you won't be sorry you did."

Lili drank it as he asked, feeling as she did so that she was out of her depth. If no English waited at the ford, would Dafydd try to take the castle back? Lili thought of her brother's men who'd made up the Welsh garrison—good men, many of them—and felt sick to her stomach. How many were dead on Gethin's orders?

Dafydd got his men moving again, in good order but riding fast. Lili held onto him tightly as the wooded hills flashed by. Dafydd's hand went to hers one more time. "A moving horse is harder to hit than a walking one," was all he said, "and I still don't feel right about this."

They rode around another hill that loomed on their left, only half a mile from the ford, and galloped through a flatter, grassy area that led down to the river. Sunlight played on the bright water, which splashed over the smooth stones of the ford.

Lili sensed movement ahead of them before her eyes really knew what they were seeing. Her heart caught in her throat, but it was only Math's company riding among the trees. They raced east along the path beside the river, and then turned north to meet the rest of Dafydd's *teulu* which was by now only fifty yards from the ford. Just as the hooves of Math's horse hit the road, Dafydd threw out a hand and reined in. Cadfarch danced sideways, his men bunched up behind him—and the ditches and trees on both sides of the road exploded with English soldiers.

"I knew it!" Dafydd pointed his sword at the sky as a signal to his men, and urged Cadfarch forward. Four English soldiers, their cloaks and helms decorated with tufts of grass and twigs with which they'd used to hide their presence, had timed their attack exactly wrong. The horse plowed through them. Dafydd's sword rose and fell while Lili, her cheek pressed to Dafydd's back, shrunk down as much as possible so as not to hinder him with a distracting movement.

"Charge!"

More Englishmen on horseback burst from the trees to their left. Dafydd didn't hesitate—or at least Cadfarch didn't, swinging wide to the right and barreling through another three Englishmen who were attempting to fight on foot. The horse leapt off the road and into the trees, chasing down a fourth man who'd turned to run away.

Lili forced her eyes to open wide instead of squeezing them shut as was her impulse. She held her knife in her left hand, prepared to protect their left side if need be. She peeked from under Dafydd's arm to see Math direct his men toward the English cavalry who had circled through a field to the west and were now coming at them from the north. Neither group had the advantage of higher ground, but Math's men had more momentum—and numbers—on their side. They crashed into the English line with devastating effect, though men and horses on both sides went down. Dafydd gripped his bloody sword in his right hand and held the reins in his left. His shield hung uselessly from a strap near her left leg.

Dafydd curved back to the road, by now only ten yards from the ford, and swung Cadfarch around to face north. Half a dozen of his men had come with him, but an equal number had been unhorsed and the road in front of them was strewn with the dead and dying. Lili had seen a battle when they'd taken Painscastle, but hadn't known what it was like from the back of a horse. She'd never felt the fear of holding onto the man she loved while he fought, praying that he wouldn't be struck down with her arms around him.

"It should never have come to this!" Dafydd's words carried above the sound of the river behind them. He urged Cadfarch back towards the center of the road, driving towards an English solder who held a Welsh man-at-arms on the ground and was about to thrust a sword through his belly. Dafydd swung his sword and decapitated the man.

In the half a heartbeat it took for the man to die, a spray of blood coated Dafydd, the horse, and Lili. Even as it arced in the air towards her, Lili shrieked and tried to cover her eyes.

"Sorry."

That one word from Dafydd left Lili gasping. It was so matter-of-fact and yet told her that he wished she hadn't seen that; he wished he hadn't had to kill the man right in front of her.

Lili didn't say, "it's okay," though the words were on the tip of her tongue. They would be a lie, however, and she was done lying to Dafydd, even about this. Instead, she clutched her arms more tightly about his waist and pressed her forehead into his back. The rough wool of his cloak, over the hard metal of his mail armor, scraped at her skin. It felt good to feel something besides her inward horror.

Dafydd cleared his throat. "It's over."

Lili still didn't want to look. Dafydd changed direction and trotted Cadfarch to the edge of the road, to where Math knelt, holding the hand of a fallen soldier. It was Owain, Dafydd's captain, wounded to death. Lili tasted ash and she swallowed hard for the hundredth time, trying not to completely fall apart in a storm of tears.

"Let me down, Dafydd," Lili said.

He gave her his elbow to hold onto. He held still, solid as a rock, as she slid off Cadfarch, and then Dafydd dismounted too. He crouched beside Owain and took his hand.

"My lord." A trickle of blood spilled from the corner of his mouth. "I failed—"

"Shh," Dafydd said. "All is well. You did not fail—neither me nor yourself."

"The English—"

"Are defeated," Dafydd said.

Owain closed his eyes. His chest rose and fell once, and then not again.

Dafydd gazed down at Owain for a count of ten and then got to his feet. He turned to Math. "Where's William?"

Math pointed with his chin towards the river. "I left him in a tree near the water."

"I'll see to him," Lili said, glad for something—anything—to do other than look at the dead men on the ground.

Only a few hours earlier, she'd forded the Wye River by herself and walked north along this very road. A lifetime ago. Lili brushed back the tears that had formed in her eyes at Owain's death. She hadn't even known the man, but that death should come to any of them ... Lili spun on one heel, wanting to run away, wanting to be anywhere but where she was.

Instead, she ran to the tree Math had indicated. William, however, wasn't in it. He leaned against the trunk on the far side, looking away from the battle towards Buellt, though the trees along both banks screened him from the castle's towers. His face was very white, and he stared straight ahead, unseeing. A dead man lay on the ground at his feet.

Lili halted beside him. He was an inch taller than she, and about the same weight. Just a twelve year old boy—with a bloody sword in his hand. Lili reached out and pried his fingers from the hilt. "This is your doing?"

"Yes." William's voice held neither anguish nor pride. It was cold and matter-of-fact. "I didn't mean to."

"Where did you get the sword?"

"My father gave it to me before we came to Wales. He said if I was to be any kind of squire to the Prince of Wales, I'd better act the part."

Lili thought he was awfully young for a sword, and to be in a battle, but she'd heard the same about herself three years ago (more because she was a girl, of course, than because she was only fifteen).

"I stayed in the tree for most of it, but then one of the English riders left the field, fleeing towards me. I-I-I dropped out of the tree right onto him. He hit the ground and ..." William gestured at the body. "I killed him."

"He would have warned the garrison at Buellt of what had happened," Lili said. "You did Prince Dafydd a great service."

Dafydd came up behind Lili. She felt him hover behind her, hesitating, and then both hands dropped onto her shoulders. He squeezed once and then moved towards William, who was bent at the waist, staring at the ground.

"Let it out, if it's going to come out," Dafydd said. "There's a first time for everyone."

William didn't vomit, though, but breathed in deeply through his nose. He straightened and leaned back against the tree. "I don't need to be sick. I'm fine."

"Glad to hear it." Dafydd's lips actually quirked. "See if you can make yourself useful among the wounded. We're not done. We must take Buellt Castle back from the traitors who hold it."

William nodded. He held out his hand for his sword, and when Lili gave it to him, he walked stiff-legged back towards the road and the rest of the men. Lili turned to watch him go, and then found Dafydd's arms slipping around her waist.

Lili couldn't make herself protest aloud or even pull away. She wanted to hold herself stiff. She *tried* to, but she found herself, leaning into him. She was *so* tired all of a sudden, it was an effort to keep her knees from sagging and making him bear all her weight. *She* hadn't done anything but ride pillion behind Dafydd. That any of these men remained upright—or could speak in a level tone without crying—was incredible to Lili.

Yet she forced herself to copy them, to not give in to her grief either. They had more work to do today. Behind her, Dafydd sighed. She felt his lips brush her hair, and then he released her. "We must move."

Lili fell into step beside him and they headed to where Math had gathered the surviving men.

"What are you going to do now?" Lili said.

"They came at us with thirty men," Math said. "Mortimer's men, though a few may have been from Buellt's garrison."

"Edmund Mortimer wants Buellt back," Lili said.

"Obviously," Dafydd said. And then touched her hand—just with one finger—but it eased the sting of his sarcasm, telling Lili that it wasn't directed at her. "Mortimer has taken the field in earnest."

"Here, he has, certainly," Lili said. "But what of Bigod, Kirby, or Vere?"

Dafydd shook his head. "I wouldn't have expected those three to league with Mortimer. They're not natural conspirators."

"Why not?" Lili stopped beside William, who was carefully cleaning the blood from his sword with the edge of a dead Englishman's cloak.

"Because the use of a sword has never come naturally to Edmund Mortimer," Dafydd said. "As a second son, he was meant for the Church and was advancing through the ranks. He's an Oxford scholar. Unlike his older and younger brothers, he's had to fight for the respect of the other barons, more than he's had to fight actual battles."

"King Edward, before he died, had delayed confirming him in his holdings because of it," William said. And then blinked. "I apologize, my lord, for interrupting."

"Apology accepted," Dafydd said, "though it is unnecessary. You are correct in your assessment." Dafydd dropped a hand onto William's shoulder. "Your father has taught you well. He would be proud of you."

5

Math

"**W**hat do we do with the dead?" Math toed the body of the closest Englishman and then glanced at his brother-in-law, who stared down at another body, his hands on his hips.

"Strip the bodies of the dead Englishmen and move them off the road," Dafydd said. "Put the armor, weapons, and other gear in a pile so we can sort through it. Send others to gather the horses, all that we can find."

"And our dead?" Lili said.

Dafydd sighed and ran his hand through his hair. He'd tossed his helmet near where he'd picketed Cadfarch; like Math, he wore it only when he had to. "We'll bury them as best we can. It's the wounded that concern me most."

"We've been doing our best, Gruffydd and I." Lili stood and stretched, and then waved a hand to indicate a man on the other side of the road, a member of Dafydd's guard whom the Jewish doctor, Aaron, had trained. William still knelt next to the man Lili had been treating, holding his hand. She'd bandaged the soldier's leg from ankle to knee.

Math observed her out of the corner of his eye. He couldn't help but notice that after they'd pushed through their initial hesitancy, she and Dafydd had stopped circling around each other. He didn't know if they'd come to a true accord during their ride, or an unspoken one. He hoped that the days of silence might finally be over. It had been a hard two months for Dafydd—and almost as hard on those he loved, who'd had to put up with his moods and his startlingly grim sense of humor.

When Math and Anna had been courting, Anna had never sent him away like Lili had Dafydd, but she'd held him at arm's length for a long while. It had taken months of patient work on his part to get Anna to talk to him about anything important. Fortunately, it had taken far less long for her to admit that she loved him.

"Now that the English numbers are reduced," Math said, "do we have a plan for taking the castle?"

"I never liked the place," Lili said. "No matter how long I stay there, it could never be home. We could let them keep it."

Dafydd smirked. "Uh ... I don't think my father would take kindly to that notion. No." He shook his head. "We have to go in and get it."

"What about gathering reinforcements first?" Lili said. "Our numbers are reduced."

Math took in a breath and let it out. When the fight began, they'd outnumbered their English attackers. Subsequently, they'd lost fewer than a dozen men; fewer than they might have if Dafydd had been less wary. Math told himself to remember this day the next time he felt a sick pit in his stomach for no clear reason. He'd gone along with Dafydd's orders willingly enough, since he'd grown to trust his brother-in-law, but Dafydd's fears had been premonition only. Without Dafydd's prescience, this could have been *much* worse.

"We continue to have the advantage." Dafydd gestured with one hand to the dead in the road. "Even if it might not seem like it."

"In numbers, surely," Math said. "If Lili's estimation is correct, the English used up most of their strength in this ambush. But we will be riding into a second trap if we go into Buellt."

"A trap of our making, not theirs," Dafydd said.

"How so?" Math said, and then his breath caught because he *knew* what Dafydd was thinking and it shook him. He stepped closer and lowered his voice. "You mean to deceive the garrison? You mean to ride into Buellt Castle as Englishmen?"

"Victorious Englishmen at that." Dafydd's blue eyes lit with an unexpected amusement. "All's fair in love and war."

Math pursed his lips. "I've not heard that phrase before."

Dafydd shrugged. "Some English guy said it, a couple of hundred years from now. I don't know that I always agree with his sentiment, especially about the love part. But war—"

Math found himself nodding. "War is something different. We Welsh, for all our disloyalty and fighting among ourselves, haven't been as ruthless as we've needed to be. We haven't fought the Normans with every tool at our disposal or we would have done better against them sooner."

"I don't understand what you're proposing," Lili said.

Dafydd looked down at her. "We ride into Buellt dressed as the English who attacked us, except for me."

"Why except for you?" Lili said.

"Because the English should look victorious," Dafydd said.

And then the rest of Dafydd's plan dawned on Math. "You will ride to the castle as yourself, with your hands tied in front of you, or seemingly so? While our counterparts on the battlements congratulate themselves on their total victory, we enter the bailey and catch them by surprise."

Dafydd canted his head. "As you say."

"What you're suggesting is a Norman trick," Lili said.

"It is indeed," Dafydd said.

"Your father might not approve," Math said.

"He is not here," Dafydd said. "And I see no reason why it shouldn't become a Welsh trick. Do you know what they say where I was born when someone reneges on a bet or a deal?"

Math's eyes narrowed. He didn't think he wanted to know.

"You *welshed* on me!" Dafydd said. "I never thought about the origin of the phrase until I came here. These Normans—and their Saxon subjects—have been belittling us for centuries. If my father had died at Cilmeri, we would have no recourse but to take it. I don't mind fulfilling Norman expectations if it means victory."

Math nodded, a quick jerk of his head, and turned to make disposition of the men. They had eight men dead and four seriously wounded, leaving him thirty-six soldiers (plus himself, Lili, Dafydd, and William) who could still fight. Each man wore an identical grim set to his jaw. In turn, they'd killed half of the English fighters, wounded or captured the rest, leaving only a handful left in the garrison at Buellt.

This was still on the condition that Lili had been right about the initial English numbers, and assuming the Welsh defenders hadn't all betrayed their country and joined the English side. Thirty-six versus half a dozen sounded like good odds to him. Maybe Dafydd wasn't so reckless after all.

"We must avenge Owain," Evan, one of Dafydd's men-at-arms, said.

"But with cool heads," Math said.

Evan glared at him, and then took in a deep breath and let it out. "Yes, my lord."

"When we rode from Dinas Bran, our minds were intent on what faced us in the south," Math said. "None of this did we plan or think would happen—"

"And that is my fault." Dafydd had come up silently behind Math. "I led you into an ambush. Even if we took steps to prepare for it, Owain's death is on me, not you."

"That isn't true, my lord," Math said. "We were the ones sent to scout the road. Why we didn't find them, I don't know ..." he shook his head.

"The English are often clever," Dafydd said. "Remember that."

Heads nodded all around.

Dafydd rested a hand on Evan's shoulder. "Which is why we are going to be cleverer than they are this time." Dafydd took in the gaze of each of his men. "Some of you will not like what comes next, for there is no honor in it."

Several men grumbled, but one spoke up: "No honor in dying on an *English* sword."

"Are we going to wear the Mortimer tunics, my lord?" Evan said. "It would allow us to trick the English guards into letting us in the castle."

Math fastened his attention on Evan. He hadn't taken much note of him before. He was a newcomer to Dafydd's *teulu*, in his late twenties and thus middle-aged for a soldier, though that meant he was the same age as Math himself. He had come from Ceredigion, the son of one of Math's many uncles on his father's side.

"That is exactly what we're going to do," Dafydd said.

"Good," Evan said. "But you should not dress as we do. To better deceive the garrison, you should ride as our captive."

Dafydd eyed him carefully.

Misreading Dafydd's look, Evan hastily backtracked. "No dishonor meant to you, my lord."

"None taken," Dafydd said. "That was exactly my plan."

Evan rocked back and forth on the balls of his toes, a look of satisfaction on his face. He bowed his head. "It could work, my lord, but it will be dangerous."

"Every day we stand in defiance of England is a dangerous day," Dafydd said.

"See that you are properly fitted out," Math said to Evan, effectively anointing him as a leader. "Too bad we don't have time to grow beards."

When the men had turned to their respective tasks, Dafydd gripped Math's arm. "Come with me. One of the Welsh traitors is in good enough condition for us to talk to."

Math turned to see where Dafydd pointed. A former member of Buellt's garrison sat with his back against a tree, ten feet off the road, bleeding from a long gash to the inner thigh. It looked serious enough that he might not live. *And he might not live anyway, if Dafydd decides that he has enough captive English in Wales already, and chooses to leave no witnesses to this battle.* Math put that thought aside. His brother-in-law would do what he had to do. Princes sometimes didn't have the luxury of mercy.

Her hands on her hips, Lili stood in front of the man, with William again beside her. Math's lips quirked to see her small figure confronting the much larger traitor, for all that he lay grievously wounded on the ground.

"Why would you do this?" Lili's voice carried across the whole of the battlefield.

The man visibly shrugged. "Coin."

"But *why*?" And this time Math heard anguish in her voice.

Dafydd approached her from behind and put a hand to each of her upper arms. "It's okay, Lili," he said. "Let me handle this."

Lili held herself stiff, and then her shoulders sagged. She allowed Dafydd to turn her away. Once Dafydd released her, however, she straightened her shoulders and marched straight towards Math. She had the look of a woman on a mission.

"You may not leave his side," she said. "Don't let him do anything he'll regret later."

"Whose side?" Math said. "Dafydd's?"

Lili nodded. She lowered her voice. "I have never seen him this angry."

Math had bent his head to look into her face and now lifted his gaze to study the back of Dafydd's head. He would have said Dafydd was determined, but the rigid set to his shoulders told him that Lili might be right. Dafydd's gentleness had been for Lili only.

Math nodded. "I wouldn't have left him anyway. See what you can do with the rest of the wounded."

"Come, William." Lili stepped away, leaving Math to do as he promised. He walked up to stand beside Dafydd, folded his hands behind his back, and let Dafydd get on with it.

"How much did your captain pay you?" Dafydd said.

"Enough," the man said. "Or so I thought at the time. My lord—" He winced and shifted, pain in his face. "A bandage ... please ... I'm bleeding out."

"I haven't yet decided to let you live," Dafydd said. "This suits me for now."

The man gaped at Dafydd. "But, my lord—"

"Am I your lord?" Dafydd said. "Because last I saw, you were among a company of men set on killing me."

The man shook his head. "Our intent was to capture, not kill."

"Your intent was to kill his companions, then," Math said.

Dafydd's jaw bulged. "That makes it so much better."

"What kind of plan did you have for keeping the Prince alive?" Math said. "Your aim was deadly."

"And why do you say, *capture*?" Dafydd said. "For what purpose?"

The man's mouth was open and his breathing shallow. "Ransom, I think. The Normans hoped to exchange you for lands in the south."

"Who gave you your orders?" Dafydd said.

The man shrugged and then grimaced in pain. "The English commander."

"And who is *his* commander? One of the Mortimers?" Dafydd said.

The man jerked his head, neither in denial nor agreement

Math leaned in. "You don't know? You wear Mortimer colors."

"Gethin said it was better that way. We couldn't wear King Llywelyn's! Better to unite under one banner."

"Mortimer's," Math said.

Again the jerk of the head. "I didn't get the impression that a Mortimer leads the Norman assault."

"Then who does?" Dafydd said.

"Norman scum are all the same to me."

"Yet you took their money to betray your King," Math said.

"A man can't eat loyalty."

"And Lord Ieuan starved you, did he?" Math said.

But the man didn't answer. He was dead.

6

25 August 1288
North of Buellt

Lili

Lili had never experienced a day like this before. She clenched the reins of her horse—it had belonged to one of Dafydd's men who would never need it again—and gritted her teeth. She needed to damp down all emotion, in hopes of also controlling her fear. She could not, however, deny the truth. She was *scared*.

She'd been a foolish girl three years ago when she'd fought in the ranks of archers at the battle of Painscastle. She'd thought herself composed and competent at the time, but she hadn't known anything about war. She hadn't known anything about men either, or the way the world worked, or why what she wanted might not be hers for the having. King Llywelyn had undermined her security in his denial of her marriage to

Dafydd. And the ambush? These last hours had destroyed whatever certainty remained.

As she waited for the men to get themselves in order, her thoughts went to her men. How did Dafydd and Ieuan live with the knowledge that at any moment, they might be required to kill another person by their own hand? She hadn't known what it was like. She'd had no real idea of what they faced every time they rode away from the safety of their castle.

Worse, *Dafydd had made a mistake.*

He'd sent Math down a different path to the ford because he didn't trust the road before him. He'd had an inkling of what might happen, and yet ... he had still underestimated his opponent. She wasn't used to thinking about Dafydd as fallible. On one hand, it made him more accessible, but on the other hand, it made the future more terrifying. From now on, every time Dafydd rode out of the castle while she watched from the battlements, she had to let him go with the knowledge that he could make mistakes.

"You will stay between Dai and Evan the whole time," Dafydd said.

"Yes, Dafydd," Lili said, for once having no intention of doing anything but what he suggested. She didn't have a sword and she'd use her bow if she could, but it wasn't a good weapon for close work, which is what they'd face in the bailey of the castle.

They'd left the surviving English cavalry behind at the ford, alive and bandaged, but hobbled. War among the Normans in their own country—Normandy—had always been a matter of capturing prisoners for ransom. Everyone knew that. But this war was about survival. If that meant Dafydd ordered the death of Englishmen who might have otherwise lived to fight again, no Welshman would have thought less of him. But he hadn't, and Lili, for one, was glad.

They crossed the Wye River at the ford and came out of the trees in good order. Dafydd had set them up as if they were English cavalry, which meant that the men carrying pole arms—spears rather than the heavier lances in this case—led the company, not Dafydd and Math. It probably made sense, though Lili heard some of the men mumbling about how it was just like the Norman lords to lead from the rear instead of the front as God intended.

As they cantered towards Buellt Castle, Lili's heart rose into her throat. The big double gatehouse which King Llywelyn had rebuilt loomed above them and they followed the road directly towards it, brazening out their deception. All of the men wore the Mortimer tunics and had their helms drawn over their faces. With their losses, and a few men left behind to watch over the English prisoners, Dafydd's company resembled the English force in number—before the ambush, that is.

The lead rider lifted a hand to the guard on the battlement. Without any hesitation, the guard waved them forward and signaled to the men below to ratchet up the portcullis. Math kept Dafydd close to him. Dafydd's head was bare and his hands were tied in front of him. As he approached the gatehouse, the men on the battlements cheered.

Once inside the bailey, Dafydd gave the English captain a chance to approach his horse, waiting through a long count of ten, and giving his entire company the opportunity to pass through the gate and into the bailey. Lili hung back, trying not to draw attention to herself amidst the much larger men. Under all this armor, she could pass for a youth, and men generally saw what they expected to see. The Englishmen who'd taken over Buellt didn't expect to see a woman among the riders, so they didn't see one.

"I count six," Lili said to Evan under her breath.

"Against thirty," Evan said. "This should be quick. We might come out of this in one piece. The key is not to be the lone casualty."

If the defenders had been paying closer attention, they should have seen that Dafydd's company spread themselves evenly throughout the cramped outer bailey, which was barely large enough to contain the thirty Welsh cavalry. The bailey remained as it had been when Lili had left that morning, encompassed by a curtain wall and accessed through the twin-towered gatehouse they'd just come through. Beyond, a motte supported a great round keep, which was defended by a small masonry wall and six towers. From the intact state of the defenses, the Welsh garrison had put up no resistance.

It seemed to Lili that even the breeze held its breath as the company reined in. The English captain came to a halt at Dafydd's stirrup. "So this is the Welsh pup? He doesn't look like much."

This had to be sheer bravado because he couldn't have been more wrong. Dafydd didn't wear his helm or his sword, but he was half a foot taller than the captain, broader, and while his face still bore a hint of the childish roundness of youth, his blue eyes held a steely glint as he glared down at the man. An Englishman underestimated Dafydd at his peril.

Fortunately, most of Dafydd's men didn't understand English or they would have risen as one against the captain. Math would not have been able to stop them. As it was, Dafydd bent forward and rested an elbow on his knee. "All is not what it seems." Dafydd straightened, dropped the ropes that he'd been holding around his wrists, and with a casual flick of his ankle, caught the captain underneath his chin with the toe of his boot.

The captain went down, a gasp of stunned silence encompassed the garrison, and then everything happened at once, like one of those explosions that took down the wall at Painscastle during the previous war. A heartbeat after the captain hit the ground, Dafydd's men were off their horses. Half ran as fast as they could towards the gatehouse that led to the keep, which had been left open, as was normal in the hustle and bustle of daily life. One of the guardsmen on the wall had his mouth open, gazing at the running men as if each had grown two heads. None of his fellows reacted any more quickly. By the time they did, the rest of Dafydd's men had targeted all the members of the garrison they could see.

Because a horse didn't provide a stable platform for Lili to bend her bow, Dafydd had instructed her to find a piece of higher ground and watch the roofs for archers bringing their bows to bear on his men. She dismounted and ran to a stump of wood, rising two feet above the ground, designed as a stand for chopping wood. It would allow her to see above the men in the bailey.

She craned her neck towards the top of the gatehouse and then ran her eyes along the battlements. A shout from Dafydd had her swinging around to look to where he pointed: an archer had appeared at the top of the keep. She raised her bow, her arrow already pressed into it, but the other archer got his shot off first.

An arrow rammed into her shoulder, throwing her backwards off the stump. The back of her head slammed into the packed earth of the courtyard and the force of the fall knocked all the air from her lungs. She lay as she'd fallen, stunned, her limbs akimbo. *Was this dying?* Lili's ears rang inside her head. All she could see was sky, the edge of the stable roof, and the shaft sticking up from her right shoulder.

She felt no pain as of yet, but stars danced before her eyes and her vision blackened around the edges.

"Lili!" Dafydd fell to his knees beside her. She turned her head to look at him, blinked hard, still confused as to why her head hurt more than her shoulder. She brought up a hand and touched the point where the shaft had gone in, feeling along it to the feathered end. Her hand came away clean. "There's no blood. Why?"

"Just lie still." Dafydd felt all around her shoulders and arms, his fingers ending up at the pulse at her throat. "Does your shoulder hurt?"

"That's the part that's confusing me," Lili said. "It feels okay, but I can't lift up my body." Lili tried again to roll onto her side, wanting to push to her knees, but she couldn't move more than a hair's-breadth. She fell back.

"What in the world—?" And then, incongruously, Dafydd laughed. Lili gazed at him in amazement, but a grin split his face from ear to ear. He felt under her shoulder where it met the dirt of the bailey. "The arrow has you pinned." He tugged and wiggled at the shaft. Then he enveloped her in an embrace, his arms between her and the dirt at her back. "Hold on." He lifted her up with a jerk.

"Ow!" Lili had been unprepared for the sudden movement. She put a hand to the back of her head and came away with blood. She stared at her fingers and then at Dafydd.

"But—" She glanced at the arrow, sticking out of her shoulder. She still couldn't feel it.

"The arrow didn't touch you." Dafydd tucked his hands under her armpits and helped her rise to her feet. He sat her on the stump, on which she'd been standing earlier. While Dafydd had been occupied with Lili, Dafydd's men had subdued the garrison. No wounded Welshmen lay on the ground.

Math had taken charge. "Get them against the wall!" Math glanced to Dafydd, who nodded that he should continue.

"It looks like Math has this well in hand," Dafydd said. "Let's get your armor off you."

"Are you sure?" Lili said.

Dafydd's looked at her warily. "What do you mean?"

"In coming to my aid, you could have sacrificed your own men!"

Dafydd stopped in the act of working at the buckle that held the top edge of the leather armor together. "The English never had much of a chance. The numbers were too uneven, exactly how I like it."

Two of Dafydd's men passed close by, herding a member of the garrison towards curtain wall. He'd been stripped of weaponry and his hands were tied behind his back. Two of the six Englishmen in the bailey were down, but four faced the wall, and soon three others, who'd been found asleep in the barracks, joined their fellows, along with the English captain. The craft workers and servants were gathered in the center of the bailey, unharmed.

"That's why you don't like it when I fight beside you," Lili said. "I distract you."

Dafydd didn't answer, just continued to work at the rest of the buckles that ran down Lili's side and held the armor on her. She raised her arms and he lifted it over her head. Because all of the mail had been too heavy and far too big for her, Dafydd had assigned her an elaborate boiled leather cuirass from one of the dead. It had included leather caps for her shoulders and upper arms. Lili hadn't wanted to wear it at all, but Dafydd had insisted that she not enter Buellt unprotected. If she'd refused, he would have left her to guard the prisoners.

When Dafydd had put the armor on her, he had laughed and commented that she 'looked like a football player'. *Whatever that meant.* She hadn't tasked him with an explanation at the time.

Dafydd snapped the shaft in half and pulled out the pieces. Together, they studied the hole the arrow had punched through the armor. "I must have turned just as he shot," Lili said. "The arrow got through the armor, but at an angle, and then it just kept going through empty air, until it reached the other side." She wiggled her finger in the hole.

"It was a very near thing." Dafydd's voice was calm but it had an edge to it and he held his jaw tightly.

81

"Did—did someone else get him?" Lili said.

Dafydd nodded. "One of the men I sent into the keep came out on the wall just as the archer loosed a second shot. My man ran him through."

Lili bit her lip. Dafydd looked into her face and then ran a finger along the line of her jaw. "Are you really okay?"

"Yes."

His teeth clenched again and he glanced towards Math. Lili recognized what that look meant. For all his genuine concern for her, she was right in what she'd said. He needed not to worry about her. He needed to focus on what he was going to do now that he'd taken the castle. That was something he couldn't leave entirely to Math.

"They need you," she said. "Honestly, I'm fine."

Dafydd nodded and stood, and then turned to face Evan and Math as they approached. "What's the cost?" he said.

"Several of our men are injured, though not severely," Math said. "Two dead among the English garrison."

"Bring me one of the prisoners," Dafydd said.

Math bowed, perhaps recognizing the intensity in Dafydd, too, and that in this moment, Dafydd was his commander, not his brother-in-law. He returned with one of the Welshmen.

"Tell me your name," Dafydd said.

"I am a loyal Welshman, my lord, Rhys ap Gruffydd." The man bowed low.

"If you are loyal, how is it you came to fight for the Normans?" Dafydd said.

"By pretending disloyalty to you, I stayed free. I couldn't help my countrymen if I was in prison with them."

Dafydd thought about that for a few moments, neither accepting nor dismissing. It might even be true. The man didn't shift from foot to foot, nor look away as if he was nervous, but kept his gaze on Dafydd.

"Who let the English in?" Dafydd said.

"The captain of the garrison, Gethin."

"Who bribed him?"

"I couldn't say, my lord—"

Dafydd crowded into Rhys and grasped him by his coat to jerk him closer. As Dafydd was eight inches taller than he, the man's toes barely touched the ground. "Tell me who?"

The man sputtered and spit, unable to get any words out.

"Who! One of the Mortimers?" Dafydd said.

"N-n-no, my lord," Rhys said. "I don't think so."

"Why, then, do the English soldiers wear these colors?"

"D-d-disguise." Rhys held himself very still, without struggling, which was brave of him, given that Lili herself felt like cowering before Dafydd's wrath. This was a side of him she hadn't ever seen, but then, she'd not fought beside him in the last three years. At Painscastle, their victory had been so lopsided and predestined, he'd not shown anger.

Dafydd glared at the man and settled him back on his feet, but didn't let go of his coat. "So you do know more."

"Only guesses, my lord, from some of the things the soldiers said."

"For the last time, if not one of the Mortimers, then who?"

"Gilbert de Clare."

Dafydd released Rhys without warning and he staggered backwards, stumbling on an errant stone that caught under his heel. He would have fallen if Evan hadn't grasped him underneath the arm.

Dafydd spun towards Math. "You know what? I don't care why they did what they did. I don't even care who ordered it. Just lock them up, as securely as you can. We have bigger fish to fry."

"But, my lord—please—" Rhys said.

Dafydd cut off Rhys with a bark. "I don't have time to determine the truth." With a nod from Dafydd, Evan hauled Rhys towards the other prisoners.

"I will send men to bring in the Englishmen from the ford," Math said. "They can stay with their brothers in the cells beneath the barracks."

"Do it," Dafydd said. "I'd prefer not to kill them, even if some might call me weak for staying my hand."

Math's eyes gleamed. "I don't think you have any need to worry about that, my lord."

84

Weak! Lili shook her head too. If anything, Dafydd had become too hard. Dafydd tipped his chin towards the men in his *teulu.* "Whom should we leave in charge? I miss Owain already."

"Evan—" Math began.

"You note his skill and measured thinking too?" Dafydd shook his head. "He's not ready yet. Or perhaps, I'm not ready to ride without him."

"I wish I'd brought more of my men," Math said, "but I left ten to garrison Dinas Bran and others to ride with Anna, thinking it better not to leave the north undefended."

"We'll have to leave at least another ten here," Dafydd said. "As those loyal to us recover, they can augment the garrison. We can't risk any of the English soldiers overpowering the guards and escaping. Or worse, retaking the castle."

"Fifty becomes thirty becomes twenty," Math said.

"Twenty will have to be enough," Dafydd said. "We ride through the night to Brecon Castle."

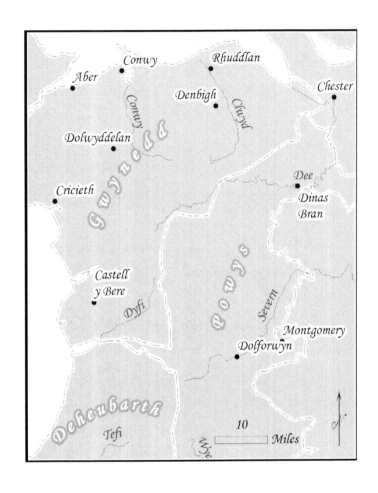

7

Anna

"How much farther?" Cadell wiggled on Anna's lap.

"Not far." Her mood lifting, Anna pointed through the trees to the looming bulk of Dolforwyn Castle, the first stop in their journey. She'd let Math go with David without protest, but had wrung from him permission to travel to Caerphilly with Cadell to be with her mother and Bronwen—and Lili if Ieuan could get her to go. *She'd* want to be in the midst of the fighting, of course, but that might require her to speak to David, which so far she'd refused to do.

Anna thought the whole thing ridiculous. Papa was behaving exactly like any other king of this time, which was to say, putting his country above the welfare of his son. *This* son, however, wasn't of this time and never would be. He wanted

Lili. Bronwen had laughingly described a conversation she'd had with her graduate school adviser, once upon a time, about the difference between *determined, stubborn, and pig-headed.* As far as Anna was concerned, both David and Papa were skating very close to the latter.

Not that she couldn't be pretty stubborn herself. Math had been reluctant to allow her to leave Dinas Bran with the onset of hostilities looming. Any loving husband, medieval or modern, would have felt the same way. But Math and Anna had been married for five years now, and Anna had pushed him into being less stubbornly protective than Papa still appeared to be. Besides which, Caerphilly was impregnable. Bohun had been sure that they had a week before Clare would have his forces together enough to begin his assault on their southern borders. That was plenty of time to reach it. She and Cadell could be safer there than at Dinas Bran.

Not that the distances between any two points were ever very great in Wales. The entire country was all of one hundred and forty miles long, and maybe fifty wide. The roads weren't always direct, however, and it was usually easier to skirt the hills and mountains than to go over them. These were the same mountains that had allowed the Welsh to maintain their independence for the last two hundred years. As it turned out, guerilla warfare wasn't invented by Swamp Fox Marion in the American Revolution, like she'd been taught in school. The Welsh hadn't invented it either, but they'd employed it for a thousand years so far, first against the Romans, then the Saxons, and now the Normans—and on occasion to great effect.

Although she thought she'd be happy to be on the road again after several months of not leaving Dinas Bran, Anna had felt unsettled from the moment they'd left the castle. Everyone in the party had felt the same way. The captain of her small company had come to her two hours ago, suggesting that they push on past the point where she might have wanted to stop, in order to sleep safe tonight at Dolforwyn Castle instead of in one of Papa's lesser holdings. He'd been nervous about how exposed they were, and that he had only ten men.

When she'd acquiesced immediately, his shoulders had sagged in relief. "Thank you, my lady," he'd said. "You have eased my mind considerably."

Now, however, even though the sun hadn't quite set (and as it was August, it wouldn't set until well after suppertime), it was time to get off this horse. Dolforwyn Castle stood on a wooded hill above the Severn valley. Papa had built it as a forward position in his territory, to overlook the Norman lordship of Montgomery which the Mortimers controlled.

The Mortimers. How Anna hated them.

It was Edmund and his younger brother, Roger, who had lured Papa into the trap at Cilmeri in December of 1282. Edmund had done it, so the story went, to prove to King Edward that he was worthy of his father's title and his lands. King Edward had withheld them for some time after the death of Edmund's father, even as the king had acknowledged the rights of Edmund's younger brother, Roger, to lands of his own.

That must have stuck in Edmund's craw, to have a younger brother in better favor with the king. At the same time, up until the death of his elder brother, Edmund's lot had fallen to the Church. Even after the brother's death, he'd remained at Oxford until his father died in the same year. Subsequently, it had been a challenge for Edmund to prove his worth as a soldier to men who'd fought in the saddle since they were fourteen.

Of course, that had been the situation in which David had found himself when he arrived in Wales and he'd done okay.

Cadell pulled out his wooden sword that Math had given him only last week and waved it at the skyline. He wore the sword in its little sheath, strapped around his waist throughout the day and had insisted on sleeping with it every night. At first, the table legs in the great hall at Dinas Bran hadn't been safe. They bore testimony to the vigorousness and enthusiasm of Cadell's assaults and his determination to master this new skill.

Watchful and ever mindful of his duties, however, Math had taken Cadell in his lap shortly after he'd given the sword to him. He'd set the weapon on the table in front of them. "A sword is a bringer of death to men," Math had said, the echo of David in his words.

Cadell was very young to understand what his father was trying to tell him, but he noted the sadness in his father's voice, and since then, had shown a greater maturity in the sword's use, though no less intensity. The table legs were safe, but every man-at-arms who walked through the great doors of the hall found himself confronted by the grim face of a three-year-old boy and a fierce, "Who are you to enter my father's domain?"

More often than not, Cadell followed this with laughter at catching yet another man unawares. And then, the man would grab a stick from the kindling pile and give Cadell the mock battle he wanted, before picking him up on one arm or throwing him over his shoulder while Cadell squealed in delight.

Cadell struggled to stand up in front of her, his feet on the saddle, but Anna clutched him tighter around the waist. "Soon. We'll stop soon."

She'd spent the last three years trying to contain her son—a child who crawled at five months, walked at nine, and spoke in complete sentences before he was eighteen months old. He was so much like David had been as a little boy, in ways that even Anna remembered, though she'd been a child herself. Meg still laughed that the best thing about David's precocity was that he understood everything you said to him. Anna would boss him around, and even at nine months, David toddled happily after her and did her bidding.

"I'll take him." One of the men at arms, Tad, rode closer. Cadell leaned towards him. "I can jump!"

Anna laughed. "No, no, no—"

"Look out!"

Ten men dressed in red and white surcoats surged onto the road from either side, swords at the ready. The horse belonging to the man-at-arms just ahead of Anna reared, dumping the unprepared rider on his seat in the road. Anna's horse, Dyfi, skittered sideways to avoid him, panicked by the uproar. Anna clutched at the reins with one hand while holding onto Cadell with the other, trying to contain him in her arms and control Dyfi at the same time.

"To arms!" Tad pulled his sword from its scabbard while his horse whinnied, trying to evade an English soldier's clutching hand. For that's who these men had to be: English. Anna would have known they weren't Welsh even without the surcoats, what with their full beards, short-cropped hair, and fringed boots.

Dyfi danced sideways and then whipped around one hundred and eighty degrees so that she faced back the way they'd come. On instinct, Anna dug in her heels, still pressing Cadell to her chest. He sent up a wail and she eased her grip. "It's okay," she said. "It's going to be okay."

Dyfi took off, heading back up the road to the north. Anna bent over the horse's neck, hanging on to the reins and

Cadell with equal intensity. She'd never become an expert horsewoman and this ride was at the limit of her skill.

"Mama! You're squishing me!"

"I know. I know. Just—"

Hooves pounded behind her, a match to her thudding heart. She chanced a look back. Two English soldiers were coming on fast. She spurred Dyfi again, would have whipped her if she thought it would do any good, but the poor creature was neither racehorse nor war horse, and couldn't maintain the speed. Even so, they held off the two soldiers for another quarter mile before the closest rider caught up with them, cursing at Anna and the horse in English. He grabbed Dyfi's bridle and forced her to slow.

"No! Let us go!" Anna kicked out at the man and Cadell did his part by swinging his little sword, nearly smacking it into Anna's arm. Cadell then brought it down hard on the soldier's fingers.

"Little devil—"

Unfortunately, the soldier didn't release the bridle and Dyfi was done running. She slowed to a walk, sweating and shaking. Anna was shaking herself and she took in deep breaths, trying to fill her lungs with air and at the same time, marshal her thoughts. One second she'd been thinking only of dinner and how put out the cook at Dolforwyn would be to find a dozen extra mouths at her table, and the next ...

93

Anna twisted in the saddle to look back down the road. A bend hid the ambush site. Anna felt herself a coward, but she was glad to be spared the sight of riderless horses and men in green and white, dead in the road. Certainly, she was glad that Cadell couldn't see them.

"Why are you doing this?" she said in English to the man who'd caught Dyfi's bridle.

"Just doing what I've been told," the man said. "No need to take more offense than that."

"On whose orders?" Anna's eyes tracked from one man to the other. They both wore surcoats with the Mortimer crest over a mail tunic, and leather armor everywhere else. Only one wore a sword. The other had a broad axe tucked into his belt. Neither wore a quiver, but then, as Englishmen—or Saxons, as the Welsh still called them—they weren't trained in the use of a bow for war.

"That doesn't concern you."

Anna studied him, unsure of what Math would want her to do or say now. Whatever it was, it needed to keep them alive. "I don't see why you would want to capture me. I'm just a woman with a young child."

"No, you're not."

Anna swallowed. He was right, of course. She tried again. "You do realize that you've violated the treaty between England and Wales to capture me? You'd best return to your own country before you find yourself on the wrong side of a fight."

The man smirked. "I'm not worried about that." He pointed with his chin, back down the road towards the south. "I believe we already took care of anyone who could counter us."

"I ask again, on whose orders have you captured us? Edmund Mortimer's?" She wanted the man to name the Norman, to give her someone at whom she could direct her anger. But, of course, it was foolish to ask, wasn't it? Who else could it be? Just as at Valle Crucis Abbey, these men wore Mortimer colors, and the road had been Mortimer territory on and off for decades—centuries even—before the Treaty of 1285 stripped them of it.

Instead of confirming her guess, the man pulled on the front of his tunic and scoffed under his breath. "This? Don't read anything into this. We serve the House of Clare. Soon, every man in England—and in Wales—will belong to our lord."

Anna chewed her lip, finding herself far calmer than she might have expected. Cadell, for his part, sat still and silent on Anna's lap, staring at the English soldier, subdued now that the race was over.

"Did he tell you that himself?" Anna said. "Clare has always been arrogant. But we have a King of England already in Edward's son."

The man smiled, showing ragged and gray teeth, and his smile was all the more sinister for it. "The child King Edward is dead."

Anna's heart sank. The boy had survived in the old world, becoming Edward II, and one of the worst kings England had ever experienced. Events were moving far too quickly. Bohun might not have reached London by now, which meant that if Clare was on hand at the young king's deathbed, he would stand in a good position to take the throne, especially if he had the support of the other regents and the Archbishop of Canterbury.

Edward I had been a strong king—perhaps the strongest since William the Bastard himself. With him dead, the crown of England had fallen to his infant son. But even with all the barons of England swearing allegiance to him, it would have been many years before he could claim the crown for himself. Those years would have been full of jostling and infighting among those very same barons for power. Although King Edward had fathered a dozen children, none of his sons but his namesake had survived him, and now this one was dead too. With the failure of the male line, Clare—young, vibrant, and powerful—would see himself as first in line for the throne, regardless of what blood ran in his veins.

Anna tightened her grip on Cadell and on the reins. "And again I say, by what right? Clare has no royal blood."

"By the only right that matters," the man said. "Force of arms and the courage of the men who call him *lord*." He reached out a hand and chucked Cadell under his chin. "Who is your father, boy?"

"Lord Mathonwy ap Rhys," Cadell said.

Gah. Anna hadn't coached Cadell not to answer that question. Neither she nor Math had ever considered that their three year old son would have to learn deceit. Admittedly, even if she'd tried, Cadell had too much of his Uncle David in him, even at the precocious age of three, to answer any differently. Ultimately, Anna couldn't regret that.

The man grinned. "A son proud of his father. Obey your mother, boy." He tugged on Dyfi's bridle to turn her around and get her heading back down the road to the ambush site.

"What will you do with us?" Anna said.

The man grinned. "Hostages taken in war can be exchanged," he said. "Your father has no hope of victory, but that's not to say a feckless nobleman won't find himself in difficult straits. To have a princess of Wales and her son in our possession will prove useful." He shrugged and looked her up and down. "In more ways than one."

Anna hugged Cadell to her. For once, he didn't complain about her tight grip. As they returned to the point where the English soldiers had come out of the woods, she covered Cadell's eyes. Dead men and horses were something he'd see often in his life, but these men had been his friends. And he was only three.

"Mama, where's Tad?" Cadell had tears in his voice.

Anna was having a hard time holding back those same tears, but swallowed them down so he wouldn't hear a tremor in her voice. "I'm sorry, Cadell."

Cadell turned inwards, towards her body, hugging her, his chubby arms tight around her neck. *My precious boy.* Math and Anna had lost a son to disease six months earlier, and that grief remained always just below the surface of her heart. Baby Llywelyn had died three months after his birth in a measles epidemic that had nearly taken Cadell as well. Anna had thought when she'd lost Llelo that her grief would drown her. The fear of losing Cadell shortly after had nearly driven her insane. Anna still didn't know how women survived losing child after child without becoming cold inside. She didn't know what she would do if one day she was numbered among them.

And still, life was unrelenting. She hadn't told Math—she hadn't told anyone—but another child quickened inside her. With effort, Anna forced her thoughts of this new baby and her fear aside. David had once explained to her that the greatest warriors were great because they fought without fear of death. It made them strong. She'd asked him how they could overcome that fear and he explained that in their minds, they were already dead.

Anna decided she could live with the fear.

"You're safe, sweetie." Anna rubbed his back. "It's going to be okay." She said this, although she didn't see how that was possible from where they now sat.

At least they were alive, and as long as that was true, they had a chance. These Englishmen knew enough not to harm her and Cadell, at least for now. How long would that last? She'd never met this Gilbert de Clare, but she'd heard of him. He was just like the rest of his Marcher peers: ruthless as they come and changeable as the wind, depending on which loyalties served him at any given moment.

Anna whispered into Cadell's ear: "I'm going to put your sword away." She slipped a hand under Cadell's cloak and carefully tucked his toy sword under it. It was wooden, but it was a weapon. The soldier had taken away her belt knife first thing. She had a second knife strapped to her calf under her leggings, however. If she saw an opportunity to free herself and Cadell, she would use it.

The Englishman walked Dyfi past the carnage and then turned onto a narrow track that curved east, just before the road reached Dolforwyn.

"Where are you taking us?" Anna said.

Her captor glanced back, that smirk permanently affixed to his face. "Montgomery."

Anna nodded. It made sense. Montgomery Castle was only four miles away, a secondary castle for the Mortimers, whose seat was at Wigmore. Far better to transport her a short a distance to a minor castle where they could hide her, rather than a greater distance to a more central castle and risk being seen. At the same time, it meant that if she could escape, she had less far to go to freedom, and to her own people who would aid her.

That was something that she *knew*. She had come to Wales with David almost six years ago as a teenager—ignorant of all but rudimentary Welsh and a few snippets of Welsh history. That she knew even that was thanks to her mother, Meg, who had tried to teach her. David had known more initially (of course he had) and done better than she, what with sword fighting and male camaraderie—and the fact that he was Prince Llywelyn's long lost son.

Six years on, however, Anna sensed it was she, not David, who felt most comfortable here. She had a husband, a child, and a community that had embraced her. Unlike David, who would be king, Anna didn't press on people. She'd learned healing from Aaron, and from the herbalist in the village of Llangollen, and carved out a place for herself. David was burdened by his station and his responsibilities. Even though he welcomed them, he chafed against them too. No wonder he'd agreed to meet Bohun at the Abbey in the middle of the night. It was just about as much recklessness as he could allow himself these days.

An hour later, they came under Montgomery's walls. It sat on its rocky outcrop, impressive and huge, glaring down at them. Anna hated that she had to enter placidly through the gates, but with Cadell to protect, she didn't know what else she could do. Her thoughts flew to Math, riding south with David. If only she had some way to get word to him, he would move heaven and earth to rescue her. But he wasn't here and he and David had a country to save. She would have to manage this adventure on her own.

After dismounting in the outer ward, her guards escorted her, with Cadell on her hip, across the drawbridge that protected the inner ward and into a lesser keep with a high tower that buttressed the curtain wall and rose two stories above it. From down in the bailey, she could see the mountains of Wales beyond the walls to the west. She felt them tugging at her. Somehow, she had to get out of here.

The guards hustled her through the tower, up three levels, to the guardroom on the top floor. A ladder came down from a trap door in the ceiling, which Anna assumed led to the battlements. Ahead was a barred door and it was there that the soldier led Anna and Cadell. He unlocked it and with his hand to the small of Anna's back, urged her forward. Anna stepped through the doorway and halted a pace inside the room. Three people—a man, a woman, and a boy, perhaps two years older than Cadell—occupied it.

Upon Anna's entrance, the man stood. He was unassuming-looking, in his late thirties and of less than average height, with black hair and no beard. He wore a white shirt, a tunic of fine wool, dyed blue, and brown breeches. Unsurprisingly, he wore neither armor nor sword. Anna gave him a sickly smile.

"Who's this?" The man looked past Anna to the guards who hovered in the doorway behind her.

"Lord Edmund Mortimer, I've brought you some company," the guard said. "Princess Anna, welcome to Montgomery Castle."

8

26 August 1288
Montgomery Castle

Anna

Anna took in the scene while her fellow prisoners stared back at her.

"We've quite a merry party now." Edmund Mortimer rested one elbow on the mantle of the fireplace.

Just the name *Mortimer* had Anna's stomach turning icy cold. Although he couldn't know it, many kings of England numbered among his descendents. Anna supposed that with the death of the child King Edward, none of that would happen now. England would have a new line of kings. She ground her teeth at the thought that the line might start with Gilbert de Clare.

"I am Anna ferch Llywelyn. This is my son, Cadell."

Edmund's eyes lit. "We have royal company, my dear Maud. What an honor."

Anna had had a long day and didn't feel like taking his sarcasm. "You find yourself in a position to mock, do you?"

They locked gazes, and then Edmund laughed, genuinely, the sound ringing around the room. "Heaven forbid that I would do any such thing. I am a prisoner in my own tower. Who am I to accuse another of failing to take the proper precautions?"

"So you really are Edmund Mortimer," Anna said.

"I am." Edmund turned to the woman. "And this is Maud de Bohun, wife to Humphrey, and their son, Hugh."

Maud, a tiny woman ten years older than Anna, with blonde hair swept up the back of her head and fixed with a thousand pins, stood. She held out a hand to Anna. Anna took it, pleased that she'd set the tone from the first and that it looked like they might treat her as an equal.

Anna was Welsh. That alone was enough to earn Marcher scorn. In addition, her Papa had fought the Bohuns and the Mortimers for years (and been allied with them too, but not recently). Neither Marcher family should have warm feelings towards Anna. But then again, if Maud knew who protected her son, William, she had every reason to be polite. Edmund, on the other hand, had tried to kill Papa six years ago. Anna didn't think anyone would blame her for not giving Edmund the benefit of the doubt, even if he had been friends with Humphrey de Bohun since childhood and he and David were cousins of a sort.

Cadell and Hugh eyed each other warily. Then, Hugh jerked his head towards the far wall, indicating that they might play together behind the only bed in the room. Anna had a snarky thought about whether it had been Maud or Edmund who'd slept in the bed the previous night, and then dismissed it. Edmund would have given it to Maud and Hugh.

Anna put Cadell down and he trotted over to Hugh. They crouched side by side to see what toy Hugh had managed to retain, even in his captivity. A moment later, explosive sounds and death rattles emanated from their corner. Despite herself, Anna smiled. Apparently, boy noises were universal.

She turned to Edmund. "I had an escort of ten, and we were within our own borders. We thought we were safe."

"That border is no more," Edmund said. "If your father and brother don't know it by now, they should."

"We know of the alliance among some of the barons, particularly those who had lands in Wales." Anna didn't tell him that she knew of it through Humphrey de Bohun. She tried to catch Maud's eye—to see if she was aware of her husband's scheming—but Maud was looking down at her hands which she'd folded in her lap.

Edmund gazed at Anna impassively, giving nothing away.

"We also had word that you might be involved," Anna said.

Edmund barked a laugh. "Obviously not."

105

"We believed it—my brother still believes it," Anna said. "And then there's Clare."

"Gilbert de Clare intends to marry Joan and take the throne," Maud said. "King Edward was a strong ruler and demanded obedience more than strength in those who followed him. Anyone who sought to gather power to himself was sat down."

"Like your husband," Anna said.

Maud canted her head. "As you say."

"With King Edward's death, the disgraced, discarded, and ambitious have been let loose," Edmund said. "I misjudged the speed at which they would act, and the force of their distrust of me."

"Did you know that the men who captured me were wearing your colors?" Anna said.

Edmund' eyes narrowed as he studied her. "My colors? You must be mistaken."

"Believe me, I'm not," Anna said. "I asked the men who captured me specifically for whom they worked. They claimed it was Clare, but they wore your colors as part of an elaborate deception."

"And with me locked in here ..." Edmund scrubbed at his hair with both hands. He turned on a heel and began to pace in front of the fire, staring down at his feet as he thought. "That Clare would dare such a thing—"

"If events go not to his liking, Clare wishes for the blame to fall on you, my lord," Maud said. "Deception comes naturally to him." Clare had switched sides during the Baron's war, just before the battle that had left Humphrey de Bohun's father dead. His defection to the crown had been a crucial turning point in the war.

"And I made it so easy for him." Edmund snorted his disgust and swung around to put his boot into a pile of kindling beside the fire. Then he set his forearm on the mantle and leaned into it, resting his forehead on his arm.

"How long have you been held captive?" Anna said.

"Since yesterday," said Maud.

"When did you last speak to your husband?"

"A week ago," Maud said. "He left for Chester with William, something about … finding allies. Hugh and I were travelling from our lands in Shropshire to Pleshey when men attacked our company and took us captive."

"Did they tell you why?" Anna said. "According to the man who abducted us, Clare would use us to ransom Normans whom my people capture."

"That wouldn't be why they captured me," Maud said. "These men are English! It must be as surety for my husband's good behavior, or because Clare intends to eliminate all of us but would prefer we languished in prison until he has secured the throne."

Was now the time to speak? Anna and Maud had been dancing around each other for the last ten minutes, never getting to the center of the matter between them. Anna turned back to Edmund. "Englishmen wearing your colors, Lord Mortimer, also attacked the cathedral church at Valle Crucis three nights ago."

Maud's hand went to her throat and her face paled. "Princess Anna." She stepped closer. "You must tell me. Please—"

Anna put a hand on Maud's arm. She glanced at Edmund, and then looked into Maud's eyes. "Your son is fine. Your husband too, last I saw him."

Maud blinked back the tears that had threatened to spill out. "You saw them both?"

"Saw them and spoke to them," Anna said.

Maud heaved a great sigh, her hand to her heart. "Thank you."

Maud hadn't matched Anna's soft tone and Edmund looked over. "Thank you for what? Whom did she see?"

Anna looked from one to the other, trying to gauge if there was a reason to continue being secretive, and decided that she had nothing to lose at this point. They were captives together. She wasn't going to get out of here without their help.

"Humphrey de Bohun and his son came to Valle Crucis Abbey, seeking an alliance with my brother and father. Humphrey told us of a plot to invade the south and retake the lands you Normans lost to us three years ago. William remained with David, and Lord Bohun returned to England."

"That's it?" Edmund's jaw was tight. "That's all he told you?"

Anna's eyes turned wary. "What do you mean?"

"Clare has more in store for Wales than an attack on the south. Surely with your presence here, you can see that? Did your brother look to the defenses on Anglesey?"

Anna brow furrowed. "He sent word to Aber of Bohun's warning—"

"It's August. The harvest is soon," Edmund said. "Anglesey is a prize."

"Clare would know that," Maud said. "What if Anglesey were to fall to him as it has fallen in the past?"

Maud was referring to the war of 1282, where King Edward had sent a fleet to Anglesey, the bread basket of north Wales, and captured the harvest.

"Clare would not have forgotten the last war," Maud continued. "You must stop him." She said this as if the Bohuns hadn't fought against Wales in that same last war. Then again, the Bohuns had always thought of themselves as a breed apart, not to mention having been in rebellion against the English crown almost as many times as the Welsh kings and princes.

"Clare would have to force the Straits if he is to do real damage to King Llywelyn's holdings," Edmund said, "but losing the harvest will cause misery this winter and weaken your father's ability to resist Clare's advance."

"Wait! Wait!" Anna said, looking from Maud to Edmund and back again. "Do you know for a fact that Anglesey is in danger?"

"I overheard our captors speak of it, not once but several times," Edmund said. "They've seen no reason to hide their plans from me. Clare is sending a force to Anglesey by boat from Chester. It has taken longer than he'd hoped to gather his forces in the north, and the delay has angered him. He wanted to attack both north and south on the same day."

"You heard Clare himself say this?" Anna said.

"No," Edmund said. "Clare has not been here. Our guards simply expressed their fear of Clare's wrath if the endeavor failed to launch on time."

"When do they hope to sail?" Anna was trying very hard to keep the panic out of her voice. She glanced at Cadell, but he was still distracted by Hugh's carved horses and soldiers and wasn't paying attention to their conversation. Cadell trotted a horse along the edge of the bed and up the post.

Edmund's face softened. "Three days' time, though with the delay in the boats, perhaps four or five. Still, there's nothing you can do about it from here."

"We'll see about that." Anna walked to the window and looked out. As she'd feared, it was a drop of at least three stories down, with a steep decline after that as the hill ran away to the west. It rose again almost immediately in grass covered slopes, however, and the forested hills beyond belonged to Wales. "I have time to ride to Aber if I leave tonight."

Maud's face paled and she gaped at Anna. "Leave? You say this as if it were the simplest matter in the world!"

Anna swung around to look at Edmund. "You and I both know that we could escape if we put our minds to it, and if we were willing to risk our lives to do it."

"Are you willing to risk theirs?" Edmund's eyes flicked to Hugh and Cadell.

"His life will be forfeit if we don't risk it," Anna said. Maud choked out a denial, but Anna overrode her, still speaking to Edmund. "Do you deny what will happen if Clare wins? What will happen to Wales under the Norman boot?"

"I cannot deny the truth of your words. I fear for my son, too," Edmund said, though his voice was so low Anna almost didn't catch his last few words.

"If I can escape, I will need a horse or my chances of warning my father's captains in Gwynedd will end before they've started," Anna said. "You have stables inside the bailey, but—"

"Even were we to escape from the tower, it would be impossible for us to reach the stables and ride through the front gate without someone stopping us," Edmund said.

"We?" Anna said. "I am not asking you to risk your life."

Edmund made a tsking sound under his breath. "It is already at risk, whether or not Maud and I chose to admit it until now."

"Edmund," Maud said. "You can't be serious. And without horses—"

"It isn't always possible to house within the curtain wall every horse whose owner visits Montgomery. I have a second stable, a half-mile distant." Edmund pointed to the west with his chin. "Just over that hill."

Anna felt a rush of relief surging through her. It was as if someone had poured cold water on her head that proceeded to cascade down her body. "Really? I didn't dare hope—"

"Do you think me as foolish as that?" Edmund said, and then didn't wait for an answer. "I haven't wasted the last six years since I became lord of my father's lands. I may have served my apprenticeship in the Church instead of on the estate of one of my father's allies, but that doesn't mean I know nothing about managing my lands and people."

Anna hadn't meant to incite Edmund's ire and moderated her tone. "I apologize. You were to be a bishop one day. I imagine the running of a diocese is at least as complicated as your father's estates."

"Thank you." Edmund dipped his head.

"How did you end up a prisoner?" Anna said.

"My brother, Roger, visited me, under the guise of familial accord. He put something in my drink—a potion to make me sleep deeply—and I awoke in here. That's all I know. Thanks be to God that my wife and our first born are visiting her family in France, or he would have imprisoned them too."

"But why would he do this?" Anna said. "I understand why your brother might conspire with Clare, but why didn't he want you to join them?"

"Roger has always coveted my lands and my title," Edmund said. "While my elder brother lived, Roger was content to be the third son. But when Ralph died, Roger resented that I came into the inheritance, when it was he who had trained as a knight. While I did nothing to deserve his animosity except be born ahead of him, it doesn't surprise me that he gave me no chance to join his cause."

Wow. It wasn't just Welsh royal brothers who warred among themselves. "And would you have? Joined him, I mean?" Anna said.

Edmund turned his gaze to Maud. "I would have been disinclined to support Clare's bid for the throne, even if your husband had not approached me with his own plans first, my lady."

Maud bowed her head. "Thank you. You have always been a friend to Humphrey."

Edmund's marriage to Maud's niece had tied the two families closer together—not that marriage always meant a lot. Edmund was grandson to Papa's sister and look where that had gotten Papa. Family ties were called upon when they were convenient, and discarded when they weren't.

"So how are we getting out of here?" Anna said.

Edmund snorted laughter. "You *are* serious, aren't you? This is a fortress and we have no weapons."

Anna's brow furrowed in puzzlement. "Wales is so close I can almost touch it." She gestured to the room at large. "We're inside *your* castle. Surely you have loyal men among the garrison?"

"Do I?" Edmund said, with a glance at her that she couldn't interpret. "I don't know that I do, not if my brother leagues with Clare."

"Be that as it may, can you get us out of the castle if we breach this door?" Anna said.

"Three men guard it," Maud said.

"And there are three of us," Anna said.

"Plus two," Maud said. "You really would risk your son?"

For the hundredth time, Anna wished that Math were with her. She missed his confidence and his support. At the same time, it was almost as if she could sense him leaning down to whisper in her ear. *You can do this!*

"I'd risk myself," she said. "But if Clare defeats my father, kills him and my brother, and wins the throne of England, I know what kind of life my son would have. Clare will cage him for the rest of his life."

Edmund looked carefully at her again. "You speak as if you know something we don't."

Anna waved a hand, dismissing his words, though they were right on the mark. In her old world, the victorious King Edward had hung, drawn, and quartered her Uncle Dafydd, and then kept his sons inside an actual cage for the entirety of their natural life, decades in the case of one of them.

"Only enough to know that we need to get out of here. Right now."

Anna had learned to bow to convention when she had to, but despite living in the middle ages for the last six years, Anna was no medieval woman and never would be.

9

26 August 1288

Montgomery Castle

Anna

"**We**'re going to keep this simple," Anna said. "I'll disable the guard who opens this door while you use my knife to skewer the one behind him."

"And the third?" The amusement in Edmund's voice was unmistakable, but Anna was deadly serious.

"I don't know," Anna said. "I figure we'll solve that problem once we're in the anteroom."

Edmund laughed. "Well that's honest, anyway. I was beginning to think that there was some truth to the rumors."

"What rumors?" Anna said, though she thought she might know.

"That you play Morgana to your brother's Arthur."

Anna grimaced with annoyance. "I hate that."

"As well you might," Maud said, "if it weren't true."

"It isn't!" Anna gestured to Cadell, who remained in the far corner behind the bed with Hugh. "And what about him? Do you think he's David's son?"

Edmund started. "What did you say?"

Anna reddened. "Sorry. I heard a hateful story about King Arthur and his sister that originated in France. It's a new one." *Or has it not been written yet?* Anna couldn't remember. And maybe in this universe, it had never been written.

Movement came from the guardroom. Anna kilted her skirt to give her legs more freedom and took her place to the right of the door, so she would be on the guard's weaker, left side (provided he was right handed—likely, but not a guarantee by any means). Edmund set his feet ten feet from the door, his hands at his sides, in an unthreatening stance. The door swung open and a serving woman entered the room with a tray of food.

A guard followed close behind. He stood on the threshold, surveying the room; then took a second step, putting him a foot and a half inside the door. "Where's—"

Before he could properly formulate his question, Anna thrust her right foot at the side of his left knee. His leg collapsed, dropping him to his hands and knees. He was bigger and heavier than Anna had hoped and though his left knee could have been broken he came back up, twisting to the left so he could see her. Her elbow met his temple, however, and though she hadn't expected that she could hit him hard enough to put him down, she must have hit him just right because he went down anyway.

To his credit, Edmund didn't hesitate or stay to watch. The instant the guard hit the floor, he leapt over him and was out the door. By the time Anna had subdued the first guard and was ready to follow Edmund into the guardroom, Edmund had driven her knife to the hilt in the second guard's chest. He'd been slow to draw his sword. His surprise at this sudden attack still showed on his face in death.

Only fifteen seconds had passed.

Maud, for her part, had clapped a hand around the maidservant's mouth to stop her from screaming. "We're not going to hurt you. We just want our freedom," she said, in Welsh.

The woman nodded and subsided. Carefully, Maud removed her hand.

"Where's the third guard?" Anna asked Edmund.

"Not here. Perhaps he went to the latrine?" he said. "His absence is a gift that we must use."

Anna crouched before Cadell, terrified that he was terrified, and that she'd scarred him for life. Spending the rest of his life in a cage in Bristol Castle, however, would have been far worse than witnessing his mother subdue their captors. Maud had blocked the boys' view of Anna's attack with her skirts, but hearing it may have been bad enough.

Cadell pulled out his wooden sword and held it with both hands in front of him. Anna touched the tip with one finger. "You okay?"

Eyes wide, Cadell nodded.

"Do you feel better with this in your hands?"

Another nod.

Anna picked him up and took him with her into the guardroom. Maud followed, Hugh's hand in hers.

"Come!" Edmund grabbed a lantern from the guardroom table and led the way out of the room and down the stairwell. Anna tried to move quietly, but it was difficult to keep her feet from thudding on the stone stairway with Cadell on her hip. Edmund shot a glance back at her when he reached the next floor down. The sound of the evening meal echoed up the stairwell from the hall, one floor below.

Fortunately, they didn't have to go down those stairs. Edmund took them into the corridor and along it to the far end. He opened a narrow door, which didn't lead onto the battlements as Anna had supposed, but into another stairwell. She wanted to ask where they were going, but decided that she wouldn't break the silence. Besides, a word from her might encourage Cadell to speak. Both he and Hugh had been far too quiet for far too long. Normally, Cadell talked nonstop from waking to bedtime, and from her short exposure to Hugh, the same could be said of him.

The stairs led down and kept on going. Blindly, Anna and Maud followed with their boys. At one point, Hugh started to ask how much farther they had to walk, his child's voice echoing among the stones, but Maud shushed him.

"It's all right, Maud," Edmund said. "My brothers and I played down here many times. We could shout and no one would hear us."

"Where do the stairs lead?" Anna said.

"Out," Edmund said, as he reached a door at the bottom of the steps.

He pushed it open. At his appearance, the lone guard in the room shot to his feet. "My lord!"

"Hello, John. I'm leaving now. Will you raise the alarm when I've gone or do I have to kill you?"

Anna knew what Bevyn would have advised her brother to do in this situation—*kill him*—accompanied by his characteristic growl. David had changed so much in the last few years, she didn't know if he would have heeded Bevyn or not.

"M-m-my lord!" John said. "I never wanted any part of thi—"

"No doubt," Edmund said, in that dry tone of his, "but you are a part of it. If I let you live, I expect you to lie through your teeth and deny that we came this way."

"Yes, my lord!" John said.

Anna hoped John wouldn't betray Edmund, whom he appeared to respect. At the same time, what did it matter? The castellan would send men after them once he discovered them missing, regardless of how they'd escaped. As long as John didn't run to the hall immediately and report their absence, they had a good head start. She longed to be free with Cadell and heading west.

"Have a look outside. We need to know if anyone is on the other side of this door." Edmund pointed to the exterior door behind the guard. "And remember, I have a knife in your back and a Welsh witch with me."

Thanks for that. Anna caught the wide-eyed look John sent her and she shot back a daggered one, first at him, and then at Edmund's back, which he, of course, didn't see. John lifted the bar, his fingers fumbling not to drop it, and pushed open the door.

The sky had darkened in the minutes since they'd left their prison. The sun had fallen behind the hills to the west and left this part of the castle wall in shadow. "I see no one," John said.

"We were never here," Edmund said.

"Yes, my lord," John said. And then added, "Good luck!"

They'd certainly had good luck up until then, though Bevyn might have argued that she'd made her own luck. Together with Maud, Hugh, and Edmund, Anna and Cadell slipped out the door. They perched on the edge of a grassy slope that descended fifty yards at a steep angle to a little valley below their feet, and then up again to a stand of trees directly opposite their position.

Following Edmund, Anna slipped and skidded down the hill, Cadell still on her hip. When she reached the bottom, she shifted him to ride piggy-back and took off up the further hill at a crouching run. Anna would have put Cadell down but he might have tripped and she couldn't have him crying. All the while, she kept her ears open for a shout from the battlements. Her footsteps pounded dully on the soft earth, but no shout came from above them. Maud and Hugh kept pace beside her, with Maud's breath coming in airless gasps by the time they reached the trees.

They entered the darkness of the woods. Anna slowed to catch her breath and rested a hand against the rough bark of a pine tree. Edmund directed a wry smile at her. "Remind me in future that a successful attempt to escape my own castle is a good way to discover holes in my defenses and poor discipline among the garrison."

"You may dislike it in principle, but I'm thanking the Lord for it," Maud said, hugging Hugh to her. "What now?"

Anna set Cadell on his feet. "We start walking. And then I need a horse."

"*You* need a horse?" Edmund headed further into the woods with long strides that Anna and Cadell struggled to keep up with. "And what of us?"

"You are Norman." Anna picked up Cadell again in order to trot beside Edmund. Maud followed suit. "Surely you don't want to come all the way to Aber Castle with me?"

"My husband is a hunted man," Maud said, gasping again between her words. "My son is in the care of your brother. Where else would I want to be?"

"We should not go to Aber, but south, to Caerphilly, and speak to your father, the king," Edmund said.

"Papa should already know about the planned attacks in the south. By the time we find him to warn him what Clare intends for the north, it will be too late," Anna said. "I'm going to Aber."

"As am I!" Maud said.

Edmund slowed slightly, glancing from one woman to the other. Even in the dim light of the forest, amusement showed plain in his face. "Then I am your guest as well, my princess. I hope you have a plan for getting us there in one piece."

10

26 August 1288
Brecon Castle

David

David's company entered beneath the gatehouse, the horses' hooves clattering on the cobbled stones, and came to a halt in the bailey of Brecon Castle. Morning had finally come, with the sun peaking over the edge of the world in the eastern sky. David slid off Cadfarch and then reached up to help Lili from her horse. She didn't need the help, of course, but he liked helping her. She had the grace to let him. He tossed both sets of reins to the stable boy who came to greet them, turned towards the keep—and stopped short.

Dad stood on the top step to the keep, gazing at him. David could feel Lili begin to slip from his side, and he grabbed her arm before she could hide herself from his father's eyes. "Oh no," he said. "You're coming with me."

"Dafydd—" she said, her tone imploring.

He looked down at her, all pretense discarded. "I need you, Lili."

At once, Lili stopped trying to pull away. Her expression softened, and yet at the same time, she squared her shoulders. "Okay."

"Good girl." David said, even as his mouth twitched at the Americanism that seemed to have taken over this world too, without him and Anna even trying. If only real conquest were so easy. He took Lili's hand and marched towards his father, who came down the steps to meet them, his hand out.

David had a moment of hesitation, but pushed through it. He reached out to clasp his father's forearm, and then his father pulled him into a bear hug. "I've missed you, son."

David held himself stiff for several heartbeats, before he capitulated and returned the embrace. "I've missed you too, Dad." And he had, every day that they'd been estranged. Even so, he pulled away. "But what are you doing here? What about Clare?"

Llywelyn brow furrowed. "What are you talking about? What about Clare?"

"Gilbert de Clare, possibly Edmund Mortimer, and Humphrey de Bohun are involved in a ..." David's voice trailed off. "My God, you don't know!"

Llywelyn had put his hand on David's shoulder, and now gripped hard. "I think you'd better come inside and explain." Then he looked past David and Lili, whom he still hadn't greeted, to David's company. "Your men are in disarray." He brought his eyes back to David's. "And you have too few. What has happened to your *teulu*? Have you been in a fight?"

"We have," David said. "With more coming."

And then, if the battles of the last day weren't enough, a lone horseman rode up the hill to the gatehouse. He entered underneath the portcullis, his horse steaming with sweat. The man, one of Math's whom they'd left to garrison Buellt Castle, dismounted. He must have left not long after they had in order to have reached Brecon on their heels.

Math started at the sight of him and trotted over to catch his horse's bridle. "What has happened? You have news?"

The messenger dismounted. "My lord, just after you left Buellt, a rider arrived from the east. He was one of your spies. The child King Edward is dead."

"How?" Dad said. He and David moved closer to the horseman.

"His illness took him," the messenger said.

Math turned to look at David, who shook his head, not voicing what they were all thinking: *Or was he helped along the path towards death?*

David pressed a hand to the messenger's shoulder. "Thank you for your efforts. You'll find food and your fellows in the barracks."

"Thank you, my lord, but there's more," the messenger said.

"Yes?" David had been turning away, but now looked back at him.

"Humphrey de Bohun has been taken."

"What did you say?" William took a step closer to the messenger. "When?"

"Yesterday, near Shrewsbury."

"He's alive, though," Math said. "You said *taken*."

"His men are dead, but rumor has it that he lives."

"So is that what those men wanted at the Abbey? To capture, not to kill?" David turned to look at Math. "If they haven't killed him, what do they plan?"

Math shook his head. "Who can say?"

The man bowed his head. "Pardon me, my lord, but your man reports that Bohun is for the Tower of London, as quickly as his captors can get him there."

"And quietly too, eh?" Math said.

David glanced towards William, whose face had paled at this news. Evan put an arm around the boy's shoulders.

"Your father sent you to us because he feared exactly this," David said to William.

"He knew his position was precarious," William said. "I should have been with him!"

"And then you would have been captured too," David said.

"Clare will not harm your father," Math said.

"Won't he?" William said. In two minutes, the boy had grown five years older. "It seems to me they already have."

"Your father is a regent of England," Math said. "That can't be lightly put aside, no matter what these treacherous barons are planning."

William's chin jutted out. "What are we going to do about it?"

David studied the boy. "I promised to watch over you, and that is what I will do. So *we* are not going to do anything. Your father is a grown man and can take care of himself. Or not. He is the least of my worries right now."

"Because Clare invades," William said.

"So it seems."

"But you have men to see to that," William said.

David snorted laughter. "Is that what war is to you? Something to 'see to'?"

William's expression turned sullen. "My father says that soon we won't need swords anymore. That you'll have your men killing from a distance, with fire and iron and steel."

David gazed down at the boy, stunned that Bohun could articulate what David had struggled to explain to his advisors. "Is that what he says? We already have what he describes. They're called arrows."

"But if you're Arthur—"

"There's no magic here, William. Weren't you at the Abbey two nights ago? Men died to protect your father because he sought to protect you."

"And now that's your job," William said.

Why did the boy look so satisfied? David pursed his lips. "It is." He gave William a wary look. "As I promised your father."

Dad had been listening to the exchange and now interrupted. "Enough, William. Your horse needs attention."

William bowed. "Yes, my lord."

Dad nodded at David. "My steward will see to your men. You need rest. Let's get inside."

David took in a deep breath. That Bohun might end up in the Tower of London was no small matter. Yet David didn't see what he could do about it. William would just have to accept that for now. It might well be the most difficult thing he would ever have to do. David turned towards the keep. For his part, he had a war on his doorstep.

11

26 August 1288

Brecon Castle

Llywelyn

Llywelyn had absorbed all that Dafydd had to tell him with a few blinks and a curse, but he'd been expecting this, hadn't he? Hadn't they all?

While the Welsh exchequer was healthier than it had been in a century, since the time of his grandfather, that didn't mean that each outlay for men and weaponry for a war as yet unfought hadn't seemed a waste of resources at times.

Not anymore.

Dafydd had shown Llywelyn what they could achieve, given enough men, money, and time. Llywelyn had given his approval to everything Dafydd had sought. And now they were going to use what they'd created. All of it. They would have an early start in the morning.

But what Llywelyn hadn't given his approval for was the one thing Dafydd really wanted: he wanted Lili. From the looks the pair had exchanged in the courtyard, Dafydd was determined to have her, regardless of what his father said. He and Dafydd had danced around the issue all afternoon, pretending that the looming wall between them wasn't really there. Llywelyn hadn't tried to breach it, coward that he was. Who would have thought that one of the greatest challenges of his reign would come in a matter of the heart—his son's heart, no less.

Dafydd's news had prompted immediate action: Llywelyn had ordered half of his cavalry south as soon as Dafydd had detailed what he knew of the coming war. Llywelyn had also sent word to every good Welshman within ten miles of Brecon that he was needed. Messengers had ridden to every cantref between Brecon and Aberystwyth to rouse the countryside and to probe how far the English menace had spread.

Llywelyn and Dafydd, however, had determined that they must delay their journey south to wait for their people to gather at Brecon. Llywelyn didn't have a standing army, and thus, it was peasant and nobleman alike who mustered for war. To give this venture the best chance of success, his people needed to see Llywelyn before they started, so that he could explain to them what they faced, and the cost to them and their country if they failed to throw the English back into the sea. To have their king ask for help directly could inspire the necessary courage in every heart to leave home and hearth to march forty miles to fight in his service.

After a long day, Llywelyn and Dafydd sat late into the evening, conversing quietly together for the first time in months. They spoke of Norman barons, of Bohun and William, and of the coming war. As Dafydd talked, Llywelyn studied his son's face. The fire in the hearth lit it and turned his face aglow. At times, Llywelyn could barely focus on what his son had to tell him. How had he let their argument fester for so long?

Dafydd turned to stare into the fire. It crackled and popped in the silence that fell between them, now that their talk of politics had ended. Nothing in Llywelyn's life had given him as much joy as this boy. Dafydd, for all his intelligence, was raised in another land and couldn't possibly understand what it had been like to stand in the clearing at Cilmeri, knowing that his life was ending, only to see his son and daughter appear to save him.

Llywelyn loved Anna—God only knew how much—but Dafydd was his son. *His son.* No Prince of Wales had needed a son more than Llywelyn, and this one had proved himself to be more than Llywelyn could ever have hoped, from that day beside the riverbank when Meg had told him that she carried his child.

And that meant he could put it off no longer. The wall had to come down. And since he was the elder of the two of them—the father—it was he who had to do it. Llywelyn cleared his throat and lobbed to Dafydd his first attempt at peace: "I never meant for things to turn out this way."

Dafydd picked up his cup of wine that had been sitting on the table between them, and took a sip. "It didn't have to."

Llywelyn's lips turned down at that. Dafydd's anger shimmered in a halo around him. And yet, could Llywelyn blame him? Llywelyn remembered what nineteen had been like for him. He and his father hadn't seen eye to eye on anything.

"So your mother has said."

Dafydd shifted in his seat, gazing into the fire and not looking at his father. "Has she? She counseled me patience."

Llywelyn's heart warmed at the thought of Meg, even has he berated himself for causing her grief and forcing her to choose between her husband and her son. He let out a sharp breath. When Meg felt something strongly enough to chastise him for it, he had already lost the argument, even if it took a long while for him to admit it. He'd been fighting a rearguard action for two years. Had he become so used to always getting his way that he'd forgotten that sometimes a man needed to retreat, in order to fight another day? It seemed so.

"I called you stubborn," Llywelyn said.

Dafydd snorted into his cup. "What did she say to that?"

"He's your son, as you may recall." Llywelyn barked a laugh.

Dafydd actually smiled. "I am your son, Dad."

Llywelyn took in a deep breath and let it out. He sent up a prayer of thanksgiving that Dafydd was willing to discuss this and hadn't gotten up from his chair and left the room. "Then Meg said, *your son loves you, my lord.*"

"Oh no," Dafydd said. "When Mom starts *my lording* you, you know you're in trouble."

Llywelyn swallowed down a laugh. The wall was thinning to the point he thought he could see through it. "And then she said, *he loves Lili. Let him have what he needs.*"

For the first time since Llywelyn had broached the subject of their disagreement, Dafydd turned his head to look at him. "And you said, *he's so damned righteous—*"

"I wouldn't have you any other way." Llywelyn gazed directly into Dafydd's eyes. "That same stubbornness will make you the greatest king Wales has ever known."

Dafydd rested his elbows on the arms of his chair and clasped his hands together, putting them to his lips. "Many times, you have said that the needs of the crown—"

"Are paramount," Llywelyn said. "Yes, I know. I shouted those words at you last we spoke. Your mother reminded me that you *are* the crown. You are my son. I had good reasons for denying your request to marry Lili, but they pale in comparison to my relationship with you. I forgot that you were a grown man, not a boy who must follow my every direction."

"Lili and I have your permission to marry, then?"

"You do." The moment the words were out, Llywelyn felt a huge weight lift from his shoulders.

When he'd told Meg that he was rethinking his refusal, her response had been, *thank God.* He'd left Caerphilly the next day for Brecon and before he mounted his horse, she'd hugged him tightly. *Thank you, thank you, thank you,* she'd said. It was worth shifting course to know that he'd reached an accord with his wife and his son in one fell swoop.

"Did you really think I would change my mind?" Dafydd said. "That I would walk away from Lili?"

"I never imagined you'd walk away from her," Llywelyn said.

Dafydd sat as he'd been, preternaturally calm. Llywelyn had hoped that he'd at least punch the air, or better yet, stand up and hug his father. But he did neither of these things. "You thought I'd take her anyway," Dafydd said. "Hoped it, even. And hoped that I would be satisfied with that."

"That is the usual way of princes, yes." Llywelyn shrugged. "I don't want to argue about this anymore. I've never wanted to argue with you about anything."

"We've only ever disagreed about Lili," Dafydd said.

"Exactly. And that disagreement is over. You have my blessing. Marry your girl, if that's what you want to do."

Dafydd still hadn't moved.

Llywelyn tried again. "I can't bear the distance between us another hour. I may not agree with this choice, for the reasons I've explained, but I trust you."

Finally, Dafydd moved, but not towards his father. He got to his feet and began to pace before the fire, one hand on the hilt of his sword, watching his feet as he strode from one end of the mantle to the other.

"What is it?" Llywelyn said. "Why aren't you pleased?"

Dafydd glanced his way. "Oh, I am pleased ... it's just that the last time I spoke to Lili of marriage, she said that she'd decided not to marry me even if you gave us permission. She sent me away."

Llywelyn studied his son. "She's a woman, Dafydd. They all do that at one time or another."

"Even Mom?" Dafydd said.

"Even your mother," Llywelyn said. "I had to bide my time until I could convince her that I wasn't a madman, much less that I loved her. I don't know that she fully believed in my love for her until she returned to Wales four years ago. If not for you, she may never have believed in me."

Even after they'd spoken words of marriage to each other in secret, Meg hadn't trusted them together, not with the scars from her first husband still healing over. He remembered the day she told him that she was pregnant. He'd seen a touch of reserve there—of fear—as if he might not be happy with the news. Llywelyn couldn't blame her. Her first husband hadn't responded like a man should when Meg told him that she was carrying Anna. Even after all these years, Llywelyn hands fisted as he considered the man Trevor Lloyd had been.

"I'm going to have to think about how to approach Lili," Dafydd said. "You may be right, but she seemed very certain that it was over between us."

"She's with you now," Llywelyn said.

"Only because she had no choice," Dafydd said. "It was her duty to find me and tell me of the attack on Buellt."

"She could have stayed there, once you'd taken back the castle."

Dafydd chewed on his lower lip. Llywelyn had never seen him so uncertain—or at least not since he'd been a strip of a boy in those first months in Wales. Even then, he'd had a confidence that shouted *Prince of Wales* to any man with functioning eyesight. Llywelyn had marveled at his son then, been proud many times, and thanked God for him every day since.

Llywelyn stood. "Let it be for now. You've said that everything happens for a reason, isn't that right?"

"It does, Dad," Dafydd said. "I just wish I didn't care so much about how it turns out this time."

12

Lili

The wind had blown hard from the west all night long—not unusual in Wales—and the morning had brought cloudy skies, and then rain. Lili stood upon the gatehouse tower, in the shelter of its roof, and gazed into the downpour. Puddles had formed in the bailey of Brecon Castle and drops staccatoed on the front steps.

"I heard that you ordered your horse saddled."

Dafydd braced his shoulder against the frame of the doorway to the stairs that led down to the guardhouse. He leaned into it, not touching her but only inches away.

Lili kept her eyes on the mountains beyond the battlements. She hadn't wanted Dafydd to seek her out; she had wanted to be alone with her thoughts. Now that he was here, however, she had to tell him the truth. "I will return to

Buellt. It was wrong of me to come with you this far when my people need me. They look to me when Ieuan leaves and I've abandoned them."

She had hoped that it would be a simple matter to slip away, while Dafydd and the king were busy with their troops. By sunset yesterday, men had started to gather in the fields to the west of the castle. She could see them now, huddling with one another against the rain. It was better to look at them than at Dafydd, whose gaze bludgeoned her with its intensity. She didn't want him to read anything in her eyes that she didn't want him to know.

"What about Bronwen? She will think you have abandoned her." Now Dafydd did touch her. He stroked the back of her hand with one finger, and then enveloped her whole hand in his.

She bit her lip. "Dafydd—" She couldn't resist looking up at him, but as soon as she did, he lifted her hand to his lips and kissed the back of it. She stared at him, drowning in him, really. The entire world receded but for his face and she couldn't hear anything but a rushing in her ears. Still, she managed to swallow her emotions. "No, Dafydd. Let me go."

He dropped her hand and straightened. "You can't go to Buellt alone and I don't have the strength of numbers to send any men back with you. Your choice is to come with me to Caerphilly, or to stay here."

"I don't need an escort—"

"Lili—"

"One man will do. I asked Math if one of the stable boys could be spared."

The wrenching up of the portcullis silenced them both. Its movement vibrated the stones beneath their feet. In unison, they looked towards the bailey to see a boy leading a horse from the stables for Lili, along with a second one for himself. Math had been reluctant to accede to her request, but she'd told him that she would not go with Dafydd, no matter what he said to convince her that she should. If Math wouldn't let her leave the castle in plain sight, she'd stay at Brecon and ride away after Dafydd left. Math had given in. But he hadn't told Dafydd about it, apparently.

Dafydd looked away and took in a deep breath. "I thought things were better between us. I love you, Lili."

Lili gritted her teeth, not wanting to answer with what was in her heart, else it break again. Because the real truth was that Lili *did* love him. She loved him with her all of her heart. But he deserved to live out his life with someone better.

Lili knew now that she'd run from him because deep down, she'd rather live without love than risk loving him and losing him. Lili's mother had died giving birth at an age only a few years older than Lili was now. Her father had left them not long after. These losses had burned themselves into Lili. It had made her afraid of giving her whole self to Dafydd as he deserved.

She'd lain awake half the night, her mind a jumbled mess of regret, recriminations, and despair. She needed to get away from Dafydd to clear her head. One moment, hope welled within her and she felt sure that all would be well, and the next, she knew that there was no way it could be.

Dafydd cursed under his breath and turned towards the stairs, just as another rider appeared in the doorway of the stables. Instead of clip-clopping sedately, however, as the other two had, he raced across the bailey towards the gatehouse. It was William.

Dafydd leaned over the balustrade. "Stop! Damn it, William. Stop!"

"What's he doing?" Lili said, but she spoke to Dafydd's retreating back. His feet clattered on the stairs and Lili flew after him, coming out into the area under the gatehouse. William had ridden through it and turned east, heading to England. He was already disappearing around a bend in the road.

"William!" Dafydd ran to the spare horse that had been intended for the stable boy and threw himself on its back, all the while cursing William under his breath.

Lili mounted her horse just behind him, and although Dafydd gave her a look that told her he was against her riding out the gate with him, he didn't stop her. He didn't have time to argue with her if he was to catch their wayward charge. Dafydd spurred the horse after William and Lili followed.

The road had become a sea of mud and the horses' hooves churned through it. Dafydd had to slow to navigate a particularly large puddle, allowing Lili to catch him. She called across the few feet that separated them: "This is a really stupid idea, Dafydd."

He shot her a grin as they picked up speed again. "At least the rain is at our backs."

His good humor got her attention. He was *enjoying* this. At first she couldn't figure out why, and then she realized that he was without a guard for the first time since he'd left his men behind in Scotland three years ago and returned to his time. Of course, that adventure, coupled with the time he was abducted from his own encampment, was why he always had a guard.

Dafydd and Lili were alone. Truly alone.

William had a head start, but as they raced along the road, Lili caught sight of him at times. It felt like they were gaining on him, but as the road began to wind among the hills, they seemed to lose ground. When they reached the crest of a low hill and saw a long straight stretch before them, there was no sign of William. They descended into a valley, crossed it, and then the road narrowed as it cut through a gap between two hills, forcing Dafydd to slow. Neither her horse nor his could maintain his headlong speed beyond the initial rush down the road.

Lili urged her horse beside Dafydd's. "I didn't think William had that great a head start."

"I didn't either," Dafydd said. "We know where he's going, though, don't we?"

"I imagine, to England?" Lili said.

"Where else?" Dafydd said. "He's going after his father. Hay-on-Wye lies fifteen miles ahead of us. Paths lead from this road, to both north and south. There's nothing to prevent him from taking one, but I don't see that we have a choice but to continue as we have been."

"Have you ridden this road often?" Lili said. "It isn't that far south from where I grew up, but I've never been here before."

"This is the region in which we raided before Lancaster," Dafydd said.

Oh. Dafydd had spoken to her of those days, and not with fond memories.

Time went by as the sun—if they could have seen it through the cloud cover—rose higher in the sky. Lili grew more concerned with every mile that passed. What would they do if they had to make a decision as to whether to continue into England, or to stop and leave William to his fate?

"Where is he?" she said. "Did he go to ground until we passed by?"

Dafydd just shook his head and kept on riding. They came over a rise and saw the town of Hay, nestled in a bend of the Wye River. Dafydd put out a hand to slow Lili and trotted his horse to the side of the road and under the trees that lined it.

He dismounted and took a water skin from the saddle bag. He took a sip and gestured with it towards the town. "We burned it, you know."

Lili dismounted too, stretching her back and legs. She'd ridden more in the last two days than in the previous two months. She brushed the wet hair from her face and looked where Dafydd pointed. Hay-on-Wye was a market town, associated with no castle, but fought over by the kings of Wales and England because of its location, ever since there was an England. Offa's Dyke, the earthen fortification that followed the length of the Welsh border, ran just to the north and south of Hay. Once she and Dafydd crossed it, they'd be in England.

Dafydd walked to the center of the road and stood with his hands on his hips, surveying the path ahead. "Where is that boy?" He turned around to look back the way they'd come. The wind blew into Lili's face as she looked west too. She sat silent, watching Dafydd. Her horse whickered and Lili patted his neck.

And then William came out of the trees to the north of the road, only ten yards from where Dafydd stood. He urged his horse to leap the ditch beside it before he noticed either of his pursuers. He pulled up, staring at Dafydd, mouth agape.

Dafydd recovered first. "A fine chase you've led us on. Come here."

"No." William's horse danced sideways as he reined him in. Dafydd stood between him and England and Lili could see William eyeing the road to Hay, estimating what it would take to get past Dafydd without Dafydd stopping him. Lili tugged on her horse's bridle to get him moving and used him to block the road as well.

Dafydd took a step towards William, who remained on his horse. "This isn't the way to rescue your father. Do you really want to ruin all his careful planning?"

"He didn't plan to be captured."

"No," Dafydd said. "But he left you in my charge in case he was."

"Exactly," William said. "Did you not tell me yesterday that I was your responsibility?"

"I did." Dafydd sighed. "Why do you think I came after you? But it is folly for me to be this close to England."

"My father needs me," William said. "You would do everything in your power to rescue your father if his enemies had captured him."

Dafydd didn't answer at first, because, of course, William was right. Then, Dafydd said, "I am not twelve."

"What difference does that make?" William said.

"Are you a knight? Do you honestly think that you're ready to face down grown men in battle?"

William swept his sodden hair from his face. He was soaked through, just as Lili was. "I killed a man at Buellt." Lili wondered from the catch in William's voice if tears wouldn't have shown on his face if the weather had been dry.

Dafydd took in a long breath and let it out. "How do you hope to rescue your father from the Tower of London? Tell me your plan."

"I have been to London," William said. "As you pointed out several times, I'm only a boy. No one will think twice about my presence if I disguise myself as a serving lad. I will bring my father a rope, and with it, he can let himself down from his window and escape."

Dafydd harrumphed. "Did you know that the old King Henry kept my grandfather in the Tower forty years ago? My grandmother brought him a rope and he tried exactly what you plan. The rope broke and he fell to his death."

That gave William a moment's pause. "Something else, then."

"Nothing else, William," Dafydd said. "Far better that you return with me to my father's castle. If we win this war, I will speak to Clare and bargain for your father's life."

William sneered. "Why should you? You would have your victory, then, and we would have nothing!"

"Please, William. It's raining." Lili didn't know what made her say that, but the skies had opened while they'd been talking and begun to pour down even harder than before.

"No!" William prodded his horse's sides and spurred towards Hay.

Dafydd reached for William's bridle as he went past him, but William swerved the horse away at the last instant and then raced past Lili too, who had no more luck than Dafydd in stopping him. Dafydd ran back to his horse and threw himself on his back. "Stay here, Lili. It's too dangerous—"

Lili gave him a disgusted glare. "You are safer with me than without me. You look more innocent with a woman in your party. We can pretend that William is my little brother and he's run away. That's why we're chasing him."

Dafydd tsked his objection, but as when they'd ridden from Brecon, he didn't do anything to stop her from coming with him. She was glad, now that they were heading into England, that she'd left her bow and quiver in the guardhouse at Brecon. It was an oversight, one that she'd been regretting during this journey, but her clothing was unusual enough without the addition of such a distinctive weapon.

Together they raced their horses after William's. At least the boy stayed on the road as it skirted the town walls to the south, rather than disappearing into Hay. In the open countryside, they had a chance to catch him. In the city, even a smallish one like Hay, he could hide and they would never find him.

"You there!"

Two men guarded the border crossing. Although the rain today wasn't unusual, it had kept people inside and there was no other traffic. The guards had taken shelter under a lean-to. William lifted his hand to them, looked back to grin at Dafydd, and continued at a gallop the last twenty yards to where the men waited. Then, he reined in.

"He's going to get himself killed, and us with him," Lili said.

"Come on," Dafydd said. "At least there are only two men-at-arms with whom we have to contend."

Lili's heart beat hard in her ears. With that and the rain, she could barely hear her horse's hooves on the muddy track as they trotted up to flank William as he waited on the road by the lean-to. Now that William had reached his objective, he sat silent in the face of the men's questions.

"I need your name, young lad." The captain glanced at Dafydd, who responded to the man's curious look by clapping a hand on William's shoulder.

"Please forgive my brother-in-law for his impatience," Dafydd said. "We're off home to Hereford."

"William got away from us." Lili spoke English with a Welsh accent. Although she couldn't disguise her Welshness, she assumed the guards knew that mixed marriages weren't unusual in the border country.

The captain laughed. "Boys do that sometimes. Just be glad you didn't run into one of Prince Dafydd's patrols. His men shoot first and ask questions later."

Lili was offended for Dafydd's sake because she knew that wasn't true. At the same time, their prejudice was hardly surprising. The Welsh had been at war with the Saxons (from whom these men descended), and then their Norman masters since William the Bastard conquered England in 1066. More than two hundred years of near constant hostilities had solidified the enmity. Dafydd had told her that seven hundred years later, in the time in which he had been born, many English still looked down upon the Welsh and thought the worst of them.

But Dafydd grinned in agreement with the guard. "We hadn't gone far inside Wales," he said. "We were visiting my wife's sister."

"Stay on our side of the border for the next few weeks." With a touch to his forelock, the man waved them on.

As they rode away, Lili said, "Was that an order?"

"Sounded like it," Dafydd said.

Lili spurred her horse to bring it beside William's. Now that he'd gotten Dafydd into England as he'd wanted, he was no longer trying to get away. "Do you realize how much trouble you're in?" Lili said. "What if Dafydd had been dressed like the Prince of Wales he is? You could have gotten him killed!"

"You didn't have to follow me," William said. "And besides, he never looks like a prince. My father told me."

"Your father has said a little too much," Dafydd said.

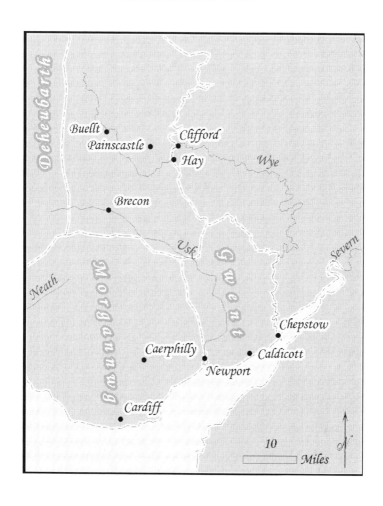

13

27 August 1288

Brecon Castle

Math

Math paced the great hall at Brecon Castle, tugging at his hair with both hands. He was alone but for the King, who stared out the door of the castle, his arms folded across his chest. The rain continued to fall—for the first time in over a week—and the hard-packed earth had quickly become muddy. Even with the rain, the men were out in it, hoods up, making the last adjustments to their gear in the bailey of the castle. It would be a wet ride to Caerphilly, though the rain shouldn't slow them down as the old Roman road they would take was still in good repair. Half of the foot soldiers would follow. The other half of those gathered had been sent to Monmouth in case the Normans chose to attack across the eastern border.

"Why didn't someone stop him?" Llywelyn said.

"*Someone* should have," Math said. "But the rain and poor sleep these last few days must have dulled the men's thinking. Dafydd and Lili were on their horses and out the gate before anyone knew what was happening. The guard at the gate didn't even report it right away, thinking that the three of them were riding to the encampment outside the walls. By the time I went looking for Dafydd and corralled the guard at the gate, they'd been gone for over an hour."

"They would have been close to England by then, if they rode quickly," Llywelyn said.

"Exactly," Math said. "God only knows what that boy was thinking."

"God knows and we do too," Llywelyn said. "He wants to rescue his father. Dafydd would have done the same for me, at his age."

Math scrubbed at his hair again. Llywelyn's assessment was all too true. William was afraid for his father. In chasing after him, Dafydd had behaved almost as recklessly as the boy. When Math had discovered what Dafydd had done, his first thought had been that it wasn't like Dafydd. After some reflection, however, he'd decided that perhaps it was exactly like Dafydd. He'd become like a caged bear these last months since Lili had rejected him. He might have followed William out of duty, but some part of him might even be enjoying his escape. Fortunately, Dafydd wasn't a boy anymore. Math was confident he knew what he was doing.

Math dropped his hands. "As it is, sire, I don't see that we can help him. We have a war to fight. Prince Dafydd will have to take care of himself and Lili."

"And William," Llywelyn said. "My son *is* capable."

"He's more than capable," Math said. "Until today, I wouldn't have called him foolhardy, however. Perhaps we've kept him tied down too tightly these last few years. If we'd loosened our hold, even a little, he wouldn't have needed to break down the gates."

Llywelyn turned on one heel to look at Math, whose face flushed.

"I apologize, my lord." Math bowed. "I did not intend to criticize your handling of him or your decisions."

Llywelyn shook his head. "No. You *are* right. Dafydd has not been himself these past months and that is my fault, at least in part."

"He loves Lili—"

"And she him, from what I saw of them together. For my part, I told him last night that he could marry her," Llywelyn said. "They have my blessing."

Math stared at his father-in-law. "But ... Dafydd said nothing about that. Not to me." He lifted his chin to gaze towards the high window in the hall that looked east, in the direction Dafydd and Lili had gone. "And when Lili came to me this morning, she gave no sign that he'd said anything to her ..."

Llywelyn's eyes narrowed. "Perhaps Lili rejected him again?"

Math's brow furrowed as he thought. "I don't think she did. He wasn't ill-humored this morning, or at least not more than usual."

Llywelyn nodded. "He has ridden after the boy because he swore to protect him. That is all."

"He swore," Math said, "but not at the cost of his own life. Not if the boy himself runs away to England on a fool's errand to rescue his father."

"My son might not see it that way," Llywelyn said.

"He clearly didn't," Math said. "But even if Lili has thrown him over, he doesn't have a death wish. He will do everything in his power to return to us if he can. And bring William and Lili back with him."

Llywelyn fell silent again, such that Math wondered if their conversation was over, even if the king hadn't dismissed him. And then Llywelyn said, "He was dressed simply, as always."

Math nodded, though Llywelyn was facing away from him and couldn't see him. "He was. And although his sword is fine, he sports no jewels. Dafydd has worked very hard to learn how to pass as an Englishman—or even as a Marcher Norman like William should the need arise."

"Does Lili speak English?" Llywelyn said.

"Passably." Math breathed in through his nose and let the breath out. He was feeling better about this escapade, even if part of him was sure he should be on his horse too, riding east to look for his brother-in-law, for Anna's sake, if for no other reason. He missed his wife, but he was glad she wasn't here. She would be worried sick about her brother. As it was, by the time she heard about it, Dafydd would be with them again and he could tell the tale before the fire for her amusement.

Evan stepped through the front doors of the hall. King Llywelyn stood a few paces away with his arms folded and Evan hesitated as he looked from Math to his king. "Do we go, my lords?"

"We go," Llywelyn said.

"I will spare two riders to inform the countryside to be on the lookout for the Prince," Math said, "and to send word if any rumor of him surfaces. It's something I'd hoped never to have to use my network for."

"And yet, for what better reason could you use it?" Llywelyn said.

* * * * *

The thirty miles to Caerphilly were some of the longest miles of Math's life. *How was he to tell Meg that her son was missing again?* And in border country at that? Still, they reached the Caerphilly before the sun was half-way down in the sky, having pushed the horses hard, and had to face what they dreaded. Math hoped that his father-in-law had thought of a way to talk to his wife so Math didn't have to.

Math and Llywelyn dismounted in the outer bailey. Of all the castles that Llywelyn had appropriated after the 1285 treaty with England, Caerphilly was the most magnificent. Gilbert de Clare had begun it back in 1268 and Llywelyn had attacked it in its early stages and destroyed it. He hadn't had the wherewithal to prevent Clare from beginning it again, however. In its completed state, it consisted of dams, moats, massive earthworks, two concentric curtain walls, multiple halls, and towers. It had cost a fortune to build. No wonder Clare wanted it back.

Math walked with Llywelyn to the main hall, though (coward that he was) Math hung back a bit. Meg was already halfway across the great hall when they entered it. "I missed you," she said. "I'm so glad you've returned." Llywelyn clasped her to him and then she moved on to hug Math. "How is my grandson?"

"Sturdy and loud," Math said.

Their eyes met. Meg had suffered with them through Llelo's death and Cadell's bout with measles. The fear for his life wasn't going to fade just because six months had passed since he'd recovered.

Math himself had been a sickly child and Llywelyn had been among those who'd worried about him, afraid that he wouldn't grow into a warrior. For a time, it seemed he was never going to be strong enough to wield a sword. When Llywelyn had taken custody of Math's ten year old self after the death of Math's father, Llywelyn had made noises about a possible career in the Church. To avoid such a fate, Math had worked harder than any of the squires at Aber, and had been saved by a growth spurt at sixteen. If he'd become a priest, he never would have met Anna. What price would he pay in the next life for that gift?

"The messenger you sent arrived yesterday. If he hadn't borne your seal, I wouldn't have believed it." Meg shook her head. "The child king dead and war on the coast. Why won't the Normans leave us alone?"

"Because they want our lands and all of them have been raised to believe they have a right to keep what they can take," Llywelyn said. "We have much to do and very little time in which to do it."

"What the messenger didn't say was *who* attacks us," Meg said.

"We're not entirely sure," Math said. "Humphrey de Bohun believed that his fellow regents, Vere and Kirby, were involved somehow, with Bigod, but exactly how many other barons support them isn't yet clear."

"It's the usual suspects, *cariad*," Llywelyn said. "Clare, Mortimer ..."

"Mortimer!" Meg's voice filled with disgust—and horror.

"It pains me too," Llywelyn said.

"When will David arrive?" Meg peered over Math's shoulder, looking towards the door to the hall. "I would have hoped he'd be with you, Math."

Math swallowed and Llywelyn stirred beside him. "He was delayed, my dear," Llywelyn said.

Meg's eyes narrowed. "Delayed? That is a delicate choice of words that has sucked the warmth from the room. What are you not telling me? What has happened?"

Llywelyn told her.

Meg's hand went to her throat, but she didn't cry out or exclaim. She was Dafydd's mother, after all. She knew of what he was capable. "And you've had no sign or word of him since?"

Math closed his eyes. He'd rehearsed this scene the entire way from Brecon. "Humphrey de Bohun put his son in Dafydd's charge. We spent only a few days in William's company, but it is within his character to believe his duty was to rescue his father."

"All by himself," Meg said.

"Yes," Math said.

"And David went after him," Meg said.

"Lili went too," Llywelyn said.

Meg brushed a loose end of hair from her face and tucked it behind her ear. "It is just like him to do this." She turned on a heel to gaze into the fire. Not that she was seeing it.

Llywelyn took in a breath through his nose and let it out. "He is my son."

Meg's shoulders fell and she bent her head. Llywelyn stepped closer and pulled her into his arms. "He was dressed as a simple knight, and his English is perfect. If not for the fact that he is the Prince of Wales, I would have used him to scout the border as a matter of course. He is the best of all the men I know for disguising himself as a Saxon."

"Did you tell him he could marry Lili?" Meg said.

"I did."

"And still he does this?" Meg bit her lip. "At least it doesn't seem he's running away from us or her."

"He's running toward," Math said. "He has a vision of the future, Mother, that he keeps close to his heart. It includes Lili, of course. It doesn't include being captured by the English."

Meg sighed and relaxed against Llywelyn. "He does what he thinks is right. Always. I have to accept that." Meg's mind was recovering and had begun to work. "What makes you think this wasn't part of Bohun's plan in the first place? He could have encouraged his son to return to England at the first opportunity. What if his plea for help was really a ploy to lead David astray and into England?"

"That would be devious, even for Bohun." Llywelyn said. "Besides which, Humphrey de Bohun himself is now captive." Llywelyn thought for a count of ten, and then shook his head.

"No. We must take his information at face value. The Norman barons want their lands back, and we must defend against their efforts."

"What do you plan to do about them?" Meg said.

Math cleared his throat. "Bohun didn't tell us very much, other than that Englishmen were gathering at Bristol Castle—"

Tudur entered the hall from a corridor to the right. "Sire! You have returned just in time!"

Llywelyn lifted a hand to him. "And brought war with me. Is Carew still here?"

"Yes, my lord," Tudur said. "We've been strategizing all night. Ieuan should have returned to Chepstow and begun marshalling the foot soldiers. You will find that we are not unprepared for whatever is to come."

"Good. Get everyone together," Llywelyn said. "I will meet with you all."

They retreated to Llywelyn's office. Clare had built the castle's private apartments, like everything else at Caerphilly, on a grand scale. Llywelyn's office here was twice as large as at Aber, making it twice as difficult to keep warm, although that wasn't a problem at present. Tapestries in shades of gold and red covered the walls. A single window, high in the west wall, caught the afternoon sun, peeking through the clouds that were beginning to abate. Tudur had already cleared the central table and laid a map on it, with weights at the corners.

"From Cardiff to Chepstow." Carew gestured with one hand. "Those are the lands which we must defend."

"And then north along the Wye," Tudur said. As he was the castellan at Chepstow, Bigod's castle built into the rock above the Wye River, it was of particular interest to him to hold fast against any assault from England.

"We've known for three years that the Normans could cross the Wye River or the Severn Estuary at any time and attack us," Llywelyn said. "That they never did so was merely a matter of being constrained by their rival loyalties."

"Or their fear of what we might bring to bear against them if they did," Carew said. "No Norman baron was willing to give another the upper hand against us. As long as they were divided, we were safe."

"But now they're not," Math said.

"All my life, they've been my companions," Carew said. "Bohun, Mortimer, even Clare, although he's ten years older than I. It was always a regret to me that our families' shifting allegiances affected our friendships at times—especially after Evesham."

Evesham had been the defeat of the baronial forces, led by Simon de Montfort, in 1265. Bohun's father had fought for Montfort and died of his wounds afterwards. Clare's betrayal of Montfort shortly before the battle had gone a long way in ensuring the royal victory.

"In 1265, Clare abandoned Montfort and me with his eyes open," Llywelyn said. "He chose the royal banner because he believed he would gain the most if King Henry was victorious." Llywelyn tipped his head at Carew. "Twenty years later, you chose to stay in Wales and side with me while he stayed loyal to the crown. Perhaps that means Clare resents you even more than he does me. All the more reason to appreciate your continued loyalty."

"I made my choice with my eyes open, too," Carew said. "I have yet to regret it."

"Let's make sure nobody has a reason to regret their allegiances, except the English," Tudur said. "We can toss these bastards back into the sea. We may not want war, but we are ready for it."

And that was Dafydd's doing, more than anyone else's, even if he wasn't here to lay his plans with the rest. At Dafydd's insistence, Llywelyn had invested huge sums in fortifications all along the southern coast, manning every high ground—whether it was a ten foot mound or forty—above the Severn estuary. Watch towers, blinds, patrol ships that could be put to sea on an hour's notice. It cost a fortune—as much as or more than Caerphilly. But it cost far less than losing one's country.

Llywelyn pointed to Tudur with his chin. "Chepstow to Monmouth. That's your charge. See to it."

"Yes, my lord." Tudur put his heels together and bowed.

"Carew. You take Cardiff to the mouth of the Usk," Llywelyn said. "And Math," he clapped a hand on his son-in-law's shoulder, "has the Usk to the Wye."

Math nodded. The distance across the Severn Estuary was less than two miles where the Wye flowed into the channel south of Chepstow. It widened to nearly three at a point a few miles southwest, where Dafydd claimed modern Britons had a built a bridge. That was plainly impossible, but still ... "You will find me at Caldicot Castle," Math said, "when I am not watching the beach."

Caldicot Castle was less than a mile from the Severn Estuary, right where Llywelyn (and Dafydd) believed the English would cross, if they were to come across the estuary from Bristol. Chepstow Castle, the base from which Tudur patrolled the Wye River until it headed east near Monmouth, was close enough that communication between the King and Tudur was a matter of a fast horse and half an hour.

"I will be at Cardiff," Carew said. "We will signal by watchtower."

That was another element to their defenses: a system of watchtowers which could communicate to each other in code, merely by covering and uncovering a light in a series of pre-planned signals.

And then there was the Greek fire. It was the most impressive, and the most terrifying, of all Dafydd's innovations. A fleet of boats had spent the last two years riding out of their dock on the Usk, with men trained to spray fire on the enemy. The idea was to defeat them before they reached the shore. Given that the boats had patrolled the Severn Estuary for nearly two years, Math didn't believe that most of their defenses were still a secret. Yet for the English to choose this avenue of attack? Perhaps even if the English commanders had heard of what the Welsh had built, they didn't believe what they could do.

And that was Dafydd's fault too. In him, myth and legend were becoming one. It was easy to dismiss who he was, and what he could do, because his very existence was so improbable.

"Go." Llywelyn said. "I will be with Math at Caldicot."

The men dispersed, at which point, Meg appeared from a doorway to the right. The door had remained slightly ajar during their conversation, though Math hadn't noticed it at the time.

"Mother," he said, accepting another embrace. They turned to walk from the room and down the hall, towards her solar.

Meg squeezed his waist. "I haven't even had a chance to ask you about Anna!"

"She and Cadell intended to ride south within a day or two of my departure." The thought had Math gritting his teeth. Anna had spoken to him of *telephones*—means by which two people could communicate a long distance. He wished for that now. He needed to know that she was safe, even if she couldn't be in his arms. If she and Cadell had left yesterday morning as they'd planned, they could be at Caerphilly in four days' riding.

"I'm not surprised she felt Dinas Bran was too far away. It would take too long to know how this falls out. And Bronwen, of course, is here too."

As Meg said the words, she pushed open the door to her solar. Bronwen and Aaron looked up as Meg and Math entered. They'd been playing chess, a game Math hated. He couldn't tell who was winning, but Bronwen had been known to hold her own against all comers, including Aaron, who prided himself on his skill.

"Math!" Bronwen was on her feet at the sight of them and Meg released him so Bronwen could wrap her arms around his neck. Math had never quite gotten used to how effusive these Americans he loved could be.

"Where's Anna?" Bronwen said, finally letting go of him enough so that he could nod his head to Aaron, who had also risen.

"On her way here, I hope." Math glanced towards the open window, checking the position of the sun. The afternoon had flown by, and he wished again that Anna wasn't riding through the countryside, even if he'd left some of his best men to ride with her. "This war might be coming more quickly than we thought. I hope they push the horses and she gets here soon."

"And Lili?" Math heard a hitch in Bronwen's voice when she said her sister-in-law's name.

"With Dafydd," Math said.

"Oh." Bronwen raised her eyebrows. "Now that's a story, I definitely want to hear."

14

David

David didn't care if it wasn't logically true: England felt different. Whether it was (what he prejudicially viewed as) the more serf-like existence of its people, the difference between being pastoral and agricultural, or something more intangible, the hairs on the back of David's neck told him that they'd crossed into enemy territory.

Now they just had to get back.

"William, slow down!" David said.

The boy pulled up, seemingly more subdued now that he'd gotten what he'd wanted. Or at least a part of it. David wanted to take the boy over his knee and paddle him.

They'd skirted the city to the south, circled around it to the east, and waited for three carts to pass. Now, they dismounted to rest the horses and stood alone at the edge of the road near a newly harvested field of grain. The remaining stalks stood up every which way. It looked as if scavengers had already picked it over.

"You should be ashamed for pulling a jester's act like this," Lili said. She'd berated him earlier, but now it looked like he was in for a greater degree of chastisement. David was perfectly happy to let Lili get on with it.

William's chin jutted out. "I have to rescue my father."

"At the cost of your honor? What would you father say to that?" Lili said.

William's expression turned mulish. "I did what I had to do."

"And that will relieve your father when he realizes that his son hasn't the integrity to fulfill his bargains?" Lili said.

"Lili—" David wasn't sure she should be taking this approach. William might run away again.

But Lili turned on him. "Don't you start! Humphrey de Bohun, and by his presence, William, agreed that he should be your squire. A squire who runs away from his master spends the night in the dungeon where I come from!"

William stared at her, wide-eyed, while David tried not to smile. Despite his initial misgivings, Lili's medieval version of good cop/bad cop—even if unintentional because she was sincere—looked like it was working. David decided to go along with her. "He's just a boy—"

169

"As he's proven today!" Lili glared at William, whose face had paled. He hadn't thought about it this way, child of privilege that he was. As Lili had known, talk of dishonor was not something a Bohun could take lightly. She continued, "If he was a man, he would have made a man's plan, in conjunction with his lord, not gone without one into England!"

David rubbed his chin as he studied William. "She has a point, William. What do you say to her? I stand before you, but if one of those English soldiers knew who I was, he would have taken me captive in a heartbeat or possibly killed me on sight and brought my head to his lord. You had—have—my life in your hands."

"I didn't ask you to come—"

"And again, that shows how little respect you have for the Prince of Wales," Lili said.

Lili had browbeaten William into submission, not that he didn't need to hear what she had to say. The boy stared down at his feet, chewing on his lower lip and digging the toe of his boot into the dirt. "I didn't think of those things."

"Obviously," Lili said.

David cleared his throat. "Do you understand that you can't rescue your father. Not today?"

Another sullen look from William. He really hated being in the wrong. "Yes."

"Do you understand that you must do what *I* say, because I say it? This is not about your father anymore," David said.

A hard swallow. "Yes."

"Good," David said. "We'll put the matter of your flight aside, then, until my father can take it up with your father. *Which he will.*"

William lifted his head and stared at David. "But if my father dies—"

"I am not abandoning your father, William," David said. "But I refuse to go along with a boy who has no plan, beyond the feeble notion of rescue and revenge. If you are to serve me, you need to live by what is in your head, not your heart."

William's temper was rising again. "This is my choice—"

David overrode him. "When one is a prince—or a Norman lord—no choice is truly ever your own."

William glared at David for a count of five, and then heaved a sigh. David sensed true capitulation. Now was the time for magnanimity.

"The issue before us now is getting back to Wales before anyone recognizes either you or me." William's mouth opened to reply but David wasn't finished. "This isn't about cowardice, William, or failure to do one's duty. This is about common sense. I have men to advise me, men who know your father, and have fought with him in the past. Among all of us, surely we can come up with a way to rescue him without the three of us going unprepared into the lion's den."

William licked his lips, his eyes on David's. Then, he pointed west with a jerk of his chin. "Wales is that way. It's a simple matter to ride to it."

"It is not a simple matter," David said. "I'm surprised you don't know it."

"But—" William said.

"We can't ride back the way we came without those guards stopping us and very likely, turning us back," David said. "Did you notice what they did after we passed?"

Both William and Lili shook their heads. "I didn't want to alarm you at the time, but two overturned carts now block the road. Perhaps we could go around their blockade, or even jump it, but I would prefer not to risk an arrow in the back if I don't have to."

"The other paths aren't any easier," Lili said. "To the north of Hay, the Wye River is more of a barrier than Offa's Dyke."

"There's a ford at Rhydspence—" William said.

"It's guarded," Lili said. "My brother told me."

"Well, then ..." William paused to think. "Further south, the Black Mountains block our way, though we could get through them given time ..."

"Not without great effort," David said. "And certainly not in time to help my father win this war."

William finally seemed to have come to true understanding. He bowed. "I apologize, my lord. I didn't think. It won't happen again."

Fortunately, Lili didn't express her disbelief, though like David, she surely must have thought about it. David gazed south and then west. "We will do what we must. The nearest southern passage into Wales along a road is at Abergavenny."

"That's twenty miles from here!" Lili said. "Plus, I'm sure it's guarded too."

"We have another option," William said. "My father rules at Clifford Castle since John Giffard died at Lancaster. That's where I was heading tonight."

David had forgotten about that particular addition to the Bohun fortune. "So you weren't going to ride all the way to London in the dark?"

William shook his head, looking sheepish. "I was hungry and it was raining ..." His voice trailed off.

"The castle perches on a cliff and guards a ford across the Wye," David said, for Lili's benefit. And then added, since English was not her first language, "which is where we get the name *Clifford*."

"It's two miles from here, if that," William said.

"Lead on," David said.

They remounted their horses and headed north along the road. Lili moved closer to David, just behind William, who led the way. "And if one of Bohun's many enemies has taken Clifford?"

"Then the conspiracy is far vaster than we anticipated. All the more reason to get back to Wales before we become pawns in the Norman game."

The castle sat on a natural knoll lying alongside the Wye River. It was a steep drop to the ford that gave the castle its name. It had belonged to the Cliffords until the line died out and merged with the Giffards. The moment the towers appeared in the distance, William pulled up.

"Is something amiss?" Lili said.

"The flag that flies above the castle is the wrong one," William said.

It looked right to David. "It's the white swan," he said.

"My father swore that until I found the crown of England upon my head, we would not fly that flag anywhere. It is his personal banner, not the standard of the House of Bohun," William said.

"Which means—" Lili stared at the flag instead of finishing her sentence.

"Which means that whoever holds the castle does not know of my father's pledge." William's color was high.

"How strong was the garrison?" David said.

"A dozen men," William said. "No more."

David exchanged a glance with Lili. "We have some experience with traitors among the garrison, do we not?"

"Money can buy many men," Lili said. "We saw that at Buellt."

"And at Aberdw three years ago." David dismounted and caught his horse's bridle. With a tug, he got him moving into the woods to the north of the road. "We need to get closer." The trees formed a buffer between the road and the Wye River and would provide them with adequate cover while they approached the castle.

As they entered underneath the branches, David's breathing eased. He'd lived in Oregon for ten years, and the last five in Wales. He felt comfortable out of doors, and in the woods in particular. He was no tracker, but his feet made almost no noise on the bracken beneath their feet. Lili, too, was nearly silent, having spent her life in her brother's wake. William tried to follow their lead, though he was somewhat less successful in keeping quiet.

A hundred yards from the castle, David stopped. Rain dripped from the leaves above his head and down his neck. But it was a warm rain and he was hot in his armor. "We should rest here until dark."

Lili shivered and David reached out an arm to pull her closer. "We're going to be okay."

"Are we?" she said. "In the last two days, I've ridden behind you in battle, stormed a castle, been shot with an arrow, and followed a wayward boy into England. The world is a far bigger place—and more menacing—than I had thought."

15

27 August 1288

Near Clifford Castle

Lili

Lili shivered. The rain had abated once the sun went down, but now a fog had moved in. She couldn't see anything at all if it wasn't moving. That Dafydd was with her was only evident by the fact that he held her hand.

"You're sure about this?" she said. "Trusting William, I mean?"

"I don't think he means to get us killed or captured," Dafydd said. "He's twelve. I was more sure of myself and self-righteous than he at twelve—until coming to Wales blew my world apart."

Lili smiled under the cover of the darkness because Dafydd was still pretty sure of himself, hence the journey into England in the first place. He could have let William go, or ordered other men to follow the boy. But no—he had to do it himself. As far as she could tell, Dafydd wasn't the least bit afraid to be stumbling about in the dark near Clifford Castle, looking for what Lili feared might be a non-existent ford, or one impossible to use if the rain of earlier had raised the level of the river past the point that it was safe to cross. Concerned, Dafydd might be. But not afraid—and even what he felt of that emotion would be more for Lili and William than for himself.

"Just a few more paces." William pulled up at the edge of the trees that buttressed the castle to the northeast.

The original builder had located the castle at a bend in the Wye River. It was hard for Lili to get her head around the geography, but the river started in the mountains of Wales, flowed southeast, then turned north past Hay. Two miles north of the town, the Wye flowed eastward before heading north again for a brief stretch (Clifford Castle had been built at this curve in the river). It then turned southeast as it wended its way through England to the sea.

Taking advantage of the winding river, the original builder of the castle had built an earthwork dam upstream from the castle to flood the little valley to the west and south of it. Thus, with water all around it, the only real access to the castle was from the northeast.

"I think it's low enough to cross." Dafydd peered through the trees towards the ford. "So much of the water has been diverted to the valley, that the dam has made the ford on the river even shallower." He had read Lili's thoughts.

"I told you we could use it," William said.

A faint light filtered to them from the battlements of Clifford Castle which towered above them. They'd gotten far closer than Lili had thought they might. The wait until the end of the day, and then the walk in the dark, had seemed endless and ultimately for no good reason. It wasn't like her to be so pessimistic, but the forces arrayed against them—against Wales—seemed far too powerful and omnipotent for them to counter. At least they hadn't gone hungry, as Lili had packed food in her saddlebags for the journey back to Buellt which she had planned to make.

Or had she always known that she would ultimately share what she'd brought? Even Dafydd had commented that she'd brought enough for the three of them to eat for a week. Could she really have left Dafydd again? It would have been for the last time, and she'd known it, even as she'd watched his face and told him her plans. She'd thought it the right thing to do. But now, the longer she was with him, the more impossible it seemed that she could walk away.

Lili shivered again, though the air was only damp, not cold. She wore her wool cloak tucked tight about her with her hood up. One hand held her horse's bridle, while her other hand was dry and warm in Dafydd's. He gripped it tightly.

"A figure moves in the upper window of the near tower," William said. "That's not a sleeping chamber. It's for prisoners. We have no dungeon because it was impossible to burrow into the rock below the tower."

Lili peered closer. The mist wasn't quite so thick in this location and her eyes picked out the shape. "I see him."

Without asking permission, William stepped out from under the trees, still leading his horse. Dafydd released Lili's hand to grab his shoulder. "No, William. Stay back. Look!" Dafydd pointed to one of the members of the garrison who paced along the wall-walk. Another few steps and William would have been out in the open for him to see.

William subsided without protest, though tense anticipation emanated from him. "But what if—?" He cut off his sentence abruptly.

Did he think the figure was his father?

"We can wait until we've established the guard's pattern before we get any closer. We're safe here. Wales is just there." Dafydd gestured to the west. "If someone ventures towards the woods, we can leap on the horses and gallop like hell."

Someone else, however, wasn't going to wait. A hand flung a rope out the window of the tower room. The twist of the loop at the end caught in the light from the torches along the battlements, giving Lili no doubt as to what she was seeing. The rope fell and swung three feet from the top of the curtain wall.

Because the tower formed one corner of the castle's defenses, once the owner of the rope climbed down it, he would find himself outside the castle proper, though hardly safe, since the drop to the ground from the top of the wall was considerable—at least fifteen feet. And since this spot overlooked the ford, not the lake on the other side, if he were to take a few steps and leap into the water, it wasn't deep enough to provide him with a cushion. If he jumped that far, the man would break his legs, at the very least.

"Dafydd —" Lili said.

"I see him." Dafydd rummaged through the saddle bags on his horse.

"What are you doing?" Lili said.

"Do either of you have rope?" Dafydd said.

"There's a length in my bag," William said. "I saw it when I was looking for food earlier."

"Give it to me." Dafydd held out his hand. William, his hands shaking as much as his voice had when he'd spoken, untied the strings on his pack, took out the coil of rope, and handed it over.

Dafydd glanced once towards the castle—the soldier who'd walked the battlements earlier had disappeared—and then leaned in to kiss Lili on the forehead. "I'll be right back."

Reeling from his touch, Lili watched Dafydd's shadow stride across the cleared space between the woods and the base of the tower. By the time he reached its foot, the man at the top had gotten himself out of the window, down his rope, and balanced precariously on the edge of the wall. No guard below him in the bailey called a warning, and no man moved along the top of the wall-walk towards them.

Her heart in her throat, Lili strained to see well enough with the mist and the distance. She couldn't make out much more than shadows and darker shapes moving in it. She did note the moment Dafydd threw his rope up to the man, who caught it. What felt like hours later, but could only have been a few dozen heartbeats, Dafydd and the man he'd rescued ran across the clearing.

"William, take Lili's horse!" Dafydd pointed the newcomer to William's horse, which was larger than the one Lili had ridden. Dafydd then threw himself onto his horse and pulled Lili up behind him. "Let's go!"

Lili peered at the man, but she didn't recognize him. "Who—?"

"No time!" Dafydd turned his horse's head and urged him out of the woods and down the slope towards the Wye River. "The alarm has been raised."

Even as their horses surged into the water at the ford, a cry came from the battlements. Lili cast a glance back. A man-sized shadow blocked the light from the tower room that the prisoner had vacated.

A voice called from behind them in English, "There! In the river!"

The sound of the rapids below the ford and the pounding of Lili's heart were so loud, Lili didn't realize that a member of the garrison had shot an arrow until the stranger on William's horse grunted and spoke in French, a language in which Lili felt more comfortable than English. "That was too close."

He plucked an arrow from where it had stuck into his saddle bag, the feathered end quivering, and spurred his horse after William, who was the first to reach the opposite shore.

The shouts grew louder, following them through the trees that bordered the Wye River. The ford wouldn't prove any more of a barrier to the English than it had to them.

"With the fog and the dark, we have a head start, at least," the stranger said, still in French.

"Do you know the area?" Dafydd urged his horse abreast of the man, speaking in the same language.

"Not as well as I might," he said. "We're in Wales, you know, and even as a boy, I didn't venture on this side of the river often."

"You weren't always at war with my father," Dafydd said.

"Be that as it may—" the man said.

Dafydd ducked his head under a low hanging branch. "Now that I think about it, I've never been here before either. Painscastle is due west from Clifford, is it not?"

"It is," William said.

"You left Bronwen's chariot only two miles to the northwest of Painscastle when you came through the last time," Lili said, speaking in Welsh for Dafydd's ears alone.

The stranger picked up on her mention of the castle, and spoke again in French. "Painscastle is less than five miles as the crow flies from here, but the passage through the Dyke might be held against us." Offa's Dyke as it stretched north of Hay, served as the treaty boundary between England and Wales. Not that the English behind them were going to respect it any more than the men who'd pursued Humphrey de Bohun.

"We won't go by the road," Dafydd said.

"Who is this, Dafydd?" Lili dropped her voice so the man couldn't hear. "Why are we helping him? Why is he riding to Wales with us when he's obviously Norman?"

"I apologize, Lili," Dafydd said, "I thought you recognized him. Meet Gilbert de Clare."

Lili swallowed hard. *The Red Earl.* Questions boiled up inside her, the first of which was *what was he doing locked in the tower of Clifford Castle?* She had no time for any of them, however, as another arrow whined past her head and lodged in a grassy tussock to her left. She looked back. The figure of a man stood out in relief on a low hill on the western side of the river. He was too far away to shoot accurately, but even so, as Clare had said earlier, that had been far too close.

Dafydd found a trail that let them pick up their pace, though how he could tell where they were going in the fog and the dark Lili didn't know. She just held on, her arms tight around his waist and her cheek pressed against his back.

He urged his horse up a steep incline and Lili tightened her hold even more. "Ease up, Lili," he said. "I won't let you fall off."

Her arms relaxed incrementally, perhaps not as much as he would have liked, but he patted her hand anyway.

"Why are we bringing Gilbert de Clare with us?" she said.

"What else would I do with him?" Dafydd said. "Leave him to be recaptured?"

"What if he means to trap us in his net? What if—"

"He didn't know that we were going to be outside Clifford Castle, just now," Dafydd said. "*We* didn't know that we were going to be there. Men locked him in, men he thought were his allies, and he got out."

"The enemy of your enemy is your friend, is that it?" Lili had heard Dafydd say that phrase during the last war.

"It's possible," Dafydd said, "though an hour ago the idea that I'd be riding into Wales with Gilbert de Clare beside me would have been a laughable one."

"At the very least, I'm in your debt," Clare said. The trail had narrowed suddenly, bringing Clare closer to them such that he overheard their conversation—even as they'd been speaking in Welsh. They'd have to be more careful about what they said to each other in private, if Clare was going to understand their words.

"They're still coming, my lord," William said from behind them, back to French.

"I know," Dafydd said. "Can you see how many?"

"No, my lord," William said. "All I know is that there are too many."

"We could go to ground?" Clare said.

Lili felt Dafydd shake his head. "With yesterday's rain, our tracks stand out plain as day."

Lili still couldn't see anything, but those following had torches and she could see how easy it would be to track them in the mud. The terrain steepened, and then Offa's Dyke rose up before them, the bulk of it evident even in the dark. Now that they had come further from the river, the fog that had enveloped them, and had helped to hide them, thinned. A pale moon shone above their heads. Compared to the murk under the trees, this was as bright as day. The Dyke showed decay in this spot, as it did in many locations along the wall. Even though it formed the boundary between Wales and England, neither side had seen fit to put effort into repairing it.

"Where are we in relation to Painscastle?" Lili said.

"North of the road that leads to it from the east," Dafydd said. "Hold tight, Lili, we're going up."

Their horse had found a path that zigzagged up the face of the Dyke. Lili clutched Dafydd around the waist and leaned forward with him to counter the sharp angle.

"How did you know this was here?" she said. "You haven't been here before."

"Not here, no," Dafydd said. "But the country folk cross the Dyke every day. You know they do. Here, at Dolforwyn, at Dinas Bran. Even when the roads are guarded, they have a way through. I was willing to travel a lot further than this to find a path if we'd had to."

"If our horses can navigate it, our pursuers' beasts can too," Clare said.

Dafydd shrugged. "By then we'll be in Wales, which means we'll be safer than they are. On top of which, I don't hear dogs. Without them, they won't know exactly where we've crossed."

The horses reached the top. On the heights, a quickening wind blew. They'd been sheltered from the west wind while climbing the Dyke. Lili turned her face directly into it, knowing by the same instinct shared by every Welsh child that the weather blew in from the southwest at this time of year.

"I don't see a way down," William said.

"I don't either," Dafydd said. "But you don't need to. Trust your horse."

Lili glanced east. The scattered clouds had parted to allow the moon to shine more brightly. Three English riders came out of the trees on the far side of the field they'd just crossed. She tugged on Dafydd's cloak. "They're coming. And surely they can see us up here!"

"Down we go," Dafydd said.

16

27 August 1288
Near Clifford Castle

David

The Dyke was comprised of mounded earth, but the turf was thick, and even what had looked from the top like a sharp drop to the bottom, didn't turn out to be quite as severe a decline as all that. David had told William to trust his horse, because he knew it was the right answer, not because it came naturally to David either. He'd had to learn it, as he'd learned so many things since he'd arrived in Wales six years ago.

The base of the Dyke on the Welsh side was fronted by a deep ditch, mostly filled in after several hundred years of wind and weather, and they scrambled up it without too much trouble. That they were in Wales would normally have given David every confidence, but the English soldiers would follow. What did they have to lose? The Treaty was dead, stamped into the mud at their feet.

David hadn't realized how angry that made him until just now. He and his father had known that the Normans would violate the Treaty eventually—of course they would. Every single Norman had heard a lifetime of slander and mockery towards the Welsh, ridiculing them as a people and condemning them for their barbaric ways. His mother's academic colleagues would have called it treating them as *the other*.

For all that, however, David hadn't been prepared for the Normans to come at them with such force and under these circumstances. And David had to admit that what maybe bothered him the most about the events of the last few days was that *he hadn't predicted any of them*. It was painful to acknowledge his arrogance in thinking that he could.

They crossed two fields, and headed into the woods on the other side, with still no sign of the English riders behind them. Maybe they had stopped at the Dyke?

"Do you know how much farther?" Clare spoke these words in Welsh, revealing a proficiency that equaled that of Humphrey de Bohun. David resigned himself to not being able to keep his communications with Lili a secret, not if all four of them could converse interchangeably in Welsh, French, and English. It was just his luck that he was associating with the only two Normans who'd bothered to learn the language of their subjects.

"No," David said. "Do you know, Lili?"

"Not exactly," she said. "But there's nothing but farms and fields between here and Painscastle."

"Then we ride as hard and as fast as we can until we reach it," David said.

Lili sniffed the air and pointed to the southwest. "We'll have more rain soon. Tomorrow or the next day, I think."

David smiled, but didn't say what he was thinking—that he didn't have to be in tune with the weather to know that in Wales, rain always came eventually.

It was only five miles from Clifford to Painscastle. They'd come half that distance already, and the remainder were the longest miles of David's life. The moon shone brightly down, illuminating every tree and hillock, but leaving too much in shadow. It felt to David as if the English soldiers that Lili had seen lurked behind every obstacle. While logic told him that the soldiers couldn't have gotten ahead of them, and that they might even have left their pursuers behind, at least temporarily, his pulse didn't believe it for a second.

Finally, they came out of a field and onto the road that looped around to the north of the castle. "I don't hear any pursuit," Clare said.

"Nor I," David said. "And now it doesn't matter. Ride!"

Never had he been happier to see the gatehouse of a castle. At a lifted hand from David, one of the members of the garrison opened the wicket gate beside the portcullis. David dismounted and helped Lili down, before leading his horse into the courtyard of the castle. Torches lit the expansive space, almost as if it were day. David opened his mouth to speak to the soldier who came to greet them—

Goddamn it!

"My lord!" The man-at-arms grabbed the bridle of Gilbert de Clare's horse, speaking in English. "W-w-we had no idea you'd be arriving tonight. Or-or-or rather, I mean ... this morning!"

David's hand went to the hilt of his sword but Lili reached around him and gripped his wrist before whispering close in his ear. "Wait."

She was right. Clare spoke to the soldier in a calm voice, also in English. "I can see that." He gestured to the refuse pile by the blacksmith's shop. "You have some work ahead of you."

The man swallowed hard. "Our captain died during the taking of the castle. We haven't had time ..." His words trailed off as Clare glared at him.

The Marcher baron waved a hand at David, William, and Lili, who crowded up beside him. "See that a meal is brought to us immediately. My companions and I have ridden hard."

"Yes, my lord." The man blinked. A more motley escort for the Earl of Gloucester couldn't be imagined. David tried to look unthreatening, but he knew he wasn't always successful, given his size.

"Did you kill all the Welsh defenders?" Clare said.

"N-n-no, my lord," the man said, back to stuttering. "Not all of them. That wasn't in our orders."

David was pleased to hear that. Clare apparently was too.

"Good," Clare said. "Where are they? I've come all this way to speak to one of them. Pray he is not dead."

The man stiffened into a more soldierly bearing. "We put them in the dungeon under the barracks, sir."

"How many men do you have?"

"Only a dozen still standing, sir. Our spy tainted the mead so we could take the castle two nights ago, but the potion didn't have the same effect on everyone and some resisted strongly. We lost several men."

Clare harrumphed his baronly disgust for this admission and dismissed the man with a sharp jerk of his head. Then he touched Lili's arm. "Come." She nodded, though she glanced once at David, who shrugged, and gave way as Clare led them towards the keep which rose above them on its motte. What else could they do, given this strange turn of events?

David tried to put on an aura of assurance as he stalked across the bailey of the castle, his hand in the crook of Lili's elbow, to make sure she kept up too. When the Welsh had taken Painscastle in 1285, the motte had been guarded by a barbican and a drawbridge. These features had been destroyed three years ago and not been rebuilt. A makeshift bridge spanned the ditch at the base of the motte and they crossed it to reach the steps up to the keep.

Given that Clare hadn't betrayed them yet, it seemed he might not and that his gratitude for his rescue was genuine. It would be interesting to see how long it lasted. David certainly wasn't going to betray Clare by informing the English soldier that he wasn't one of *them*, any more than David was, and that David had picked the Marcher lord up while Clare was escaping from Clifford Castle.

Whoever the main conspirators on the Norman side were in this war, they didn't seem to have communicated their chain of command to those below them beyond the barest minimum. The soldiers at Valle Crucis Abbey had thought Mortimer was their commander. The soldiers at Buellt had claimed it was Clare, despite wearing Mortimer colors too. Now, these at Painscastle took Clare's appearance at face value, even though a third party had to be behind the Norman invasion.

At the same time, David didn't know what game Clare was playing. For now, it was enough that he hadn't pointed out to these soldiers that David was the Prince of Wales. If Gilbert de Clare was a prize, David was the whole carnival.

Plus, if Humphrey de Bohun was really on the way to the Tower of London, then the capture of William would have been well-received also. The boy, however, had done well. He hadn't betrayed himself or them, and had uncharacteristically kept his mouth shut since they'd returned to Wales.

David glanced at the boy. William's head was down and he looked neither left nor right as they walked up the thirty or so steps that took them to the top of the motte. David hadn't ever seen William this subdued, not even after the attack outside Buellt. David hoped it wasn't a precursor to another rebellion. In William's mind, they had to moving backwards and now were further from rescuing his father than when they'd started.

Clare took them to the entrance to the great hall, through it, and to a doorway at the far end. Beyond, a short hallway led to several rooms. He entered the first one, which proved to be the castellan's study. Like David, it seemed that Clare had been here before. Clare stood with his back to the door, staring out of the window.

David gestured Lili around the only table in the room, to the stool behind it, while David perched on the table's edge. Nobody said anything until two servants appeared with food and drink and left again. David gestured to William to close the door behind them. He obeyed unquestioningly, and then leaned his back against it.

The four accidental companions gazed at the food for ten seconds before Lili said, "I'm hungry."

"May I join you?" William said.

Lili nodded and William tugged a bench from its position near the door towards the table, and sat. The two were similar in size and David couldn't help smiling at their similar dishevelment. Lili still wore the same boy's breeches she'd put on to shoot in at Buellt, but her entire outfit, like William's, was definitely the worse for wear.

David grabbed one of the small loaves of bread and a hunk of cheese and walked to stand beside Clare. Only one of the window shutters was open. David pulled open the second one, peered into the darkness, and then closed it again. "We're forty feet above the bailey. Nobody can hear us," he said.

Clare walked to the table and plucked one of the loaves from the tray. He gestured towards David with it. "What have we got ourselves into?"

The *we* and Clare's evident good humor had David feeling remarkably cheerful all of a sudden. For now, it *was* 'we'. Allies, no matter how unlikely, should always be made welcome.

"I met with Humphrey de Bohun three days ago. He warned us that you Normans were moving against Wales." David eyed Clare. "Your name came up."

Clare snorted. "I can see why Bohun might suspect my involvement. Ever since Evesham ..."

It might have been twenty years ago, but certain things cannot be forgiven. Even so, David let it go. "English soldiers took Buellt Castle two days ago. We took it back, but it does seem that whichever baron is moving his pieces on this board, he has a well-conceived plan. It's not his fault that certain elements didn't go entirely according to his intention."

"That would be because of Lili, my lord, and you," William said.

"And you, in truth," Lili said. "While I hate to admit it, your flight into England hasn't been without benefit."

"Certainly to me!" Clare said.

"But who is it that plots against Wales?" William gestured with his belt knife to Clare. "My father suspected you, my lord, it is true, but Buellt *was* taken in your name."

"My name?" Clare froze in the act of popping a roasted mushroom into his mouth. "Have my enemies sunk that low?"

"So it seems, my lord." William poured each of them a cup of mead from the pitcher. He handed the first cup to Lili, who smiled at him as she took it.

"And yet, those same English soldiers wore Mortimer colors," David said.

"Which Mortimer?" Clare raised his eyebrows. "Young Roger, surely. Edmund conspires with Bohun if he conspires with anyone."

That was news to David and something Humphrey de Bohun had neglected to mention.

"We had assumed it was Edmund," David said. "But it didn't matter in the end because it was your name on their lips."

"It does seem that we have found ourselves caught in a complicated plot, doesn't it?" Clare said. "Too complicated, if you ask me. Every moving piece raises the risk that one weak point will bring down the whole."

"And where do you stand, at present?" David said. "From the behavior of the men out there, they think you are one of the conspirators in this war. Why *aren't* you?"

"I'm as mystified as you as to why my captivity was kept secret," Clare said, "though surely grateful for it as well. But Valence has many plots and stratagems up his sleeve. Who's to say that playing one baron off another isn't useful to him? You thought I was with him until you found me hanging from a rope outside of that tower."

"D-d-did you say, 'Valence'?" David said, stuttering just like the English captain had when they'd entered Painscastle.

Clare's eyes turned wary. "You didn't even know that William de Valence was involved? It is his mind that is behind … well …" Clare gestured expansively, "all of this."

"No, we did not," David said.

Clare let out a deep breath. "Valence has more power and reach than any other lord in England. I'm sure that the commander of my knights, Ralph de Quincy, betrayed me to him. Ralph is the only one of my men who could command unquestioning obedience from the rest, all of whom would assume his orders came from me. Valence must have bought him."

William de Valence had been uncle to King Edward. He crusaded with Edward before he became king and as the former Earl of Pembroke (he'd lost his lands to Wales, too, with the Treaty), was the most powerful man in England who wasn't a regent, with the possible exception of Clare himself, whose estates were spread across twenty-two English counties.

That Valence wasn't a regent had more to do with his upbringing in France, and the bad influence (from an English perspective) of his French relatives, than his lack of actual power. His Pembrokeshire base had been the jumping off point for King Edward's 1282 campaign against David's father. In fact, it was he who had replaced Clare as commander of the English forces in Wales towards the end of 1282. The two men openly despised each other.

That Valence hadn't been at Lancaster when King Edward died was pure luck. And surely, the man thanked God every day for it.

Lili had been looking from Clare to David and back again. "Please—who is William de Valence? Bohun didn't mention him, did he?"

David turned to Lili. "No, he didn't. Valence was King Edward's right hand man, up until the day of his death. We've had no indication that Valence was involved until now."

"That must have been his intent," Clare said. "Valence is in a perfect position to orchestrate men and events according to his desires. In order to ratify the Treaty with Wales, the regents had to appease him by compensating him for his loss of Pembroke, with lands to the north and west of London, else he ruin all. He has courted Archbishop Peckham to the point that the Archbishop thinks the sun shines out of Valence's arse. Never doubt that Valence has his ear."

"So, it was Valence who imprisoned you in the tower at Clifford Castle?" Lili said.

"His men ambushed mine," Clare said. "I recognized Valence's commander from past wars in Wales. Despite the natural assumption made by the soldiers here that every Norman in the March supports this war, Valence and I rarely see eye-to-eye. I am not one of his conspirators."

"Why not?" David said. "You've worked with people you despised in the past."

Clare shot him a dark look. "I want Caerphilly back—you know that."

David nodded. Of course, Clare did.

"But the plan as Valence explained it to me was not what I would have chosen. I was willing to wait a little longer, for the right moment to make my move. Not Valence's move. *Mine.*"

David found the bread he was eating sticking in his throat and he brought down his hand without taking another bite. "You were going to wait until my father died. Your idea was that I would be weakest then. You were going to test me."

Clare shrugged. "Be that as it may, I did not see any benefit to being hasty when great loss could come from it. In

Valence's conspiracy, I would have been one of several rival lords—and late to the game at that."

David could see Clare's point. Conspiracy was nothing new to Clare. Twenty years ago, Clare—then a young man of twenty-two—had conspired with Simon de Montfort and David's father (who at the time was still a vassal to the English crown) to divide England and Wales among themselves. The size of Clare's ego had never been in doubt.

"But I underestimated their resolve," Clare said. "I received an invitation from Humphrey de Bohun to visit Clifford Castle and discuss alternatives." He spread his hands wide. "Needless to say, the message wasn't from Bohun."

"Who is himself on the way to the Tower of London," David said.

"Is that what you heard?" Clare's eyes went to William's face. "Ah," he said, in response to what he saw there. Defiance, David thought. Or guilt. "Were you in England with the Prince of Wales on your heels because you thought to rescue your father all by yourself?"

William flushed red to the roots of his hair.

"We've been over that," David said. "Did you know that Bohun had spoken with me?"

"No," Clare said. "But seeing you together with young William put the pieces in place. Bohun *does* have an alternate plan. I find it very interesting that he has formed a counter one so quickly. Valence is right to be wary of him—and of me."

"Indeed," David said.

Clare canted his head. "You are not concerned to be with me in a castle held against you, with no plan for getting out?"

"You don't have a plan that includes me? I felt sure you did," David said. "You've gotten us this far, haven't you?"

Clare studied David. "Tell me what you think we should do?"

David shrugged. "There are men loyal to Wales here, albeit imprisoned. I say, we break them out."

17

28 August 1288
Painscastle

Lili

"**W**hy haven't they killed our men?" The question had niggled at the back of Lili's mind from the start.

"I don't know," Dafydd said. "I've wondered that too. The English soldiers killed Welshmen in taking the castle, but once victorious, they rounded the defenders up, both here and at Buellt."

"It's because Valence plans to actually rule Wales, not just conquer it," Clare said.

"What a remarkable idea." Dafydd picked at his upper lip as he gazed at Clare. "And he thinks by showing mercy to a handful of Welsh soldiers, he's taking a step in that direction?"

"He needs the loyalty of all the people in the region, both Welsh and English, once he establishes his puppet Prince of Wales," Clare said.

"You've lost me," Dafydd said. "What are you talking about? What puppet Prince of Wales? Certainly, not me."

Clare snorted laughter. "No." He canted his head. "You don't know that either?" And then at Dafydd's steady gaze added, "You really don't know."

"Tell me," Dafydd said.

Clare's look of amusement set Lili's teeth on edge. Dafydd had managed to keep his face serene but he had to be cursing Clare inside. She hated it when older people—men in particular—looked down on Dafydd because he was only nineteen.

"Valence has the eldest son of Owain Goch, King Llywelyn's older brother, in his pocket."

"He hasn't!" Lili said.

Dafydd barked a laugh. "Of all things for you to say, I never expected that. I didn't know my uncle Owain had a son."

"Didn't you?" Clare seemed genuinely surprised—and amused, as always.

"I didn't know he fathered any children. My father has never spoken of them, and even when my uncle Dafydd was alive, before my father publically claimed me as his son, it was always Uncle Dafydd who would be his heir."

"Your uncle Dafydd certainly wouldn't have mentioned it, would he?" Clare said. "He wouldn't have wanted to distract attention from his own inheritance. Your existence was offensive enough."

"My uncle Owain spent much of his life in prison," Dafydd said.

Actually, Lili knew that statement hardly conveyed the magnitude of what had been done to King Llywelyn's brother, Owain. From the age of eighteen, he'd been imprisoned in succession by his grandfather, his uncle, the King of England, and his brother, for all but the last five years of his life. The 1277 treaty released Owain from Llywelyn's custody. Subsequently, he had retired to his estates in Gwynedd. He died before Dafydd had come to Wales.

"But he was not kept in seclusion," Clare said.

Dafydd scrubbed at his hair with both hands and then pulled at it. The ends stood straight up. Dafydd didn't do anything to smooth them, just dropped his arms in resignation. "Apparently not." He paced towards the window and back. "Today is definitely not the day I would have chosen for a long-lost cousin to come out of the woodwork, especially not a son of my father's intemperate older brother."

"I would be very surprised if your *father* doesn't know of him," Clare said.

Dafydd grimaced. That was something he would want to take up with his father, undoubtedly. Dafydd hated being surprised, and to Lili's mind, for Llywelyn to omit that Dafydd had a cousin was tantamount to lying.

Dafydd pursed his lips. "Where did Valence find him?"

"He's lived his life in England," Clare said. "He speaks no Welsh and has never set foot in your country as far as I know."

"You've met him?" Dafydd said.

"Yes," Clare said. "Valence trotted him out when he was trying to convince me to join him."

Dafydd made a sound of disgust. "I would guess, if Valence has a prince of Wales to place on my father's throne, that an important part of his plan is the death of my father and me."

"Yes," Clare said.

"What's this man's name?" Lili said.

Clare had obviously enjoyed the imparting of his news to his incredulous audience, and continued to answer patiently. "Hywel. He was born in 1248, which makes him twenty years older than you, my lord, and the heir to all that your father kept from his older brother when he left him to rot in Dolbadarn Castle for so many years."

"So—Valence thinks that by showing mercy to some Welsh soldiers in a few border castles, the populace as a whole will be more likely to accept Hywel?" Lili said.

Clare shrugged. "Better than not showing mercy. Though you Welsh seem to delight in keeping rebellion alive."

"That must be it." Dafydd turned to Lili, ignoring Clare's inflammatory comment. "If Valence is going to trot out his puppet prince after this war is over, he doesn't want to have the legacy of the murder of every man in every garrison in Wales to contend with."

"If Valence wins," Clare said, "Painscastle would, of course, return to Norman hands, but a resentful local populace could prove a handful for an upstart prince, and a rallying point for a new prince—even Dafydd, here, were he to survive and retreat into the mountains with a handful of men to support him."

"He'd have more than a handful," Lili said.

"Clever of Valence to think that far ahead," Dafydd said.

Lili didn't think it was clever at all. Evil, maybe. Wales had often been torn in two by rival claimants to the throne—usually brothers. For all that King Llywelyn had only fathered two children, it was a relief that only one was a son. Lili hoped for Dafydd's sake that the child Meg carried now was a girl. Even twenty years younger than Dafydd, a younger brother could prove troublesome when he grew up.

"Valence and Hywel are holed up in Bristol Castle," Clare said, "overseeing the southern advance."

Now, Lili was confused. "I thought Bristol Castle was—"

"Mine. Yes." Clare's words left no room for further questioning. He glanced at Dafydd. "Bohun was to be taken there, not to the Tower."

"Was he?" William's eyes lit. He'd been keeping very quiet, focusing on the food before him as any good twelve year old boy should. At the mention of his father's name, however, he woke up fully. He looked at Dafydd. "That's far closer to where we are now than London."

Dafydd's face took on a look that Lili knew. The wheels of strategy were spinning in his head. He had an idea. "I agree. It changes everything."

"Why does it?" Lili said.

"It really does?" William said.

"I believe so," Dafydd said. "But I don't want to get ahead of myself. Let's get our men free from their prison here, and then we'll decide what to do about Bohun, this upstart prince, and the Norman who holds his leash."

Clare didn't press him, though William opened his mouth to ask for more. Clare prevented that by heading for the door. He jerked his head at Dafydd before opening it. "What if you play the role of my nephew, with Lili as your wife, and William as your wife's brother. Do you have any problems with that?"

Dafydd took Lili's hand in his. "No problems here."

William glanced at Dafydd and Lili and stood. "Okay," he said.

"Then, let's go," Clare said.

Lili didn't protest either. It was what she had suggested they tell the guards at the border crossing. She *wanted* to marry Dafydd. She just didn't see how it would ever work, not with him destined to become the King of Wales. Who was she to be a queen? The thought was ludicrous. It wasn't that she thought so little of herself, but King Llywelyn's concerns were valid. Dafydd *should* marry a woman who could help Wales politically. Her head told her that, anyway, even if her heart denied it.

Lili trotted beside Dafydd, whose long strides followed hard on Clare's heels. Clare nodded to the guard at the top of the steps to the keep as they went through the main door.

"Rain's coming, my lord," the man said as they passed him.

Lili, too, had forecast rain during their journey from Clifford Castle, and she felt in her bones that it was coming, but there was no sign of a storm yet.

While they'd been talking and resting inside, dawn had come. The motte at Painscastle rose above the surrounding countryside, according them a spectacular view beyond the curtain wall. The sun shone brightly on the green fields all around. Although the wind still blew, no clouds filled the western horizon.

As before, Clare showed that he knew his way around. He strode across the bailey and into the barracks. Upon his entrance in the doorway, the men lolling in the mess hall leapt as one to their feet. "My lord!" one of them said, a smart-looking Englishman with close-cropped hair and beard.

"As you were, men," Clare said. "I have business with one of the Welshmen whom you're keeping in here."

"Yes, my lord!" the same soldier said. "This way."

Clare accorded him a nod and the four companions followed the soldier down a short hallway to a set of stairs. The stairs led to a long but narrow guard room, twenty by ten, fronting five doors. Each door was made of solid oak, with an iron-barred window and a heavy lock.

Dafydd released Lili's hand to come abreast with Clare as he faced the two guards who occupied the room. With a scraping of chairs on the stone floor, they stood to greet Clare. Lili halted on the bottom step, William right behind her. She turned slightly to speak to him. "Why would the former castellan of Painscastle have occasion to imprison so many people that he needed five cells?"

"It does seem an unusually high number, doesn't it?" William said. "I can't recall a time when my father has needed more than one." He had answered her in English and Lili realized that she'd spoken in Welsh. From his position behind Clare's left shoulder, Dafydd shot her a worried look. She should have known better than to speak Welsh in what was now a Norman castle.

Fortunately, the two soldiers who'd drawn the duty of guarding the Welsh prisoners had been busy talking to Clare, who covered for Lili by saying something she didn't catch but that made them laugh.

"Yes, my lord," one of the guards said. He bowed to Clare, nodded at Dafydd, and approached the stairs where Lili waited. William had already stepped past her to quarter the room, perhaps trying to act more grown up and contribute to their endeavors—and perhaps to make up for the fact that it was because of him they were here in the first place.

Lili moved to the side to allow both guards to climb the stairs to the hallway above. The initial soldier who'd brought them downstairs was the last to leave. He glanced back at Clare, his brow furrowed.

Clare lifted a hand to him. "All is well. I won't be a moment."

"Yes, my lord," the man said.

Lili wished she could tell what the soldier was thinking. "They didn't mind leaving the prisoners with no guard?" she said.

"I assured them that we could handle them." Clare eyed Dafydd up and down. "They seemed impressed with your husband's size."

Dafydd smirked. "I loosened my sword in its sheath and looked at them grimly. What could they do but give way?"

As most people gave way before Dafydd, Lili wasn't surprised, but it was probably equally likely that Clare's authority convinced them. Who would believe that Gilbert de Clare could work with the Welsh, especially with all that had happened in the twenty years since Evesham? And yet, Valence should have known that Clare had always put himself first. He had spent those twenty years supporting King Edward, true, but just because Valence was stepping in to fill the hole left by the king's death, didn't mean that Clare had any intention of following him.

"Did they leave the keys too?" Lili said.

"Over here." William lifted a thick ring off a hook on the wall.

Clare held out his hand for the key ring, and then dropped his arm before William could hand the keys to him. "You release them, Prince Dafydd. I'll watch the stairs."

Dafydd didn't question Clare's reasons. Clare was probably right that releasing Welsh prisoners was a task better left to a Welshman. Dafydd took the keys from William and went to the first door.

"They'll need weapons." Dafydd shot the comment over his shoulder as he stuck the key in the lock, and then added, "Lili and William, see what those chests over there contain."

Lili went to the closest one and opened it. "It's a jumbled mess is all," William said, looking with her. They pawed through it, but other than a dull belt knife, the contents consisted of worthless items: broken earthenware cups, a pitcher, two ragged cloaks, and a couple of helmets.

They moved on to the second chest, which proved to have more satisfactory contents. It was nearly full to the brim with real weaponry: knives, swords sheathed in worn scabbards, and even an axe with a finely honed blade.

Lili and William each took two swords and brought them to the table. Meanwhile, Dafydd opened the door to the first cell. "Is everyone all right in here?" he said.

"A few bruises, nothing more." A heavy-set, dark haired man stepped through the door, followed by five other men. They gazed around the room, taking in the four companions. William handed the first man a weapon and he grinned as he took it. "Who are you?" he said.

William didn't answer and Dafydd moved on to the second cell. "Be as quiet as you can," he said to the six men who filed into the main room.

Two went to help William and Lili with the weapons they'd unearthed. "Excuse me ... uh ... Miss," said a youth no older than Lili herself, looking her up and down.

"We're getting you out of here," Lili said, ignoring his surprise at what she was wearing. At the bottom of the trunk, she found a quiver of arrows to match the three bows that someone had propped in the far corner. One of the bows looked small enough to suit her.

Dafydd got stiff nods from the newly freed men, some curious looks, but otherwise, no resistance. By the time Dafydd got to the fourth cell, the guardroom was crowded with relieved men, hastily buckling on weaponry.

"Hurry!" Clare said. "We shouldn't linger."

"Last one." Dafydd unlocked the fifth cell, pulled the door wide, and then stopped. The cell contained only one man, who lay slumped on the floor.

Dafydd hurried forward and crouched before its occupant. Lili took a lantern from its hook on the wall, without Dafydd needing to ask for it, and brought it into the cell.

William followed. Before the boy could shout, Clare, who'd noted Dafydd's attention and had left his post at the foot of the stairs, came up behind him and clapped a hand over his mouth.

Before them lay Humphrey de Bohun, regent of England.

18

28 August 1288
Painscastle

David

Ignorance, stupidity, and blind luck. The phrase had
been one of David's high school history teacher's favorites,
referring to how often the course of history was changed by
events unforeseen by any of the players in it. The words went
through David's head as he stared down at the damaged body of
the Earl of Hereford. Humphrey moaned and David gently
lifted him up so he could sit with his back to the wall.
Humphrey painfully stretched out his legs, one by one, and only
then did he open his eyes.

"Father!" William gasped as he fell to his knees beside
Humphrey.

"I thought I recognized your voice," he said to William,
speaking in French, "but I was sure that I was dreaming."

"That this is a dream does seem more probable than us finding you here," David said. "We had word that you'd been captured, but that you were to be taken elsewhere."

"They killed all of my men. Savages!" Despite his weakness, Humphrey spit out the word.

"What have they done to you?" William gazed at his father, taking in his damaged face and weakened limbs.

Humphrey put out a hand to William. "I'm all right, son. Nothing but cuts and bruises. I'll mend."

David looked over at Clare, who stood silhouetted in the doorway. "This is a slight complication."

"A minor one," Clare said. "Not insurmountable. And leastwise saves you a journey to Bristol Castle."

David leaned down to grip William's shoulder. "You and Lili should stay with your father," he said. "The sooner Clare and I—and these men—move, the better."

Humphrey squinted towards the door, his eyes reacting to the glare of Lili's lantern. She lowered it and half-blocked it with her body to ease his transition from darkness to light.

"What's your plan?" Humphrey said.

"We've freed the Welsh garrison," David said. "We're going to take the castle back."

"Wait." Humphrey bent forward, one hand to the floor, and very painfully got to his feet. He stood, one arm wrapped around his ribs, and the other using William's shoulder as a crutch. "I need to see whom they imprisoned down here."

David accommodated him, though surely they were short on time. The guards on the floor above would soon begin to wonder how long Clare meant to spend with the prisoners.

The members of the Welsh garrison—all twenty of them—gazed at Humphrey as he staggered out the door of his cell, one arm over William's shoulder, with David holding onto him from behind. The boy was the perfect height to help his father, who wove back and forth in the doorway. He settled, finally, with weight on both feet and his shoulder resting on the frame of his cell door. He surveyed the men before him. "Is this all there is?" he said, in Welsh.

"Llelo's just here," one of the men said, helpfully moving aside to reveal a man squatting against the wall by the guard table.

"That's the man I want," Humphrey said.

Llelo made a break for the stairs.

David started forward. "Stop him!"

One of the men closest to Llelo grabbed his leg as he tried to disappear up the stairs. Llelo fell to his knees on the stone steps and then turned onto his back, kicking out with his free leg at the man. His foot connected with his captor's chin and he fell back, but other hands grabbed Llelo and dragged him down the stairs. Llelo fought madly and managed to get away from his handlers long enough to pick up one of the two spindle chairs in the room. From a far corner, he held it, legs out, like a lion tamer. "I'll shout a warning if you don't let me go!"

"If you were going to, you would have already done it," Humphrey said. "You're a spy, but one who can be bought, is that it?"

The man opened his mouth to shout and then ... *thwtt!*

An arrow appeared in Llelo's throat, cutting off whatever sound he'd hoped to make. Lili had loosed one of her borrowed arrows. With Llelo only fifteen feet away, it had been the easiest shot she'd ever taken. And maybe the hardest. She lowered her bow.

Llelo dropped the chair, staggered back, and fell to his rear. His hands scrabbled at the shaft. He didn't have the strength to pull out the arrow, and it wouldn't have saved him to do so anyway. He collapsed onto his back. The other Welshmen who'd been his companions observed him, their expressions ranging from surprise and horror, to cold belief.

It was a dangerous moment, perhaps more dangerous than when Llelo had tried to shout. David had assumed all would be well once he released the prisoners, but Lili had just killed one of their own. Blood began to pool under Llelo's head.

"Lili," David said, keeping his voice low and gentle. "Give me the bow."

She didn't move, didn't relinquish it. He stepped closer to her and put a hand on her shoulder. She didn't look at him but kept her eyes on Llelo. Her face was pale and her hands shook. David wanted to put his arms around her and comfort her—but he couldn't, not in front of all these people, not when they had so little time.

The same burly soldier in his late thirties who'd come out of the first cell David had opened glared towards Bohun. "You name Llelo a traitor?"

"And you are?" Humphrey said.

"Madoc," the man said.

"I do, Madoc," Humphrey said. "This is the man who opened Painscastle to the English."

"How do you know?" David said, forcing his attention away from Lili to pick up his responsibilities again. "Although from his behavior, we should have no cause to doubt you."

Humphrey twitched, pain written in his face. William helped him to the remaining chair, with the Welsh soldiers moving aside in cordial silence. David didn't know if they would have been quite as respectful if they knew Humphrey's name. Humphrey let out a sigh as he sat. "Llelo was chained to me, up in the keep. The English commander found it amusing to put us together. I expect Llelo didn't get the treatment he thought he deserved."

"We thought our captain was the traitor," Madoc said.

Another sigh from Humphrey. "Llelo killed your captain before he opened the gate."

"But you're a Norman," Madoc said. "We can't trust you."

Humphrey pointed with his chin to David, who had returned to Lili's side, his shoulder to hers and his arms folded across his chest. "You trust *him*, do you not?" Bohun said.

Madoc eyed David, who returned his gaze with a mild one of his own. "And who are you?" Madoc said.

"Dafydd ap Llywelyn, the Prince of Wales." Clare stood at the bottom of the stairs again, one eye on the door above them. "And I suggest you do exactly as he says."

A wave of surprise coursed around the room. Men who'd been leaning against the wall straightened, and the two who'd found seats on the bench by the table stood.

"My lord!" several of the men said, in unison. Everyone bowed, whether it was a quick nod of the head or a complete bend at the waist.

David raised a hand in acknowledgement, not sure, even after all these years, that he would ever get used to men's obeisance.

Clare nodded, viewing their behavior as normal and expected. "We're running out of time, my lord."

"At once." David leaned in to Lili one more time. "Will you be okay if I leave you for a few minutes?"

"Yes," she said.

David still hesitated, but as he looked at her, Lili's eyes cleared. "Go. Do what you must. I will be waiting for you when you're done."

David looked to Madoc. "Twenty-two able-bodied men can take back this castle, can they not?"

The man's shoulders went back. "Yes, my lord! The only reason those English bastards took it from us in the first place was because of the traitor, and a potion in our mead. The key is to get into the keep before they can hold it against us."

"And how would you do that?" David said.

"If we clear out the barracks first, since we outnumber them and have the element of surprise, we can then make a run at the keep."

"We don't need the keep," David said. "We just need to contain those within it."

"True. But we should try," Clare said. "I have a plan."

David swiveled on one heel to look into Clare's determined face, and then back to Madoc. "Leave the keep to Clare and me."

"Some of us should go with you, surely," Madoc said.

"You're supposed to be in a cell," David said. "If you come, we lose that very element of surprise which will aid us. The English soldiers don't know that Lord Clare on our side or we wouldn't be here."

"*Is* he on our side, my lord?" Madoc lowered his voice so it didn't carry to the Norman lord.

"He is today," David said.

"I suppose that's what counts," Madoc said. "I will do whatever you ask."

David turned to Lili. "Please stay here with William and Humphrey. Will you, for me?"

"Yes, Dafydd," she said.

And David thought she really might.

Clare waved a hand to David, indicating that he should come with him.

"Give us a short head start," David said to the men.

David and Clare trotted up the stairs, followed immediately by the freed Welshmen. These men would wait until David and Clare had left the barracks, and then ambush the guards whom Clare would order to return to the guardroom. David and Clare took long strides down the short hallway that led to the mess hall, which still contained half a dozen soldiers. The front door to the barracks stood open.

"They're all yours," Clare said as he headed for the door.

"Yes, my lord," one of the guards said. He tapped one of his fellow soldiers on the shoulder and they started down the hall towards the stairs.

David assumed Madoc would do what needed doing and turned his attention to the keep. When he and Clare reached the porch of the barracks, they pulled up short. The bailey was completely deserted. "This can't be right," David said.

"God smiles upon us," Clare said. "Don't question His blessings and follow my lead."

"You said you had a plan?" David said. Their boots sounded hollowly as they loped along the stone pathway through the bailey, across the bridge, and up the stairway to the keep.

"No time to explain," Clare said.

Reluctantly, David gave way and pushed open the big double doors to the great hall, acting as Clare's second-in-command. Clare nodded loftily at David's gesture that Clare should precede him, and stepped first through the door.

"Come with me now." Clare's voice echoed around the room. "I need to speak to you all together."

The man who'd greeted them in the bailey when they first arrived straightened from where he'd been leaning on the mantle by the fire, talking to another guardsman. "Everyone, my lord?"

"Yes," Clare said. "Now."

His voice held a timbre that men obeyed. The soldier shrugged and waved at the other three men in the room that they should accompany Clare.

"Is anyone else in the keep?" Clare said.

"No, my lord. We're spread thin, as I said. The rest of my men are on the wall-walk or in the barracks."

"I will speak to them separately." Clare urged the men to take the stairs ahead of him, with David bringing up the rear. They entered the second floor corridor and Clare pointed them to a room at the far end. "Go on inside."

The men obeyed, but Clare and David stopped in the doorway. The room held a bed with a plain, brown blanket and a trunk set under a thin slit of a window in the far wall. The captain's face flashed concern when the knowledge that something wasn't right hit him full force—before Clare slammed the door closed and dropped the bar. It was the only room in the hallway that locked from the outside. David wondered how Clare had known about it.

"My lord!" The four men hammered on the other side of the door. "What are you doing?"

"Taking over the castle," Clare said, through the door. "Best make yourselves comfortable."

"We can't watch the door," David said. "And they'll get through it eventually. One of them left his sword leaning against the table downstairs, but the others have their weapons on them." David didn't say what he was really thinking: that Clare's plan was hardly a plan at all. He didn't know that he'd have gone along with it if he'd known what it entailed.

"I admit this is sloppy," Clare said. "But we don't need them contained long—just for the time it takes to subdue the rest of the garrison."

"We'd better split up," David said. "I'll have a look in the kitchen. I hope none of the servants are spies for the English. Perhaps you can make sure the captain didn't count wrong and leave someone lurking at the top of the keep."

"Done." Clare headed towards the ladder that jutted down from a trap door in the ceiling above their heads.

David took the stairs at a fast trot, passed through the great hall, and then continued down a second flight of stairs into the kitchen. It took up the first floor of the keep and had its own doorway out the back.

David caught the door jam to stop himself from hurtling into the room. Three servants and a cook looked up from their food preparation. "You are Welsh?" he said, without preamble.

"Yes," the cook said.

"All of you?"

"Yes." The cook's chin firmed. "And what are you doing with that Norman lord if you speak our tongue so well?"

"He is with me," David said, "not the other way around, and we are taking the castle back." The cook's mouth dropped open. David didn't care to explain further, so he dashed past the cook to the rear door. He poked out his head and saw no one.

"Wh-who are you?" the cook said.

"Never mind that." David drew back his head, blinking away the transition from bright sunshine to darker interior. "The English captain and three of his men are locked in a room on the upper floor, but the bar on the door won't hold them long."

"There's another solid door that separates the kitchen from the great hall," the cook said.

"That will keep you safe for a while. Bar it after me." David threw the words over his shoulder as he took the stairs back up to the hall two at a time. When he reached the stairs to the upper floors, the door to the kitchen closed behind him and he heard the bar drop into place. Just then, a shout and a clash of swords came from above. The door had obviously not held the English soldiers for as long as Clare had hoped.

David continued up the stairs, pulling out his sword as he hit the top step. The English soldiers had backed Clare into a corner, behind the ladder to the battlements. Clare held them off only because the space was so small only one man at a time could reach him.

David's feet pounded along the corridor. He reached the closest Englishman before the man realized he was coming and could marshal an effective counter. David skewered him through the gut. *One down.* The next soldier David confronted was the one without a sword, though he held a wicked-looking dagger.

He edged away from David, which allowed one of his companions to turn from Clare, who had his hands full with the English captain. The two Englishmen closed in on David together, forcing him to back up. He pointed his sword from one to another, trying to look at both men at the same time. In unison, they pounced.

David parried the sword of the first man, who swung so wildly he didn't allow his companion to get the edge of his blade near David. Feeling he had very little time before this turned bad, David switched his sword to his left hand. Continuing to direct it at the first soldier, he rushed the one with the dagger. David's armor deflected a poorly aimed blow as David hit the man with the heel of his right hand directly on the bridge of his nose.

The man screamed and dropped his dagger, both hands over his face. He fell to the floor and onto his side, blood gushing from between his fingers. The move could have driven a bone into his brain and killed him. David had known that when he'd hit him, and had hit him anyway.

The hallway was still too crowded, even if the sides were now even. Clare countered the English captain blow for blow. David faced the fourth English soldier, whose wide eyes flicked from David, to the exit at the end of the hallway, to the open door of the room behind him, which lay opposite the room with the splintered door that he and his companions had destroyed. It looked like one of the soldiers had put his boot through it.

David stepped towards the man-at-arms, who took that instant to make up his mind. "No!" His voice hit a note David's hadn't reached in four years. The man leapt towards the room behind him and slammed the door shut. This door didn't have a bar. David could have broken the latch with a hard thrust from his shoulder, but it was a better idea to take care of the English captain first.

"Stand down!" David said, in English.

The Englishman half-turned from Clare, his sword out to hold both Clare and David at bay. He backed towards the opposite corner.

"Glad you could make it," Clare said.

"Glad you were still alive when I did," David said.

That was enough banter. "I was just coming down the ladder when they burst through the door," Clare said. "I couldn't get back up it and fight at the same time."

David lifted his chin to the Englishman. "Drop your weapon."

"No."

David sighed and flicked the point of his sword towards the trap door. "If you leave your sword here, I will not kill you. Take the steps up."

"What about my men?"

"They will each make their own decision about whether to live or die," David said. "They are no longer your responsibility."

"I'll go." He dropped his sword and moved towards the ladder. Before he could reach it, David stepped in, grabbed his arm and twisted it up behind his back while at the same time, putting his knee into the back of the man's knee. The captain's leg collapsed. A second later, David had him on the floor.

Seeing what David had done, Clare stepped into one of the rooms and grabbed the sheet from the bed. He tore off a strip with his teeth and tied the man's wrists behind his back.

While Clare finished, David took a page from the captain's book and put his boot into the door behind which the last soldier had hidden himself.

"Don't hurt me!" The man cowered on the floor, his hands over his head.

David didn't like to see any soldier so unmanned, but it didn't change what he had to do. David grabbed him, wrestled him out the door, and onto the floor beside his captain.

Then Lili appeared at the top of the stairs. "A rider has come from the south. From your father."

Clare looked up. "I wouldn't have thought the King knew you were here?"

"He doesn't," David said. "He must have sent the message for the castellan of Painscastle." David placed a foot between the second man's shoulder blades to keep him down while Clare tied his wrists. "Tell me, Lili."

"The English are moving in the south. He expects them to come across the Severn Estuary tomorrow."

"Tomorrow!" David focused on Clare. "Could you return to the barracks and oversee what's happening there? We need to hurry. My father needs me."

Clare nodded. He nudged the downed Englishmen with the toe of his boot. "Get up." Neither could manage it from their present position, so David and Clare had to help them to their feet. With his sword out and prodding them in the back,

Clare urged them down the corridor past Lili, who moved off the stairs to let them go by.

For the moment, David and Lili were alone, except for the dead, of course.

"Are you okay?" David took a step towards her.

"I'm fine," Lili said.

David kept asking her that and she continued to give him the same answer, but he wasn't sure if it was a true one. He fixed his gaze on her and as she met his eyes, her face crumpled. She ran forward. He spread his arms wide and she fell into them, weeping. He caught her up, his hand brushing at her hair to soothe her. "You're safe with me," he said, though the truth was, he felt like weeping himself.

Years ago, when he'd first come to Wales, Anna had spoken to him of how killing would change him. She'd been right. He was changed. He knew it. He didn't want that for Lili, even if she'd thought she wanted it for herself.

"I know, I am." Lili dried her tears on David's cloak. "I'm sorry." She tried to step away but David kept his arms around her.

"Talk to me, Lili. I can't go on like we have been. I love you."

"I know that, too, but I don't know why you care for me, Dafydd."

David eased up on his grip so he could look into her eyes. "What on earth do you mean by that?"

229

"I sent you away because I was afraid of losing you! It's easier not to love you than to care so much my heart breaks every time you leave me." Lili gripped his shoulders. "What kind of person am I that I would treat you that way?"

"*Cariad*, there's nothing wrong with you. I have a hole in me, too, that only you can fill." He swept a tear off her cheek with thumb. "That's what loving someone is all about."

Lili took in a deep breath and let it out. She bent her neck and pressed her forehead into his chest while her arms came around his waist. "Are you sure?" The words came out muffled.

"I'm sure," David said.

Lili didn't answer for a long moment, to the point that David wasn't sure if he should say something more or not. And then Lili's shoulders rose and fell once. She turned her head and rested her cheek against his chest, such that the underside of his chin rested on the top of her head.

"It is my turn, I think," Lili said, "to ask you to marry me."

David's heart skipped a beat. He opened his mouth to accept—or to laugh—or even to shout, but Lili barreled on before he could. "But I'm out of my depth with your father. You said before that you'd marry me without his permission, and if that's what you want, I want it too. If you want to wait until he changes his mind, I'll wait with you. I won't send you away again. All I ask is that you speak to him about us one more time to see if he will bend."

"Ah, Lili." David lifted her chin with one finger and bent his head to hers, touching her forehead with his. "I already have."

19

26 August 1288
Near Montgomery Castle

Anna

Anna kilted her skirts to free her legs, swung Cadell onto her back, and ran. Beside her, Maud panted, still holding onto Hugh's hand, while up ahead, Edmund Mortimer's long strides soon outpaced them. Anna didn't have the breath to shout to him that she and Maud were getting too far behind—and wouldn't have wanted to shout if it meant calling attention to them anyway. Fortunately, when Edmund crested a rise, following a narrow path between two trees, he stopped and waited for them.

"Let me take the boy," Edmund said.

"That's oka—"

Before she could finish her denial, Edmund had lifted Cadell from her back and swung him onto his own. "Hold on tight."

Cadell obeyed, clutching Edmund around the neck. Anna rubbed Cadell's back. It was so dark, she couldn't see his face and she hoped he really was okay. He had never been frightened of strangers, and Anna didn't know that she would even put Edmund into that category anymore, Norman or not.

"The stables are just ahead." Edmund trotted forward, Cadell bouncing on his back and the two women redoubling their efforts to keep up. He turned into what Anna would have called a driveway in her old world, with rail fences on either side, and then into a clearing in front of a long low building that had to be the stables.

The big double doors were pulled wide—it was summer so the horses were plenty warm enough—and Edmund poked his nose into the darkened building. It smelled of horses, hay, and alfalfa. "Hello?"

Anna caught up with him, gently tugged Cadell from Edmund's back, and set the boy on his feet. She held Cadell's hand, finding that this was one of the few times that her son clutched her hand tightly too, with no interest in exploring or getting away.

Scuffling came from the back of the building and a young man in his early twenties loped out of the darkness, holding a lantern. "Yes?" When he saw Edmund he stiffened, his shoulders squaring, and came to a halt in front of the Marcher baron. "My lord!"

"I'll need three horses, Andrew, just as soon as you can."

"Of course, my lord," Andrew said. "Is something wrong—?"

A shout echoed from the road they'd just come up. Anna couldn't hear hooves, but that didn't mean riders weren't minutes away.

Edmund gripped Andrew's upper arm. "You have always served me well, Andrew. Will you again? These men who look for us must not find us."

Andrew didn't hesitate. "Of course, my lord."

Cadell released Anna's hand and wrapped both arms around her thigh, pressing his face into the fabric of her skirt. "Mama—"

Anna caught him up in her arms. He clutched his legs around her waist and his arms went around her neck. "Don't talk now, sweetheart," Anna said. "We're going to hide—like when we play hide and seek at home. You have to be really quiet, okay?"

Andrew led them down the central aisle, past a dozen stalls, only half of which contained horses, to an empty one on the left. Andrew scraped his boot across the floor to sweep aside the hay that covered it. Beneath the hay lay a ring to a trap door. He bent, grasped it, and pulled it up. It came free with no squealing of hinges and revealed rickety stairs leading down.

Edmund patted Andrew's shoulder as he passed him.

"Thank you," Anna said, as she, Maud, and their boys followed into the darkness below.

"This way." Edmund led them towards the front of the barn and stopped directly underneath the front door. He tipped his head back, listening hard for the sound of their pursuers.

Cadell pressed his face to Anna's neck. He was frightened now—perhaps more so than he'd been since the ambush. Anna tightened her arms around him. Back at the stairs, Andrew closed the trap door so it was once again flush with the floor. She could hear the sweep of his boot as he brushed the hay back over the ring to disguise that the door had been used—or even that it existed at all.

Maud settled onto an overturned bucket, with Hugh between her knees and her arms around him. Anna still held Cadell close, though her face was upturned like Edmund's, looking through the thin slats in the ceiling above them. The light from Andrew's lantern pierced through the gaps—and then went out.

"They'll question him," Anna said.

"Yes, they will." Edmund sounded resigned. "We'll see how good an actor he can be."

They didn't have long to wait. The trapdoor had been closed for no more than a minute when horses' hooves sounded on the gravel in the driveway. The lead rider reined in at the doorway and dropped to his feet with a thud that rang hollowly on the wooden floor of the barn. "Anybody here?"

Edmund's shoulders jerked at the voice. Anna stood only inches away from him, and although she couldn't see his expression, she sensed his dismay. She wished she knew what it was about the man that had startled him.

Their hiding place was darker than the barn itself, and through the slits in the wood above her head, Anna could just see the shadow of the rider's arm as he waved his men off their horses. "Spread out and search. This is where'd I'd come if I were running."

Andrew appeared out of the back, lantern in hand as before, and strolled towards the questioner. "May I help you, my lord?"

Above them, the man said, "I'm looking for my brother, traveling with two women and their children. Have you seen him?"

So that's what had shaken Edmund. It was his brother, Roger, personally doing the looking. It was a good thing that emotions weren't visible. Anna could feel the anger rolling off of Edmund in waves.

"It's been quiet here," Andrew said, "except that one of the horses got out about two hours ago—his stall wasn't latched properly—and I had quite a time catching him. That was before full dark, though. If Lord Mortimer passed through here then, I wouldn't have seen him."

The knothole above Anna's head gave her a good look at Roger. He looked away from Andrew, gazing west and chewing on his lip. Andrew peered past him to the empty saddles of his companions. "Your men are welcome to search, if they like."

"They are already at work," Roger said. Just then, one of the other men came around the corner from the north, took the lantern from Andrew without asking, and headed for the stalls behind him. For a moment, he stood on the planks just above Maud's head. None of them moved. Anna feared that her heart was beating so loudly that he could hear it. Thankfully, he detected her fear no more easily than Edmund's fury.

Then he began moving from stall to stall. "Were these empty all day?"

"Yes sir. We're not often full." Andrew looked back at Roger. "What's this all about, my lord?"

"Nothing that need concern you." Roger walked the length of the barn. At that point, Edmund put a hand to Anna's shoulder and pushed her into the shadows of the side wall, next to one of the posts that supported the ceiling and augmented the earthen foundation. He had a finger to his lips.

Anna nodded. Cadell's eyes were closed, his face hidden in Anna's hair, which had come down from the bun at the back of her neck in their journey from Montgomery Castle. He appeared to be asleep, or close to it. *Thank God.*

The men walked back and forth through the barn for what seemed like an eternity, though their search was something less than thorough if they never thought to look beneath their feet. One of the men did climb the ladder to the loft and declare it empty.

"All right." Roger spun on his heel and marched back to his horse. "We can't waste any more time here." His companions followed, one handing the lantern back to Andrew as he passed him.

The other horsemen had returned, too, with rueful shakes of their heads. "Nothing in the woods," one said.

Lord Roger had removed his riding gloves when he arrived and snapped them into his palm, punctuating his dissatisfaction. "Either he didn't come this way, or he went to ground."

"We'll keep looking, my lord," one of the other riders said.

Roger mounted his horse, but bent towards Andrew once he was seated. "If they arrive here, I'll need you to reassure them that they are safe, and then contact me at the castle."

"Yes, my lord," Andrew said.

They rode away.

Anna leaned in to Edmund. "Do we stay here or flee? Will they keep a watch on the stables?"

Edmund still had his head tipped back, looking up at the ceiling. "It disturbs me that Roger assumed Andrew's loyalty was greater to him than to me."

Anna didn't know what to say to that. This had not been a good day for Edmund Mortimer.

The trap door pulled up. Andrew's feet, and then his face appeared, illumined by his lantern. "They're gone, but they may well be back. I can set you on your way by quieter paths than the main road, but you should leave now."

Edmund nodded. "If we stay, they'll find us eventually. Roger knows about this cellar, and will recall it given time. We should risk it and go."

* * * * *

The wind whipped into Anna's face, screaming out of the western skies, unrelenting. At the same time, it kept her on the right track. Safety was to the west. They could lose the men who pursued them in the mountains that rose before them. She clutched Cadell to her. He slept as only a child could, sprawled across her lap. The urgency that Anna had felt back at Montgomery had increased tenfold. It pounded in her temples and affected her breathing. *The English were coming to attack Gwynedd.* She needed to hurry so she could warn the defenders at Aber and on Anglesey before they did.

The four of them—including Andrew, who had refused to abandon his lord and return to the stables—had ridden twenty miles in the dark and the wind, always heading northwest, picking their way from one track to the next until they found the old Roman road that led to Caer Gai. They had turned due north sometime after what Anna gauged to be three in the morning, and then fought onward towards Dolwyddelan, fifty miles in all. From Dolwyddelan, the castellan could send a fast rider to Aber to warn the garrison of the English approach.

Anna felt at times that if it weren't for Cadell sleeping in her arms, they could have walked the distance faster than they were riding. By the early hours of the morning, Maud was also nodding in the saddle, while trying to contain Hugh who rested against her chest.

Thankfully, it was August, not cold, and they were in Wales, which meant that sunrise came only ten hours after it had set, instead of sixteen like it did in the height of winter. Anna had never been so grateful in her life to see the first rays of the sun shoot above the eastern horizon. The warmth of it was short lived, however, because soon after, the wind that had blown unceasingly up until then, brought a wash of rain with it. Anna hunched with Cadell over her horse, trying to keep both of them as dry as she could.

"How much further?" Edmund said. "It has to be soon or we will need to find a place to sleep."

Anna was loath to stop. "We'll be there by noon," she said, hoping her internal calculations were correct. She felt responsible for Hugh and Maud. It was she who'd provided the impetus to get them out of Montgomery. "We could sleep in a shepherd's hut if we have to, but I'd rather push on."

Edmund didn't argue. "The threat of war is a great weight."

He had that right.

They passed a derelict croft not long later, one that seemed to be standing only because a tree had grown close to a side wall, supporting it. Anna didn't turn aside, even though it had begun to rain harder. This journey reminded her of another one—another ride—although that one had been in winter after a traitor let the English into Castell y Bere. Now, instead of Gwenllian, her little sister, she held her own son, warm within the blanket she'd appropriated from the stables.

Maud turned her head and looked at the hut too—longingly, Anna thought—but when Anna opened her mouth to apologize, Maud wouldn't allow her to get the words out. "I'm afraid of pursuit too," Maud said. "It seems unlikely that they'd search this far from Montgomery, if they haven't already found us, but we don't know how far your brother's ambition stretches, my lord."

"Far enough for me not to want to stop either," Edmund said. "He might put great effort into recapturing me, if only because I've hurt his pride." He urged his horse closer. The wind whipped his hood from his head and instinctively Anna tucked hers tighter in response. "Are you well, my lady?"

"Well enough," she said. "I am more thankful than I can possibly express that we are no longer in Montgomery Castle."

Edmund barked a laugh that the wind caught and blew away east. "I feel the same, for all that the castle has belonged to my family for three generations."

"Have we lost our pursuers, do you think?" Maud said. Hugh, who rode before her in the saddle, began to wiggle and she gripped him more tightly. "If Roger returned to the stables—"

Edmund reached out a hand and patted Maud's arm in reassurance. "We rode south and then west. Andrew knew what he was doing when he said that he would help us to escape my brother's clutches. With every mile, we head deeper into Wales." They were following the old Roman road which provided the most direct path through the mountains. It was the high road—and one Roger might assume they'd take, but Anna also breathed more easily with every hour that passed.

"Thank you for aiding us," Maud said, turning to Andrew who brought up the rear.

"It is my pleasure, my lady," Andrew said.

Anna glanced at Edmund who turned in the saddle to gaze past his servant to the direction from which they'd come. The road behind them stretched into the distance. Not a soul moved on it. "We left no sign of our presence," he said. "Perhaps Roger decided not to waste any more effort in catching us, an effort that would be better spent elsewhere. Even though I am his brother, you are Bohun's wife, and Anna, a princess of Wales, we are only five people. Six, now, with Andrew. We are not worth his time."

"Roger has a country to win," Anna said.

"We are safe in Wales, Maud," Edmund said, and then added tactlessly, "unbelievable as that may seem."

Anna didn't know if she should get up the effort to take offense or not. It had been Edmund, after all, who had tried to murder Papa. It was his men that Anna and David had driven into at Cilmeri almost six years ago, saving Papa's life. Anna looked away, knowing she should let it lie, but in the end spoke anyway, though only loud enough for Edmund to hear. "Don't think I've forgotten."

Edmund glanced at her. "I would never presume that, my dear. Does it help if I tell you that Cilmeri was my brother's idea?"

That was easy enough for him to say now, though given Edmund's present situation, it could be the truth. "Papa is your uncle," Anna said.

"I know," Edmund said.

He didn't elaborate and Anna didn't press him. No present accusation could change the past. Besides, Edmund owed her now, just like Humphrey de Bohun owed David for keeping his son safe, even though they still weren't clear as to the threat against him.

Finally, as the noon hour approached, Dolwyddelan appeared out of the rocks in front of them. It was here that

Anna had fled with Gwenllian after the English had burned Castell y Bere. Anna hoped the precedent boded well for her today.

It should have been a relief to ride under the gatehouse, but all of them—horses and humans—hung their heads in exhaustion. Anna felt like throwing up. Whether that was because of the child she carried inside her, the lack of sleep, or what might be happening on Anglesey just then, she couldn't decide.

"My lady!"

All of a sudden, the day grew brighter. The steward of Dolwyddelan, a stout older knight by the name of Marc, came out of the keep. He was followed by its castellan, Goronwy, her father's right hand man since they were boys. *Thank you, Lord.* Anna sent up a prayer and kissed the top of Cadell's head.

He squealed and reached for Goronwy, who came to a halt at Anna's stirrup and took up the boy as a matter of course. "What are you doing here, Anna?"

Anna would have teased him for not giving her a *nice to see you* or *how are you?* but the concern in his eyes had her biting back her retort. Cadell wiggled and Goronwy set him down so the child could gather up one of the unsuspecting barn cats. Even though nobody else in Wales seemed to have the same tolerant view of pets that she did, Anna had taught Cadell not to chase them.

"It's a long story," Anna said. "Can you help me down? I can barely feel my feet." Anna was numb all over from the ride and she was comfortable enough with Goronwy not to hide her discomfort.

"I missed you, my girl." Goronwy caught her up in a bear hug before her feet touched the ground. "But I have a feeling that whatever news you're bringing isn't going to be something this old soldier wants to hear."

"No, it isn't." Anna gestured to her companions. "You've met Edmund Mortimer, of course."

Goronwy's jaw dropped. His eyes had been only for Anna but now he turned to Edmund. "I can't say this is a pleasure."

"Nor for me," Edmund said, in Welsh, "although I'd appreciate it if you do not pass judgment until you hear what I have to say. I find I am in your princess' debt—one that I may never be able to repay." Anna, Maud, and Edmund had spoken mostly in French up until this point. His Welsh was better than Anna would have expected. But then, his grandmother had been a Welsh princess, daughter of the great Prince of Wales, Llywelyn Fawr.

"Come inside and tell me." Goronwy took Anna's hand and kissed it. He lowered his voice. "You look exhausted. Are you with child again?"

"Goronwy." Anna put her hand to his cheek. "I could never keep a single secret from you. Please don't tell anyone. Even Math doesn't know."

"Not a word. But I worry for you."

"And I for you," Anna said.

The steward's wife had hastened out of the keep after her husband. "May I draw a bath for you, my lady?"

Anna put a hand to her head, her lack of sleep catching up to her between one breath and the next. "Yes. Thank you. We can ride no more today."

"How far have you come?" Goronwy said.

"From Montgomery," Edmund said. "Under some duress."

"All of you?" Goronwy tightened his grip on Anna's hand.

"Thus, the tale we have to tell," Edmund said.

Anna glanced at Edmund. He was back to his old form, with dry tongue and bemused expression. Anna herself felt short-tempered and hag-like. Cadell, of all of them, was feeling the most cheerful. Still holding the cat, he ran with Hugh to the stables where they'd spied three puppies playing in the hay.

"I'll watch them, my ladies," Andrew said.

Anna nodded, accepting his offer, though he had to be tired too. She made a note to herself to speak to Marc about finding someone to relieve him soon.

"Eat or bath first?" Goronwy took Anna's arm to escort her inside the keep.

"Bath," Maud and Anna said in unison, and then smiled at each other. Anna had been impressed with Maud's fortitude over the last two days. Separated from her husband and older son, she'd escaped from Montgomery and trekked across the spine of Wales without complaint. And her son hadn't complained either. They raised them tougher in the March than Anna's prejudice against Marcher lords would have given them credit.

They reached the room off the kitchen intended for bathing. A fire burned in the hearth, heating water, which the servants poured, a bucket at a time, into the wooden tub. Magnanimously, Anna allowed Maud to bathe first, while she plunged her hands into the warm water of a nearby basin and washed her face. "You and Hugh will be safe here," Anna said.

"I know," Maud said.

Anna glanced at her. "You do?"

Maud turned to her. "My dear. Out of nothing, you conjured our escape from Montgomery, found horses for us to ride, and led us through the wilds of Wales to this castle. I have no idea how you managed any of it, but after my initial fear of what the guards might do to us if we were discovered, I've not been afraid."

Anna swallowed. She hadn't considered how Maud might feel about all of this. Truthfully, she'd barely considered

Maud at all. It had been along time since she'd met a woman of this time with whom she could carry on a conversation that felt *normal* to Anna, one in which they talked about ideas, or politics, or something other than the specifics of child-rearing or household management. Most of the time, she didn't try.

"I'm sorry about your husband," she said. "I don't know what we can do for him."

"He has always looked further into the future than I could see," Maud said. "I wouldn't count him out just yet."

The women took turns bathing, but the water cooled quickly and they finished sooner than Anna would have liked, since she wanted nothing more than to laze in the tub until she fell asleep. They arrived in the great hall just as Edmund was concluding the story of their escape.

"—and the princess led us here."

Anna felt Goronwy's eyes on her as she sat down. She looked back at him and smiled. She'd only been two years old when they'd met. They'd missed each other for a long gap of fourteen years during which Anna had grown up in the modern world. But the connection between them remained tangible. Goronwy had not married or had children (at least none whom he claimed). He viewed Cadell as a grandson.

"Your father will not be pleased to learn of what has happened to you," Goronwy said.

"You're too polite," Anna said. "That's a gross understatement. Fortunately, it was David's task to tell him about the English invasion, not mine."

"I will send a rider at once to inform the garrison at Aber of the threat they face," Goronwy said.

"They should already know about the threat to the south," Anna said. "Come to think of it, you should already know about that part too. Math sent a rider to warn you days ago; he left Dinas Bran within an hour of us knowing ourselves."

"We have heard nothing from him," Goronwy said.

An ache settled into Anna's belly that had nothing to do with the baby. "Ask your rider to continue on to Anglesey," Anna said. "Bevyn must hear of it too."

"A man will leave within the hour," Goronwy said.

"And we should follow in the morning." Her heart sank at the thought. The last thing she wanted to do was get on a horse again. *Ever.*

Goronwy canted his head and studied her. "You, at least, need not travel more. Dolwyddelan is safer than Aber. For the sake of your family, you should stay here."

"Isn't the crown stored in the treasury there? And the piece of the true cross in the chapel?" Anna said.

Goronwy looked discomfited. "Of course."

"Then if Aber is at risk, we can't leave them there. If the English capture the castle, possession of our House's most sacred relics will give them a terrible hold over Papa."

Goronwy couldn't deny it. Anna herself knew it from what King Edward had accomplished in her old world. With Papa's death at Cilmeri, they'd stolen the relics from their hiding place at Aber, and in the seven hundred years that had passed between 1282 and the twenty-first century, had never given them back to Wales. That the heir to the crown of England was called the *Prince of Wales* from then on, Papa's former title, made mockery of all that the Welsh—her people now—had fought for and sacrificed.

Anna studied her old friend. "I would let you go in my stead, but you cannot ride that far, Papa told me. As much as I hate to admit it, we can't leave this to anyone else."

"I am not so enfeebled that I—"

"Don't even start with me," Anna said. "You can't ride until your wound heals. I will go with an escort, and then I will come back, as quick as I can." She turned to Maud. "If you will care for Cadell for me—just for two days?" Anna didn't like leaving him. At home at Dinas Bran, there were times when she had been called to attend a birth—and sometimes the birth lasted for two days. She always fretted about him when they were apart, but would return to find Cadell content and see that he'd been spoiled by everyone in the castle in her absence.

"Of course," Maud said.

Goronwy's chin jutted out as if he would protest, but at Anna's look, he closed his mouth. She'd used the word 'wound', but Goronwy suffered badly from hemorrhoids, such that sitting, even at the high table, was painful much of the time. Riding was intolerable. He would ride, of course, if he had to and if it came to open battle. When Papa returned from the south, Goronwy would get himself to Aber, come hell or high water and if he had to walk the whole way. But not today. Not with any kind of speed. It was only twenty miles. She could reach Aber in a half a day and return the next.

"You are too headstrong, just like your mother." Goronwy grumbled under his breath. "I will strip Dolwyddelan of its manpower for this endeavor. As soon as Bevyn hears of this, he will rouse Anglesey and marshal more men than I have at my disposal. With the garrison at Caerhun, we should have enough soldiers to protect Aber and the surrounding area."

Edmund leaned forward in his seat, positioned on Anna's other side. "You can't protect the whole coastline."

"Of course not. Nor can King Llywelyn defend the whole of the south," Goronwy said.

"But the countryside will fight for us," Anna said.

"And we have not been idle these last three years," Goronwy said.

Which put down Edmund very nicely without telling him anything at all. David had hoped that the threat of what he might throw at the English would act as a deterrent to whatever invasion plans they might think to concoct. He hadn't tried to squash the stories that came out of Wales, only to prevent the actual details from leaking out. But maybe the Normans hadn't heard enough rumors—or if they had, hadn't believed them.

"I will ride with you, of course, Princess Anna," Edmund said.

Anna eyed the Norman lord. "There is no need—"

"There is every need," he said. "I am in your debt, which feels uncomfortable enough, given past events. I will not add to it by allowing you to ride into danger without me. Your father would have my head."

As if he wouldn't anyway. But Anna didn't say that.

Edmund grinned. "Besides, I'm looking forward to seeing some things I shouldn't."

Goronwy growled at that. Edmund, his eyes alight with mischief, saluted him.

20

27 August 1288

Dolwyddelan Castle

Anna

"Edmund is a spy," Goronwy said. "Dafydd would warn against riding with him."

The remains of dinner lay on the table in front of him. Anna had shooed Cadell off to bed, with a maidservant to watch over him in case he woke and was confused by sleeping in a strange place. Maud and Edmund had also retired. But Anna felt restless. She knew she needed to sleep, but the danger the Normans were bringing to Wales weighed on her.

She brought her fingers to her forehead and pressed hard, trying to drive away the incipient headache that had plagued her since they'd arrived. At least she was inside and warm. The wind had blown all day here, too, whistling through the cracks in the old stones and whipping down the gap between the stables and the keep, making even Cadell reluctant to play outside. The skies had cleared, but Goronwy rubbed his knee—an old war wound. It would rain again soon. Anna feared that when it did, she would be out in it.

"You're talking about my brother, right? The man who met with Humphrey de Bohun in secret in the middle of the night and accepted charge of his eldest son?" Anna said. "William is a spy. Maud is a spy. Edmund is a spy. Even Andrew is a spy. What any of them learn in the next few days may help the English defeat us in the next war, but I can't worry about that right now."

"I sent a pigeon to Bevyn on Anglesey," Goronwy said. "If they invade his shores, he'll be prepared."

"Only one pigeon?" Anna said. Goronwy's fondness for his messenger pigeons was well known. If he allowed one out of his sight, it had to be for a good cause. It was the reason he'd spent the summer at Dolwyddelan in the first place, because this was where he bred them.

"I will send one a day until such a time as I hear from you." Goronwy leaned closer to put his arm around Anna's shoulders and hug her. "My girl."

"I am your girl," she said. "I always have been."

Goronwy bent his head to look into her eyes. "I have loved you since you were two years old and I carried you from your mother's chariot. I'm not going to lose you now. You take care of yourself."

"I love you too, Goronwy." Anna felt her eyes fill with tears and fought them back. "I will stay as safe as I can."

* * * * *

Anna had barely gotten to sleep, or so it felt, when she awoke with a sudden start to find Cadell straddling her, his hands on her shoulders. "Mama! Mama!"

Anna wrapped her arms around him. "*Shh, shh,* what is it, *cariad?*"

"The puppies! The puppies are going to die!"

Anna came fully awake, though it seemed Cadell was still dreaming. She grasped her son around the waist to move him so she could sit up. "What's wrong with the puppies?"

"The stable roof is on fire and the puppies are inside!" Cadell sobbed into her shoulder. "I saw it."

Anna scrambled to her feet. "Show me."

He pointed to the window that overlooked the bailey. It wasn't midnight, as she'd thought, but nearly dawn, and a faint light filtered through it. Anna ran to the window, pulled open the shutter all the way, and saw instantly that what Cadell said was true. She ran back to him and scooped him up. "We have to wake the castle."

With Cadell in her arms, Anna dashed into the hallway. She hammered on each door along the corridor as she ran down it. "Fire! Fire! Wake up! Fire!"

She didn't wait to see if any of the occupants responded, but swung Cadell onto her hip and clattered down the stairs to the great hall. She burst through the doorway. It was deserted. Something was very wrong, and not just because the stables were on fire. How could it be that she and Cadell were the only two people awake in the castle?

Dolwyddelan's keep consisted of the two floors above the hall, plus the kitchens, which had been cut into the foundation itself. The stables and the West tower, constructed by Papa, housed the armory, offices, and barracks for the men. It lay across the courtyard from the keep.

Anna hustled down the next flight of stairs to the kitchen, where she found a dozing kitchen boy and the cook, yawning over his bowl of bread. "The stables are on fire!"

The cook looked up, his eyes half-lidded. "Wha—?" Perhaps he didn't think he'd heard her correctly. The sight of the princess of Wales in her night shift with her son on her hip, however, was enough to have him pushing up off the table. He weaved in front of her, but managed to reach out a hand to the sleeping kitchen boy. "Wake up!"

Anna pushed past the cook and flung open the door to the outside. Across the courtyard, the roof at one end of the stables had gone up in flames. The fire was dangerously close to jumping from there to the West tower. While the tower was made of stone, the roof was thatch and wood, as were many of the fittings.

"The puppies!" Cadell said.

Anna turned to the kitchen boy, who like the cook, wasn't standing solidly in front of her. "I see two of you, my lady," the boy said.

Anna stared at him, and then decided he was all she had to work with so he would have to do. "I don't know why none of the garrison is awake, but you must run to the West tower and raise the alarm."

The boy nodded, his eyes wide and his pupils too large. He left by the back door. Anna thrust Cadell into the cook's arms, which went around the child instinctively. Anna put her hands on either side of Cadell's face. "Mama is going to help the puppies. Can you stay here with Cook and have a biscuit?"

Cadell was used to adults and their comings and goings, for all that Anna had always been his constant. He nodded. Anna headed out the door.

"What are you going to do?" the cook said, clutching Cadell to him.

"I'm going to free the horses if I can," Anna said. "And the puppies."

Anna ran across the courtyard. The flames had consumed the back half of the stables, not surprisingly since that was where the hay was stored. Fortunately, the stables were long and low, without a hayloft above. If these stables had been built in the same way as Edmund Mortimer's extra barn, the burning hay would have dropped right onto the horses

257

below them. As it was, the roof had collapsed in the back, but hadn't yet destroyed the whole.

Anna ripped off the hem of her nightgown, dunked it in the water trough outside the stables, and tied it around her head so that it covered her face and nose. Then, braving the smoke, she plunged through the main door. The horses neighed and stamped their hooves. The puppies, fortunately, had been sleeping at the entrance to the stables and she scooped up all three at once and dumped them into the arms of a lone craft worker who had appeared, staggering and not fully awake.

Anna ran back into the stables and pulled the latch of the first stall she came too. The horse reared and pitched, but sensed freedom when Anna opened the door. He galloped past her, going in the right direction, away from the fire and towards safety.

"Yah! Yah!" She slapped the rear of a second horse and he galloped away. Smoke billowed past her hair and she crouched lower, hardly able to see beyond her hand and knowing that she didn't have much time before she might succumb to the fumes. The stables housed thirty horses and every stall was full. She had a lot more animals to free.

She started tugging out pegs that held the doors closed, not worrying about whether or not the horse inside the stall had the sense to depart. Fortunately, at that point, other helpers appeared, passing her, hurrying, but she couldn't make out their faces for the smoke. Then an arm came around her waist and tugged at her, trying to haul her towards the stable door.

She pulled against the man, but he wouldn't let her go. "What are you doing? We have more horses to save!"

"Other people can save them, Anna." It was Edmund. Of course it was.

She coughed hard, her hand to her chest. He stopped trying to coax her away and just scooped her up and ran for the door. The air outside was smoky too, but it felt clean to Anna after the interior of the barn. Once Edmund sat her down on one of the steps to the keep, which hadn't been touched by the fire, she took in deep, heaving breaths. The wind blew into her face, still coming from the southwest, and she turned into it, letting it blow the smoke from her lungs.

It was the weather, in fact, that had saved the West Tower. Even the fierce blaze couldn't jump the thirty feet between it and the stables, not against the wind. The keep lay to the south of both, and thus the wind had protected it too. The rest of the outbuildings weren't so lucky. All of the craft huts and stalls had sat downwind of the stables and were smoking wrecks. It could have been—it might still be—a horrible loss of life.

The cook, who'd been watching for Anna, approached with Cadell in his arms. Tears spilled down Cadell's cheeks and Anna pulled him to her. "The puppies are safe, Cadell," she said. "One of the workers has them."

Edmund stood with his hands on his hips, gazing down at them. "I can see to that, at least."

Anna didn't know what he meant by that, but he came back two minutes later with a wriggling puppy in his hands. He set it gently on Cadell's lap and Cadell hugged and petted it while the puppy licked his face. It was a particularly ugly mutt, spotted black and brown, with a flat face and floppy ears. He obviously had a friendly disposition. Anna gazed up at Edmund and mouthed the words, *thank you.*

"I think thanks to you are in order, rather," Edmund said. "I hear you raised the alarm."

Anna shook her head. "Cadell woke me, worried about the puppies. He'd seen the fire."

"Lucky he did," Edmund said.

"Do we know what started it?" Anna said.

Edmund glared at the burning stables. "Not a single guard remained on duty." He shrugged. "I'm sure Lord Goronwy will get to the bottom of it."

Maud's hand was to her throat as she looked at the destruction of Dolwyddelan. She settled herself on the step above Anna with Hugh beside her. Andrew was among those in the human chain that ran from the well to the stables, passing buckets of water hand to hand to contain the fire. Anna felt she should be among them, but she was *so* tired.

"Betrayal. That's what this is." Goronwy strode up to them. He sent a hard look at Edmund, and then at Maud.

Anna followed his gaze. "Edmund and Maud didn't have anything to do with this, Goronwy."

"Didn't they?" Goronwy said. "I'm surprised you would defend a Mortimer."

"Only this Mortimer," Anna said.

"How could all the guards fail in their duty?" Goronwy said.

Anna sighed at having to be the one to say it, but her admittedly cursory evidence couldn't be denied. "Were they dosed with a potion to keep them asleep? In the mead perhaps? Cadell and I had none of it." Anna hadn't drunk any mead because she was pregnant. And although some mothers allowed their children mead, Anna was not one of them.

Goronwy nodded, though grudgingly. "Most are still struggling to wake." He glowered again at Edmund. "All the more reason to suspect treachery from the Normans in our midst."

"If my intent was to murder everyone in the castle, would I have stayed to witness it?" Edmund said. "And to be accused of it by you?"

"Probably the culprit has slipped away by now," Anna said. "I would count the men in the garrison, and the servants, and determine who—if anyone—is missing."

Goronwy took in a deep breath and let it out. He pinched his fingers at the bridge of his nose. "You're saying that the presence of Normans at Dolwyddelan is coincidental to the fire?"

"I'm saying exactly that," Anna said. "Wales is under attack on many fronts. It is why Edmund and Maud are here. It is why someone tried to burn Dolwyddelan to the ground. Surely you don't believe that Maud would risk the life of her son?"

"No." The word came out abruptly, but without hesitation.

"We can't stay here now," Edmund said. "Any of us."

"No, we can't," Anna said, "even if a few hours ago, I couldn't have imagined a safer place in Wales to leave my son."

"Surely you're not suggesting that we ride anywhere today?" Maud said. "Perhaps if we stayed in the village—"

"We can't, Maud," Anna said. "It's neither safe nor healthy for the boys to stay here, not with what they've been through."

"Every mile I travel that brings me further from England makes me feel like I will never return," Maud said. "Where is Humphrey in all this?"

Anna could understand that particular question because she felt the same way each time Math went away. She missed him every second they were apart. Anna hoped that he was safe, and that she would see him again, standing well and whole in front of her. She put her hand on Maud's. "We'll be okay. Humphrey will be okay too. My brother will see to it."

Maud shook her head. "You Welsh and your optimism. Nobody born in the March would ever say that, because life is rarely, if ever, *okay.*"

Anna didn't correct Maud, didn't tell her that it was the American in her that had brought the word, and the concept to Wales. Somehow, neither she nor David, despite all that had happened to them, could abandon the idea and the hope that little word gave them.

21

28 August 1288
Dolwyddelan Castle

Anna

The destruction at Dolwyddelan would take weeks to clean up. Goronwy left Marc in charge of it. He confessed in an aside to Anna that the burning of the castle, coming hard on the news of a danger to Anglesey, had lit a fire under him he hadn't felt in years. He was the same age as Papa and had entered semi-retirement, but all of a sudden, he wasn't quite ready to hang up his sword.

It was shortly after noon on the day of the fire that they arrived at Caerhun, the fort that guarded the passage across the Conwy River. The garrison captain, a man named Alun, came out to greet them, his face grave. He'd been prepared for their coming by a second rider in the last twenty-four hours, who warned him of what had happened to Dolwyddelan Castle.

One look at Goronwy's face had Alun grabbing Goronwy's arm while the older man dismounted. "My lord, let me help you."

Anna had ridden beside Goronwy the entire ten mile journey from the castle. Any movement of his horse or a shift in the saddle had sent a pain through him that Goronwy couldn't entirely disguise. By the time they reached the Conwy River and turned north to ride along the west bank, his face had turned as gray as his hair.

Goronwy shook his head. "I don't need your help. I'm not bedridden yet."

He dismounted and glared at Anna, who dismounted too and set Cadell on his feet, still clutching his new puppy, who'd fallen asleep in his arms during the ride. Anna stepped close to Goronwy, lowering her voice to protect his pride. "You can't ride another yard, Goronwy."

His jaw bulged with denial. "You can't talk me out of going with you—"

"Maud, Hugh, and Cadell should not ride to Aber," Anna said. "You can keep an eye on Maud while I watch Edmund."

Anna didn't think that ploy would work and it didn't.

"You should stay here," Goronwy said. "Edmund and I will ride to Aber."

"Cadell will be more comfortable staying at Caerhun if you do." Anna didn't feel guilty for one second about playing the grandfather card. She glanced over her shoulder at the two

265

boys, who naturally had glommed together again. Hugh was as bright and cheerful as Cadell—he'd even gotten one of the other puppies so as to match his new friend—but Maud wove in the saddle and her dismounting was matter of falling off the horse into Edmund's arms.

Anna turned back to Goronwy. "We've been over this. I am perfectly well. It's a skip and a hop to Aber—another ten miles. With all that I've been through since I left Dinas Bran, that's nothing. Your men will ensure my safety on the way there, we'll sleep at Aber tonight, and return in the morning. What could be simpler?"

Goronwy still hesitated. He looked west, in the direction of Aber, though he couldn't see it from where they stood. The road to her father's seat followed a path over the high hills, through the pass at Bwlch y Ddeufaen and its ancient standing stones, and then curved north to the Irish Sea. After a moment, Goronwy nodded his grudging admission and turned to Alun. "How many men can you send with her?"

"Twenty, prepared to mount immediately and ride to wherever you wish," Alun said. He was a wiry man, though firmly muscled, without an ounce of fat on him. "As soon as your messenger arrived yesterday afternoon, another twenty rode north to defend the coast and rouse the countryside."

"Good," Goronwy said.

Alun lowered his voice. "The rider I sent to Aber has not returned with word of the status of the garrison there. That fact doesn't surprise me, necessarily, and he could be on the road even now, but you should know before you send her that all may not be well to the west."

Goronwy grunted his acknowledgement and eyed Anna. "I wish I could go with you."

"I'll be fine," Anna said. "Alun and his men can take care of me. With Alun riding with me, you'll have more than enough to do here at Caerhun."

An hour later, after a bite to eat and a lullaby to settle Cadell for a nap (at which point Anna had almost fallen asleep herself), Anna mounted a fresh horse. She was the only woman in the company, which wasn't unusual for her. The men kept her boxed in the middle of their mass, riding three abreast across the high hills to Aber.

Just before the road jagged north, heading past Aber Falls to Aber Castle, the two men that Alun had sent ahead to scout their route came galloping back, in the company of a third man whom Anna would have recognized from a hundred yards away, if only by his mustachios.

Bevyn.

Alun spurred his horse to greet him and Anna followed. They reined in twenty yards ahead of the rest of the company.

"My lord!" The lead rider's horse skittered sideways as he tried to control the headlong rush. "Aber has been taken!"

Alun's face blanched. "By whom?"

"Normans." Bevyn's eyes tracked to Edmund, who'd trotted up after Anna, and they narrowed. "What is *he* doing here?"

Anna urged her horse closer. "Edmund was made captive in his own castle, by his own brother. He is here because I was captured too and the men who'd ridden at my side killed. He helped me to escape from Montgomery Castle." When Bevyn continued to glare at Edmund, Anna added, "Goronwy allowed him to ride with me."

Bevyn subsided, though his face remained set in grim lines. "Does your husband know where you are?"

"No," Anna said.

Bevyn's nostrils flared, but what else could she say? It was the truth.

"Did the rider that Math sent reach you?" Anna didn't want to argue with Bevyn. She put out a hand to him and he lowered the volume on his glower enough to clasp it. Despite Bevyn's gruffness and the tenseness of the moment, Anna's heart had lightened at the sight of him.

"No," Bevyn said. "But Goronwy's pigeon did. I rode for Aber as soon as I got it. At worst, I would waste a day. At best ..."

"David has long trusted your instincts, Bevyn," Anna said, "and since they've proved prescient yet again, I'm grateful for them. Please tell us what you know."

"Not here," Bevyn said. "We've set up camp at the foot of Aber Falls."

Bevyn led the company from the high road they'd been traveling on, down into a cleft in the hills that came out among trees that grew below Aber Falls. Anna couldn't see Aber Castle from here, which comforted her, since whoever had taken it couldn't see them either.

"Aren't we too close?" Anna said. "Surely the English have sent out scouts."

"Not that we've seen," Bevyn said. "They wouldn't have wanted to, especially if they are wary of the local populace."

"As they should be," Alun said. "Do they fly a flag?"

"No," Bevyn said. "But they were mistaken if they thought they could take the castle unnoticed. The village is all abuzz with the news."

"Many villagers work in the castle, of course," Alun said.

"Those that went to work today haven't been allowed out," Bevyn said.

"They must be frightened." Anna had spent many months at Aber and knew most of the inhabitants of the little village, which lay just across the Aber River from the castle. "What are they saying?"

"That the garrison was lax," Bevyn said. "A few Englishmen disguised themselves as peasants and entered the castle in disguise. When night came, they overcame the few guards on watch and let the rest of their companions in."

Anna took in a deep breath. "At least we have no word of traitors among my father's men."

"How many men do you hav—" Alun cut off the sentence. They'd entered the camp. Bevyn had only six men with him.

"I could have brought twenty, but I thought the English threat to Anglesey was greater," Bevyn said.

"How did you get here without being seen?" Anna said. "Not over the sands?" The Lavan Sands stretched across the Menai Straits between Anglesey and the beach at Aber. For millennia, travelers had crossed them at low tide. They were easily visible from Aber's towers.

Bevyn shook his head. "We came across the Straits at Bangor."

Edmund had been listening closely to their conversation. "We have nearly thirty men. That's enough to encircle the castle. Unfortunately, it's not enough to lay siege to it."

"We don't need to lay siege to it," Anna said. "Provided we can get inside undetected."

Edmund eyes grew wary. "And how are we going to do that?"

Bevyn didn't balk at the *we*, even if the expression on his face indicated he wanted to. Instead, he pointed to a cluster of trees to the east, in which a barnlike building stood, bearing a striking resemblance to the shepherd's hut Anna had rejected as a stopping point on their journey north. The barn was so rickety it looked like the next wind storm would bring it down.

"We'll enter through the tunnel," Bevyn said.

22

28 August 1288
Near Aber Castle

Anna

Edmund had never heard of the tunnel beneath Aber Castle. He was offended that he hadn't.

"This is the one of the things you're not supposed to know about," Anna said, "though it's an open secret among the people of Gwynedd."

Edmund raised his eyebrows, clearly expecting more of an explanation. Anna glanced at Bevyn, who gave her a slight nod. "Aber is built on a Roman site," she said, "with hypocausts and a bathing room. Plus two tunnels: one that leads north to the beach, and a second that comes up over there." She pointed to the barn.

"So ..." Edmund looked from Anna to Alun to Bevyn, "we're going to enter Aber through the tunnel?"

"They'll never even know we're coming." Bevyn rubbed his hands together and grinned wickedly.

"Is Princess Anna participating in this dangerous venture?" Edmund said.

"Of course, I am—" Anna said, while at the same time, Bevyn scoffed, "Of course, she's not—"

Edmund's face held a bemused expression as he looked from one to the other. "Which is it?"

"I've come this far," Anna said. "When the queen of Deheubarth remained behind while her husband rode to Gwynedd to enlist allies, the Normans attacked. She rallied her men and defended her country. Do you think me less capable of playing a part in the defense of my country than she?"

"As I recall, the Normans hung her from the battlements when they captured her castle," Bevyn said. "I don't think that's the story you're looking for."

Anna tried again. "If you left me here, you would lose some of your strength in protecting me. Am I more likely to get into trouble out here, or in the tunnel? Edmund and I will hang back, won't we Edmund?"

"It seems so," Edmund said, back to his near-perpetual state of amusement. He bowed to Bevyn. "I will protect her."

"I don't like it," Bevyn said. "Your husband—"

"—isn't here." It wasn't recklessness that drove Anna. Motherhood had rid her long ago of whatever sense of it she possessed before she came to Wales. It was, rather, the knowledge that she *could* help. And thus, she should. It may be that she wasn't trained to wield a medieval sword. Yet she'd proven back at Montgomery that she knew how to fight.

One of Bevyn's men, a man named Gruffydd, approached with a boy of about twelve. "He says that the English took Aber with twenty men, no more," Gruffydd said.

"Rode right in," the boy said, "once their spies opened the gate."

Bevyn looked hard at the boy. "You've done your job, have you?"

"Yes, sir." He scuffed at the dirt with his big toe. "Both north and south. My mum is still inside—"

"Nobody has forgotten it," Bevyn said. "We can only pray that none of our friends have been hurt. We will rescue her just as soon as we can."

"How many patrol the battlements?" Bevyn said.

"Ten," Gruffydd said.

"Archers?" Edmund said.

Gruffydd shrugged. "Not that we've seen."

"So they are English," Edmund said.

"That surprises you?" Anna said.

Edmund pursed his lips. "So much of what has happened diverges from first appearances. You tell me that men wearing my colors entered Wales near Dinas Bran, though they were not my men. Who is to say that the English who took

Aber are really English? What if Clare has paid mercenaries from Germany to do his dirty work?"

"Or even Welshmen," Alun said.

"That has often been the way of it in the past," Bevyn said, admitting without apology what they all knew to be true.

Anna lifted one shoulder. "Since Uncle Dafydd died at Lancaster, fewer Welshmen have fought on the other side, or so Papa has thought. Not to say you're wrong, but maybe it doesn't matter just now. We have to take Aber back regardless of who took it from us."

Bevyn snorted under his breath: "We."

"You, then," Anna said. "But we cannot allow the Normans to fortify it against us."

Alun lifted his chin. "The sun sets. Who knows if the English are sending more men to fortify the castle, now that it's taken? We should be in position before dark, even if we don't go in until midnight."

"How are we to get from the tunnel into the castle?" Edmund said. "Surely the entrance is barred and guarded."

"If King Llywelyn were in residence, it would be. None of the men of Aber's garrison will tell the English of it," Bevyn said, "and the boy ..."

Edmund slowly nodded, as comprehension filled his face. "You thought of this, of course, long since. This was what you meant when you asked the boy if he'd done his job."

"What are you talking about?" Anna said.

"Treachery is always the easiest way to take a castle," Bevyn said. "The kings of Wales have planned for this day since Arthur built his fortress on the ruins of the Roman villa."

"When the boy saw the English enter the castle, he left by the very tunnel through which you now propose to enter it," Edmund said. "But what's to stop the English from discovering the unbarred door?"

"They might eventually, if they have time to explore, but he left the door closed, along with the trap door that leads to it," Bevyn said. "Chances are, we'll get inside safely if we move soon."

And then the men were all action. Anna left Bevyn to scout the entrance to the tunnel, arrange the men at its entrance, and come up with a viable—if hastily conceived—plan with his captains. She, in turn, took care of all that she could, specifically food, clothing, and rest for herself, in that order.

Anna begged a spare pair of breeches and a leather coat off one of Bevyn's smaller soldiers whose daughter worked as a serving maid inside the castle. She acquired a small loaf and a portion of dried meat from the soldier tending the smokeless fire. While Anna was strapping a second knife to her calf, Edmund planted himself in front of her.

"You are Morgana," he said.

Anna snorted in disgust. "Not that again. I am not. I'm tired of people saying it, much less thinking it. I am no more or less than a princess of Wales. How about we leave it at that?"

"And your brother? He *is* Arthur returned."

Anna glared at him. "Think what you like. He puts on his breeches one leg at a time just like you do."

That prompted a cough of laughter from Edmund, but it stopped him from talking about the legend anymore. While they waited for the rest of the company to ready themselves—or do whatever Bevyn needed them to do—the pair sat in front of the fire. Anna dozed off and on, her head resting on her knees as the hour drew closer to midnight.

Edmund leaned his shoulder into Anna's, jostling her gently. "It's time."

Anna opened her eyes. It *was* dark. She must have slept more than she'd thought. "I'm ready."

Anna and Edmund hung back at the end of the line of men as they approached the tunnel. The entrance lay beneath a trap door set in the floor of the old barn, which had been deliberately built over the top of the entrance. Anyone who didn't know what to look for would have passed it by, such was the genius of the disguise. The whole building leaned ten degrees off center and Anna wasn't sure if the vines trailing up one side were the only thing preventing its total collapse.

Edmund swiveled to his left and right, studying his surroundings. Anna stepped in front of him. They would be the last to enter through the trap door and she let the rear guard disappear before she spoke. "You aren't allowed to use our secrets against us later."

Edmund's eyes narrowed. "Excuse me?"

"I mean it. After this, whatever your past allegiances, whatever your future ones, I'm trusting to your honor that you will not use what you know of us to plot against Wales."

Edmund cleared his throat as he hovered with her on the edge of the hole in the floor. "We don't have time for this—"

"This is the one thing we do have time for." Anna pulled her knife from her belt and held it at waist level, pointed at Edmund. "You may not continue with us—you may not be a part of this—if I do not have your word."

Edmund stared at her. "Is this really necessary—?"

"If you can't swear to it, then you should go back to England now. Better that, than I leave you dead right here on the floor," Anna said. "You saw me fight at Montgomery. I could do it."

Edmund lifted up both hands, palms out, and stepped back. "What good is a man's word if it's given at the point of a knife?"

Anna swallowed hard, amazed at herself. As she'd made for the tunnel, a wave of unease, and yet—certainty—had flooded through her. She'd realized that she had crossed some kind of threshold and after today, she would never be the same again.

She straightened, resheathed her knife, and opened her hands to Edmund. "See. Gone."

Edmund nodded, and then surprised her by stepping closer and catching her chin in his fingers. He gazed down, into her face. The light from the lone torch left to them reflected in his eyes and the gold flecks in the brown glinted at her. "You *are* Morgana and I will not cross you. I swear that I will never plot against your brother."

Close enough.

He released her. Anna swallowed hard, shocked at her audacity in challenging Edmund Mortimer. Before she said something she might regret, Anna turned from Edmund, bent to grab the top rung of the ladder, and climbed down to the floor of the tunnel. Edmund followed.

Inside the tunnel, the line of silent men stretched into the distance. The path sloped downward as they headed north towards Aber and as they went along, the height of the ceiling increased another foot. Even David could have walked comfortably under it without fear of scraping his head.

The light from the torches bobbed and weaved ahead of them. Although she knew the way, since she and David had explored the tunnel back before Anna had married Math, Anna was glad to have so many men with her. The tunnel creeped her out with its dampness and echoing stones. It bent and turned to avoid the winding Aber River (or rather, creek, in this location) that flowed beside the castle. As when she and David had explored it a few years ago, water seeped continually down the walls of the tunnel, but the wooden beams and stone pillars

279

still managed to hold up the tons of earth pressing down upon them.

"This is a marvelous feat of engineering." Edmund paced steadily beside her.

"The Romans have left so many things that we haven't discovered." Anna was glad they were back to being politely civil. "That this has lasted for a thousand years is amazing."

"But surely it's been improved upon since then," Edmund said.

"The last king of Wales before Papa, Owain Gwynedd, rebuilt all of Aber in stone and included the tunnel in his refurbishment," Anna said. "Llywelyn Fawr and my Papa continued his efforts. It's not easy keeping it up, you know, not with the rain we get here."

The quarter mile to the castle took all of ten minutes. Anna and Edmund approached the tail end of the line of men. Anna could feel the excitement among them. Here was *action*. They hadn't faced much since 1285. Even David had remarked (being careful not to complain) that men without challenge lost their edge. For Anna's part, her pulse pounded, the beat so loud it hammered in her ears. She clenched her fists. She wasn't a warrior. She had a three year old son to care for and a husband who'd have gone all authoritarian on her and put his foot down if he knew what she was doing. This was *crazy*. But at the same time, she was *here*. She wasn't going to let Bevyn down.

Up ahead, Bevyn swept a hand in an arc above his head, signaling a halt. He'd arrived outside the door to the castle. Anna pictured what was on the other side: a dim guardroom and a steep stone stairway that led to the trap door which opened into the southernmost tower of the curtain wall.

"Everything turns on this moment," Edmund said, his voice low in Anna's ear.

Anna couldn't see past the press of men in front of her, but she felt the pull of fresher air in her face as the door opened on silent hinges. The only sound was the scrape of boots on stone as the men filed into the anteroom beyond the door. This was the bottom floor of the tower, sunk twenty feet into the soil. The space was less than fifteen feet on a side—the size of a large bedroom. Once through the door with Edmund still at her side, Anna hung back, keeping to her word not to get involved if Bevyn didn't want her to.

"If the English have a guard, he'll be on top of the trap door," Bevyn said.

Anna swallowed hard, and she was pretty sure she wasn't the only one. For some of the men, this might be their first real encounter with an English force.

Edmund shook his head. "With less than two dozen men, even if the English commander knows of the tunnel's existence, he might not waste a man on it."

"It depends on whether or not one of their Welsh spies told them what to look for," Anna said. "If I were an English commander and I *knew* about the tunnels, I'd place half my men here, and an overturned table on the trap door to stop us from lifting it up.

"The English don't know," Edmund said—again, as if he weren't one of them. "We're far west, here. North Wales has always been a hotbed of resistance to the English crown. Finding a Welshman to betray your father isn't as easy as it used to be."

Anna took some comfort in Edmund's words—that and the fact that the English *hadn't* posted a guard down here. Hopefully, they had their hands full with the inhabitants of the castle, of which there were dozens, even without the king in residence. She hoped the invaders hadn't killed all the members of the garrison.

Anna didn't know if Alun and Bevyn had talked about it, or had come to an unspoken understanding, but Alun had relinquished command to Bevyn. Thus, Bevyn had organized the men into groups before they'd entered the tunnel. Bevyn lifted his chin to Alun who obeyed his unspoken command.

Alun waved a hand at his group and the set of five climbed to the top of the stairs. Alun's head nearly touched the trap door and he stood with one hand flat against it, pressing up. At four feet square and heavy, with blackened metal fittings, the effort necessary to move it would be considerable. Alun pushed up on it, ever so slightly. The door lifted up an inch.

Bevyn stood at the bottom of the stairs, looking up. Alun glanced down at him, and Bevyn nodded. Alun pushed harder and one of the soldiers beside him bent his head to use the back of his neck and shoulders to help push the door up. As it swung wide, another man surged up the steps and caught the trapdoor before it banged flat onto the floor above.

They were in.

Anna's group consisted of herself, Edmund, three men she didn't know, and Bevyn. They were the last through the trap door and crowded into the too small space with the other men.

"We can't hope for secrecy beyond the next few minutes," Bevyn said. "We move *now*, before any chance of discovery." He stabbed a finger at each group's leader in quick succession and sent them on their way. Alun's group climbed the tower to the battlements above, the rest spilled out of the entranceway and into the gap—ten yards wide at most—between the curtain wall and the great hall.

One group headed towards the gatehouse. They were to open the gate. The remaining two groups were tasked with eliminating all the English soldiers in the barracks, gatehouse, and exterior buildings. Bevyn's group took the great hall and the apartments associated with it.

Bevyn led his men (and Anna) to the right, towards the kitchen entrance in the rear of the hall. Unlike the guardroom, the kitchen was a cavernous space. Along with its pantries and butteries, it took up nearly the same amount of room as the great hall, one floor above it.

"Sir!" Ado, the cook on duty, saluted Bevyn as they entered through the rear door. Bevyn had known him for years, of course, even if Ado was preparing food for his new masters today. Bevyn didn't offer any recriminations, just clapped him on the shoulder as he went by.

At the sight of the cook's familiar paunch and nearly balding head, Anna smiled.

"My lady!" Ado kept his voice down this time, and moved around the table on which the makings of today's breakfast waited for the dawn.

Anna moved to his side and put a hand on his arm. "Are you well, Ado?"

"Yes, my lady," Ado said. "They've not harmed any of the folk but a few who resisted."

"And where is the garrison?" Anna said.

Ado's chin stuck out but he couldn't meet her eyes. "Most are dead, cut down in cold blood after surrendering their weapons. The four the English didn't see fit to kill are in the barracks."

Anna put a hand to her mouth. "Aber's garrison was twenty strong at least! They're all dead?"

"All but those four, my lady."

Bevyn had signaled to the men to quickly run through the pantries while Anna questioned the cook. The only other servants in residence were two teenage boys who were found in a lower basement. Bevyn leaned in. "Are we correct that the English have twenty men?"

"Three fewer now, sir," Ado said. "The only reason they overcame the garrison at all was because they were let in by mistake, bided their time, and then surprised us. Even so, our men fought hard."

"Where are the rest of the servants?" Anna said.

"Two men who worked in the stable are dead," Ado said. "They picked up their pitchforks to join the fight, but were overcome. Other than that, none were harmed."

Anna patted Ado's arm. "Thank you. We'll be going now. Keep your head down."

"Yes, my lady," Ado said, but he held his knife in such a fashion that Anna thought he might wield it this time, if he had to.

Bevyn jerked his head to his men who formed up with him. The moment any of them set foot on the stairs that led up to the hall, they were committed to the fight. It might well be hand-to-hand in the great hall. Anna was glad that Papa wasn't there to see it. It had been a long time since blood had been spilled at Aber.

Anna pulled out one of her knives. It had belonged to Math's father, who had sharpened the tip to a needle-fine point. She went up the stairs last, hanging back as she'd promised. She had no interest in killing anyone or even fighting. Before she reached the top step, the sound of clashing swords came from the hall and Anna gripped the knife tighter. With gritted teeth, she trotted through the anteroom that separated the stairs from the hall, the door to which opened immediately behind the high table. A man screamed and another shouted.

Just as she peered through the doorway, Bevyn said, "Hold!"

He stood atop the high table, his sword pointed towards the ceiling. Bevyn had five men, the English eight. But all had been asleep or drunk and Bevyn's men, including Edmund, had overwhelmed them. The last two Englishmen had decided that surrender was the better part of valor.

Edmund stood over a body and prodded it with his toe. He stared down at it without speaking.

Anna walked to him. "Did you know him?"

"What?" Edmund came out of his reverie. "No. No, I didn't know him, but ..."

"But what?"

"I have never killed a man with my own sword before," Edmund said, still looking at the fallen Englishman. "I'd never killed anyone at all before you gave me your knife at Montgomery."

Anna was glad that Edmund wasn't looking at her because she couldn't keep the surprise out of her eyes. She blinked it back and then said, "I thought you fought in the 1282 war?"

"You forget, I was still with the Church up to two months before the incident at Cilmeri." Edmund barked a laugh. "Everyone thought I would have a great career, perhaps even become archbishop. And then—" He shrugged.

"—and then your father died."

Edmund nodded. "I conspired with my brother at Buellt in an attempt to convince King Edward to grant me my inheritance, which he'd so far refused. Did he think me unworthy?" He paused. "Perhaps I was. That was the first day I wore a sword at my waist. I hadn't even held one in seven years. Yet, I hadn't earned it and my peers knew it."

Bevyn jumped off the table and came forward. "You did well, then. The second man you engaged surrendered because he was afraid you'd kill him."

"There's nothing more terrifying than a man who is himself terrified." Edmund said this without apparent embarrassment. He turned to Anna. "You weren't afraid, were you?"

Anna bit her lip, realizing that her external calm had genuinely reflected what had been going on inside her. "No." Edmund snorted under his breath and Anna hastened to add. "But I don't know why."

"Because you've faced much worse and lived," Bevyn said. "Besides, the odds were in our favor and God is on our side!"

287

The door to the courtyard beyond burst open at the hands of a young man whom Anna hadn't seen before. He skidded to a halt and gazed about him, taking in the dead men on the floor and the Englishmen whom Bevyn's men had forced to lie face down on the floorboards. He pushed back his hood, revealing sweat-matted hair and bright blue eyes. "I've just come from Caerhun. The men at the gatehouse let me in." He swallowed hard. "The beacons have been lit!"

23

29 August 1288

Near Caldicot Castle

Math

Dafydd hadn't found the resources to implement all the weapons he knew how to build, so Math and Llywelyn stood on top of what Dafydd had laughingly called a *gun emplacement*, but which really was a protective hide for archers. Math faced the sea and held the binoculars to his eyes, gazing across the Severn Estuary. Dafydd had brought them home from the twenty-first century three years ago and Math had always thought them a singularly useful item.

Up until now, Llywelyn hadn't known either the number of boats the English were prepared to launch or their intended landing site. The English had been very savvy, developing plans within plans within plans. But the Welsh had put some thought into this too. Once the king's spies had reported a gathering of boats across the Estuary a few days ago, the assault became easier to prepare for and track.

"How much longer, do you think?" Math said.

Llywelyn leaned over and took the binoculars from Math's hand without asking. Not that the king needed to ask, or that Math minded giving them up. In the dawn fog, he couldn't see anything anyway and they'd been serving as a foil to his feverish thoughts, the most pressing being not the disposition of the English army—but the whereabouts of Anna and Cadell.

He had hoped, even assumed, that his wife and son would have arrived at Caerphilly by now. Admittedly, to have done so would have meant Anna had left Dinas Bran when she thought she might, pushed the horses, *and* taxed Cadell's tolerance for sitting still. At the same time, his wife was full of common sense and could easily have chosen to stay safe at one of her father's lesser holdings rather than travel further with war so close. Or that's what he was trying to tell himself, anyway.

"If I were the commander of the English forces, I would launch the attack now," Llywelyn said, unaware of what was really on Math's mind. "Low tide is the best time to cross the Estuary. It will give them enough beach upon which to land."

At first glance, it might seem that the English could have come across the Severn Estuary anywhere. They could have forced the Wye River above Chepstow too. But the landscape limited both their ability to maneuver and their choices. The Wye had no good ford until Monmouth, some fifteen miles as the crow flies north of where it met the Severn. It was too far to move so many men without the Welsh detecting them long before they passed into Welsh territory, and the terrain was too rugged to cross anywhere closer.

Caldicot Castle lay opposite several possible crossing points of the Severn Estuary near Bristol. The choices included the shortest expanse of water west of the Wye River, a little over two miles from shore to shore, but the union of the Severn and the Wye had created few beaches. Instead, it had fostered mud flats, sand flats, rocky platforms, and islands that made it impossible to successfully bring an army across in most places. It also had some of the highest tides in the world—routinely fifty feet from low to high tide. If this were the solstice, the tides could have been even higher and had the potential to generate a wave that traveled upstream against the river's current.

Even with no wind, the force of the tides made the water turbid and brown. The English could cross several miles of water here, or aim for a spot further west, even one past Newport, thought to do so would mean they'd face more than twice the distance, if less turbulent waters.

"Sound travels in the mist," Math said.

"But it's difficult to gauge distance and direction," Llywelyn said. "It may be a day or two earlier than he intended, but this fog is a gift to Clare—or at least he will think it so. He will come now." Llywelyn turned his head to gaze behind him. He was looking for Dafydd. The king had looked over his shoulder so many times in the last hour that Math had to stop himself from doing it too.

But for better or for worse, Dafydd had gone after William. He wasn't here and wasn't coming. Math had to trust that Dafydd knew what he was doing, and that Llywelyn—and Tudur, Carew, and Ieuan—and Math himself, could manage this assault without the prince.

A creaking sound echoed over the water. As Llywelyn had warned, Math couldn't tell from which direction it came.

Apparently, Llywelyn could. "Our fire boats were to have launched. They should be leaving their harbor even now."

Math listened hard, waiting, as everyone on the beach was waiting. The Englishmen in the boats out on the water were waiting too, with probably the same thumping in the chest and pounding in the ears every soldier felt, every time he went into battle.

"Hmm." Llywelyn lifted up the binoculars and looked east, and then west. The fire boats still didn't appear out of the mist. "What's keeping them?"

One of the longest half hours of Math's life passed and still no fire boats appeared. Then a soldier hurried up to King Llywelyn. "Sire!"

Math and Llywelyn turned to the man. His face was pale. The news wasn't good. "I—" He stopped, unable to get the words out.

"Say it," Llywelyn said.

"All four fire boats have foundered just off the dock."

"Good Chri—" Llywelyn cut off the last word, loath as always to curse openly. "Those boats have patrolled the rivers and coast for two years. They've kept the English off our backs for two years. Why now?"

"It has to be sabotage, my lord." The man looked pained.

Llywelyn turned to Math. "Gather the men. The English are coming. We'll have to do this the traditional way."

"Now?" Math said, surprised at the king's ability to shrug off the sabotage of his fire ships.

"The loss of the fire boats is disappointing, but not devastating," Llywelyn said. "Dafydd viewed them as a method to weaken the English minds, rather than as the lynchpin in our defenses."

"But—"

"Listen." Llywelyn pointed out to sea.

And then Math heard the echoes, so many that they had to be coming from across the Estuary. "I do hear them." He listened some more. "It sounds like they could already be halfway across!"

"Only a third, perhaps." Llywelyn said this with no anxiety in his voice. Math couldn't match his preternatural calm. This is what they'd planned for, waited for, for three years. Part of him couldn't believe that all that effort hadn't actually gone to waste, that the Normans had really—and after all this time—marshaled themselves for an attack.

All along, the problem for Wales had been that the Normans had choices for this assault, and the Welsh were forced to defend themselves against whatever they threw at them. The Welsh border, from Chester to Chepstow, was over one hundred miles, with a further seven hundred and fifty miles of coastline. They couldn't defend it all.

But Dafydd and Llywelyn had endeavored to try, through intimidation backed up by superior weapons of war. Their goal had always been to narrow the possibilities of where the assault might come. Or *assaults*. In this case, the Normans had attacked Buellt in concert with this southern advance.

In 1282, the English had gone first for Anglesey to capture the harvest. After they'd failed to force the Menai Straits, the Mortimer brothers had tried to assassinate Llywelyn. They'd failed. In Anna's old world, however, they hadn't failed. They'd murdered him, and then taken down the Welsh castles which Llywelyn had controlled, one by one. The Normans had conquered all of Wales that way, using each captured castle as a base to capture the next one. Ultimately, their ability to defeat the Welsh depended on persistence and resources, and overwhelming numbers.

Today, the English faced a different task, though one no less difficult: to gather enough men in a location close enough to Wales to invade successfully, but in such a way that the Welsh wouldn't know of the attack until it was too late. Bristol Castle was such a place, just across the Severn Estuary from Wales. The same ridge that prevented Math from seeing the castle on a clear day could also hide thousands of men only a few miles from Wales. The only reason the English weren't going to succeed today was because of the information Humphrey de Bohun had given them. *That* was something Math had never thought he would say.

Even though the city of Bristol was fewer than ten miles from the Welsh shore, at heart, it was much further. The Welsh and the English in the March had mingled freely for hundreds of years, swapping daughters and sons more easily than lords, and just as frequently. Not so for the English in Bristol, though Math couldn't say exactly why. The Severn Estuary had always been a barrier to communication, if not commerce.

Llywelyn clapped a hand on Math's shoulder. The two men looked into each other's eyes for a heartbeat, and then Llywelyn nodded. "Go. We'll combine our companies for a stronger force."

Math raced down the path from the lookout to the place where his *teulu* waited, behind the sand dunes that lined the shore of the Estuary in this location. He'd ordered his men to stay alert and together as a matter of course, but he'd been thinking he would use them for clean-up work, or if some of the English boats survived the attack from the fire ships and made it to the beach. Now, they would lead the Welsh defense.

"Two must ride to Tudur at Chepstow." Math stabbed a finger at his two best scouts. "Tell him that the English are coming here. Maybe elsewhere, we don't yet know, and we will fight them on the shore." He threw himself onto Gwynfor's back and turned her head towards the path to the beach. "Where's Lord Ieuan?"

"I'm here." Ieuan trotted his horse forward. He'd worked like a madman to organize the foot soldiers and get everything in order, and now would lead them.

The Welsh had set up camp two hundred yards behind the dunes, awaiting the English assault. Overnight, the populace had arisen and come to fight for Llywelyn. Math had hoped for it, but not dared expect it. The southern cantrefs had lived under the Norman boot for two hundred years, on and off. Some had grown to like it. Some had thrived under their Norman lords and had resented their new masters, even if they were of the same blood.

The men of Monmouth were known for their skill with a bow, and distances being what they were (short), the few days Ieuan had been given was all the time he needed to marshal a force of four thousand foot, five hundred cavalry, and a thousand archers, spread out in small units along the coastline from Chepstow to Cardiff.

Each of the companies had captains and commanders of every rank, plus workers to insure that the horses were cared for and the men fed. It was costing Llywelyn a fortune, but not as much as it would cost to lose.

"How did the English get to our boats?" Math said to Llywelyn, once he'd led his men to the rendezvous point on the path back to the dune. Between them, they had a total of one hundred and twenty men. That would have to be enough. No more could fit on the narrow beach.

"Paid a Welshman to do it, probably." Llywelyn said, briefly allowing his disappointment to show. "Isn't that always the way?"

"The lead boats are only half a mile off shore!" A rider swept up to Llywelyn, his voice going high in his excitement. Llywelyn had sent fishermen to watch the English advance. They knew the vagaries of the Estuary better than anyone.

"How many boats do they report?"

The man swallowed hard. "At least two hundred."

Two hundred. My God.

A stiff wind had sprung up in the last few minutes and blown away the fog as if it had never been, revealing high clouds skittering across the sky, heading for the sun which had risen over the horizon to the east. Math couldn't see the English boats from where he sat on Gwynfor's back, but those in the blinds, higher up on the dunes, could be gazing at the end of Wales as they knew it. And with the rising of the sun and the dissipation of the fog, the English would be able to see the stretch of beach for which they were aiming.

Math took in a huge breath of air. "Give me a moment to evaluate what we're facing."

Llywelyn nodded his approval and Math urged Gwynfor up the path to the sand covered blind. He dismounted behind it and stepped into the little room formed by canvas on three sides, which protected the men inside from the elements. "Is it as bad as it looks?" Math said, before peering through the hole that gave him a view of the whole Estuary, without the English knowing that he was spying on them.

Yes, it was.

"They have many boats," the scout beside him said.

It was no good pretending what they faced wouldn't be devastating if they allowed all those men to successfully navigate the beach. Watching the boats bob on the waters in the distance caused tendrils of anticipation—not to mention a touch of fear—to curl in Math's stomach. He swallowed hard, got a grip on himself, and said, "Keep me posted."

"Yes, sir," the scout said. Math turned to leave but the man caught his arm. "Wait. That's not all."

Math's shoulders didn't even fall. The certainty and grit that he cultivated before a battle was settling into him. "What else?"

"A storm is coming."

Math's brow furrowed. He hadn't noticed. He threw back the flap at the entrance to the blind.

The scout jerked his chin towards the southwest, from whence the weather always came in August. "That," the man said.

The sun still shone, rising ever higher to the east, but the same wind that had blown away the fog was bringing clouds with it. Dark ones. At the rate they were heading up the Estuary, soon they would cover the sky from horizon to horizon. They grew darker even as Math studied them.

An older man stood a few feet away, sorting through the arrows in his quiver. He was of an age with Llywelyn, perhaps, if not older, bent and gray. His bow rested on the pack at his feet.

In a gesture similar to the one the scout had used, the man pointed with his chin to the southwest. "This time of year, that means trouble. If those English are going to beach their boats safely, they have less time than it will take me to finish sharpening my arrowheads to do it."

"How do you know this?" Math's heart, already pumping hard, began to race as the implications of the man's observation occurred to him.

"My family has fished these waters since there were fish in the sea."

Math didn't wait to hear more. He made an instant decision that might not have been his to make, but he felt that every second counted. He pointed at the lead scout who'd come with him out of the blind, and then at the chief of archers who stood with his captains twenty feet below him, conferring. "Take this blind down! Get the archers in position and have them stand in a long row on the top of the dune so the English can see them!"

"On the dune, my lord? But—"

"On it!" Math said. "The time for secrecy has passed. We need to show them what they face! Move!"

Math scrambled on top of the sand dune himself, his sword unsheathed, and waved it in the air to gather the attention of every man within hailing distance. One of the scouts had a horn at his waist and Math grabbed it and winded it (not well). Disgusted, he thrust it back into the man's hands. "Blow!" The man gazed at him wide-eyed, not understanding Math's sudden lack of secrecy, but then he brought his horn to his lips anyway.

The call reverberated down the beach. It was a good horn. Maybe Tudur could hear it at Chepstow.

"Let them know that we defend this beach!" Math used all the air in his lungs to rouse his men. "To your positions. Now!"

Math bounded from the top of the dune, threw himself onto Gwynfor's back, and raced her to where Llywelyn waited.

The king's face showed puzzlement, maybe amusement, but not anger, for which Math was grateful.

"The plan has changed, I see," Llywelyn said.

"We need to form up on the beach. Show the English that they won't take this land without heavy casualties."

"The lead boats are two hundred yards off shore," Llywelyn said, "with the bulk of the fleet well back in the channel. They could alter their plans at the sight of us and head west to land at Newport."

Math grinned from beneath the helmet he'd just crammed onto his head. "They could have done so if they'd started an hour earlier. Now, they can't. The tide is going to turn very soon and will start running against them."

"And against us," Llywelyn said, patience in every word. "We could never move enough men that far by sea—or by land for that matter—to counter them in time."

"We won't have to," Math said. "All we have to do is make them second guess themselves long enough so that they dither in the channel before deciding."

"You've lost me, nephew. Tell me what you're thinking. I don't understand." Llywelyn studied his son-in-law. "The plan was to let the English beach their boats and then surprise them."

"Not anymore, Father." Math pointed his sword at the clouds that loomed so large now, even the English couldn't miss them. "Look at what's coming. If the English head west, they head into the storm."

Llywelyn glanced upwards. "The storm—" Then he held out his hand as the first raindrop splattered onto his palm.

24

29 August 1288

Aber Castle

Anna

Anna didn't know when she'd last been this tired. She felt as if grains of sand had caught under her eyelids. But she kept her eyes open. With the spectacle before her, she was in no danger of falling asleep just yet.

The Irish Sea was nothing but chop, the white crests evident on every wave. Below and behind them, the men who'd remained at Aber to defend it cleaned up the English mess, working through what was left of the night and into the morning. She'd doctored those she could save and looked away when Bevyn had hung the single Welsh traitor who'd helped the English into Aber. She had been glad that she couldn't see the gallows, built in the marsh to the northeast, from where she stood. Bevyn had made everyone but her march out to see the death. *Summary and swift justice in medieval Wales.*

The watchers on the coast, whom Goronwy's rider had warned, had done their duty. They'd lit the beacons on the Great Orme, and by so doing, sent a signal along the coastline between Aber and Conwy, long before they'd sighted the English ships. Exactly as David had planned, the beacons had raised the countryside to arms. David had hoped that because of the warning, the defenders would have enough time to counter whatever threat the English were bringing to bear. The beacons themselves were an old idea—not invented by fantasy authors—but had never been used in Gwynedd until today.

Only twenty minutes earlier, a fleet of English vessels had hove into view, coming around the Great Orme and heading towards Anglesey. They only had a few miles left to go, but the boats were fighting the wind, tacking back and forth in their attempt to progress. One third of the thirty craft had the shape of Viking longboats and had reefed their sails. Anna's eyes weren't as good as David's—she certainly couldn't see the oarsmen rowing low in the water—but someone with far worse eyesight than she had couldn't miss what was before her.

"Look at them, Bevyn!" Anna said.

The old soldier stood on the battlements beside Anna. He raised a hand to the men below them. "Come here, my lads. When you dangle your grandchildren on your knee, you'll be able to tell the story of this day."

Anna kept glancing to the west, and then back to the boats, and then to the west again, unable to contain her horrified fascination.

"They have to know what's coming," she said.

"Do they?" Bevyn said. "Though if they were smart, they would have hired Welshmen to sail them here—traitors that such men might be."

"Plenty of English sail out of Chester," Anna said. "Even they *have* to know the size of this storm."

"Maybe they did before they sailed," Bevyn said. "Maybe the English captain was arrogant enough to override any naysayers."

And that sounded like a viable *maybe* to Anna. The confidence that the Normans had shown in this last week was stunning. It reminded her so much of King Edward's tactics that a shiver passed through her. *Could he have somehow survived Lancaster?*

But no—enough people had seen his body—and seen it buried, for him not to be haunting them from the dead. This was someone else. But who? Not Edmund, obviously. Was Edmund's brother, Roger, that clever? Bigod or Clare? It looked to Anna as if the man, whoever he was, had mortgaged his future on the chance of victory. The expense of all these men and materials had to be as enormous as her father was spending to defend against them.

But perhaps as Math had said, back at Valle Crucis Abbey, it didn't matter who it was. They had to defeat him, regardless.

The sky drew darker to the west until the storm covered all but the eastern tip of Anglesey. Aber itself was due south of Puffin Island, the closest land the English could reach, if they were going to reach land. It seemed as if the tip of the island reached out a finger to the English boats. All it had to do was crook it to bring them to safety.

The lead boat seemed to reach out too. Anna's heart was in her throat. Would it make it safely? But no. The lead ship foundered and swung sideways, in the face of the wind. Then as one, the ships turned tail. They pointed their bows east, flying before the wind, their hulls surfing over the surface of the water as fast as their masters could ride them. There was a danger in that too, but it looked like most of the ships had turned away in time.

Bevyn nodded. "Safer to head south and beach themselves on the Great Orme. That's where ships always wreck."

"I was hoping they'd try to beat the storm to Anglesey." The first drops of rain spat on Anna's head.

"No such luck," Bevyn said. "Let's move under the gatehouse."

They stood together and watched the storm overtake the English ships. First came the waves that pulled the boats apart from one another; then the gale winds that they'd been fighting the whole time, but that now threatened to upend them if they didn't pull down their sails.

As the clouds loomed over them and the rain began to fall, a few of the boats seemed to lose their bearings and founder—perhaps taking on water. The rest, however, had the look of reaching shore.

And then the weather boxed Aber in. Anna could see nothing but black clouds and driving rain. It *poured* down on them, as if someone had turned a fire hose on their heads. It gave a hint of what the English were experiencing in their open craft. They would find little shelter on the beach, and even less when the men of the garrison at Caerhun, along with volunteers from the villages that lined the Irish Sea, penned them onto that beach and slaughtered them.

If that was indeed what Bevyn had planned. Anna didn't really want to know.

Anna eyed her old friend. He hadn't said and she hadn't asked what was in store for the English. It wasn't that Anna didn't care about their fate, but she understood this world she lived in a little more clearly every day.

Anna stood under the gatehouse roof with Bevyn for another minute, feeling the thunder of rain on the wooden planking above their heads. "I know you received Goronwy's warning," she said. "But you had to think that he'd warned

Aber too. Why did you come? Why didn't you stay to defend the Anglesey shore?"

Bevyn turned his head to look at her and when she met his gaze and smiled at him, he guffawed a laugh. "Not much gets past you, does it, girl?"

"I like to think not," she said. "Though you don't have to tell me if you don't want to. I'm only guessing."

"Guesses can be worse than the truth." Bevyn laughed again. "It was luck, is all. Luck brought me here."

"What do you mean?"

Bevyn's eyes lit. "I have a son, did you know?"

"I knew your wife was expecting a child," Anna said. "I didn't know that he'd been born. How old is he?"

"Three weeks." Bevyn didn't temper the joy in his voice.

"And—?"

"My wife's mother came to visit."

Anna laughed. The sudden surprise and amusement burst from her and felt good. "You don't like your mother-in-law? *That's* what brought you to Aber?"

Bevyn managed a sheepish expression, despite his enormous mustache which to Anna's eyes made him look more like a revolutionary than a contrite husband. "My wife suggested I patrol for a few days with my 'lads', as she called them. She even pointed me here." He paused. "She has a touch of the *sight* sometimes."

Anna canted her head as she looked at him. "In addition to knowing you very well, she loves you."

"I hope so," Bevyn said. "I love her."

Anna didn't press him beyond that remarkable admission. "So you came to Aber."

"And found it held against us. Luck, as I said."

"But not luck that we could enter through the tunnel," Anna said. "This eventuality has been long planned, I gather? You expected the boy to do as he did."

"From the days of King Llywelyn's grandfather, at least," Bevyn said, "and maybe since the time of Arthur, those tunnels have made us vulnerable. They are a weak point in our defenses. At the same time, they have long been a comfort to the residents of the castle. Sometimes it's better to flee in the night in order to live to fight another day."

"Have the Normans ever attacked Aber before today?"

"Not that I know of," Bevyn said. "Perhaps not since the time of Arthur."

Anna knew that in her old world, after Papa's death at Cilmeri, the Normans had taken the infant Gwenllian from Aber. They'd locked her in a convent for the rest of her life, so that she couldn't produce an heir to threaten England. By then, all but a handful of castles had already fallen to the Normans and she'd had nobody to protect her. Gwenllian was six years old now, safe with Mom and Papa at Caerphilly. But still, Anna shivered at the thought.

"How's Dafydd?" Bevyn hadn't asked that yet, and in retrospect, it showed how careful Bevyn was to have put the life he'd led before behind him.

"In the south, I hope," Anna said, not really answering his question. She didn't actually know if her brother was well or not. "The English may be crossing the Severn Estuary even now."

"I was going to say that I wish I was with him," Bevyn said. "But I don't. My place is here."

"David misses you," Anna said. "He's said so. But I agree. You were needed here."

25

29 August 1288

Near Caldicot Castle

Llywelyn

Rain dripped down the back of Llywelyn's neck. In his haste to prepare for battle, he hadn't gotten the leather collar of his helmet and his mail to overlap properly. He could have worn his mail coif but he hated how it restricted his vision and movement, so instead he wore a mail shirt with supplemental plate on his chest and a tin cup helmet (as Meg called it).

The moment he thought of her, he brutally forced aside the image of her face that rose before his eyes. It was battle that he had to think on. The English had wavered, as Math had hoped, caught between the storm and the beach. In the end, they'd split in two. Those in the tail of the fleet had fled back to the English shore, and the rest had decided take their chances on the beach.

Llywelyn had overheard two of his soldiers discussing which water passage was more dangerous: the Menai Straits or the Severn Estuary. Llywelyn knew the truth (the Menai Straits, of course, his home ground), but the argument had been heated and Llywelyn had to admit that the southern man had some good points, particularly in regards to storms.

The Menai Straits was a narrow passage between Anglesey and the Gwynedd mainland. When crossed in front of Aber Castle, the Straits stretched two miles to the Anglesey shore. At Bangor, however, the distance was only three hundred yards and was proportionately more perilous. The water could shift direction without warning at the change in the tide. At least on the Menai, however, a boat had a chance of reaching shore. Out here ... Llywelyn shook his head to see the bulk of the English fleet still half a mile from the Welsh beach, facing Llywelyn's army if they went forward, and only more storm between them and safety to the rear.

When he'd come out of the blind, Math had been in his element. Given the way he'd rallied the troops into action, he must have gotten some Berserker blood from a hither-to-unknown Viking ancestor. Math had flung himself onto his horse and put himself in front of the Welsh cavalry before their charge. Llywelyn could see him now, fifty yards ahead, heading down the beach towards the English soldiers who'd managed to land their craft before the storm hit.

By their position in the fleet, these men had been eager to be the first to assault the Welsh position, but now with the menace of the storm, had been unlucky enough to find themselves first onto the beach. One of the young men from Llywelyn's *teulu* reined his horse and shot Llywelyn a grin as he fell in beside him. "God is with us, my lord!"

It seemed just so much hubris to agree, but an exhilaration rose over Llywelyn. *By God, He is!*

Llywelyn hung back with two dozen of his men. Their job was to form a defensive wall to the southwest of the main Welsh force, to prevent the English from fleeing down the beach in their direction. One of Llywelyn's men glanced over his shoulder to make a comment to his neighbor, and his jaw dropped.

Llywelyn looked too. It had been raining hard for half an hour now, but it was nothing in comparison to what was coming. A wall of rain was driving up the Severn Sea towards their beach.

"They have a hundred heartbeats. No more." Awe resonated in the man's voice. He, too, had grown up in the north, in Gwynedd, where the mountains dominated the landscape as much as the sea. For Llywelyn's part, he'd never been on the sea during a storm. Hearing about the one that had shipwrecked Meg was bad enough.

Llywelyn tightened his grip on his sword. His horse's legs were splayed, bracing against the wind that threatened to blow Llywelyn right off of him. Further up the beach, Math's men drove into the English soldiers who'd left their boats.

And then the storm hit.

It was only then that Llywelyn saw the real danger—not to the boats out at sea, though that was certainly bad for the English—but to his own men. The storm and the tide were almost perfectly synchronized, with the tide turning at the same moment that the storm was hitting. From what the southern soldier had boasted, the sandy beach on which they stood could go from dry, to two inches deep in water, to waist height two waves after that. And it was already happening.

"Retreat!" Llywelyn grabbed the horn his banner bearer carried and sounded it himself. "By God! Retreat!"

The men ahead of him didn't stop. Either they were too caught up in the blood lust of battle to think of anything else, they refused to accept a retreat when victory was right before them, or they honestly didn't hear the horn call over the storm. Llywelyn shoved the horn back into the man's hands. "Make it sing!" Llywelyn had barely been able to hear it himself over the sound of the rain pounding *rat-a-tat-tat* on his helmet.

Without waiting for the standard bearer to obey, Llywelyn spurred his horse towards Math. His guards followed as a matter of course, rather than because they had any idea what the king was doing. Llywelyn circled around the fighting to the north. Math's men were actively engaged with the former occupants of at least twenty boats that had reached the shore, though a handful had attempted to escape back into the Estuary once they saw the size of the force that greeted them. Perhaps that was the safest place to be right now, but Llywelyn didn't see how anyone could think that, even if they were English.

Men seethed near the shore, but further back, the Welsh cavalry danced on the margins of the fight, their horses skittering and everyone nearly blinded by the rain. Llywelyn thrust through a gap to where Math had pulled up, watching the storm come in and the English boats fall back in disarray. Already, bodies floated in the shallows, some with open wounds, the blood mixing with the salt water. More were caught up with every wave that drove onto the shore. Some of the English boats must have capsized further out.

Llywelyn grabbed Math's arm. "We must get off the beach!"

"What?" Math turned to him. His color was high, but at the sight of his father-in-law's grim face, some of the light in his eyes faded. "What's wrong?"

"With the storm breaking and the turning of the tide, we'll drown where we stand."

Llywelyn didn't need to say more. Math may have been a child of the mountains, but with that upbringing came a healthy fear of the sea.

"Back! Back! Back!" Math stood in his stirrups and sounded the retreat, first with his voice, and then with a high, piercing whistle. That caught his men's attention when the horn hadn't. At last the men began to obey, turning their horses' heads and making for the dunes that lined the beach to the north.

Llywelyn glanced to the southwest. The waves surged ever higher. A moment ago, his horse had been standing twenty yards from the water. Now he was five. The men who'd been engaging the English noticed the change too and broke off the fight. Some of the men who'd been unhorsed or come to battle on foot had lost their footing and fallen into the water, while their horsed companions struggled to save them.

Llywelyn risked a delay to collar a man-at-arms—a boy really, he couldn't have been older than Dafydd was when he came to Wales—and haul him upright.

"Thank you, my lord." The boy coughed and sputtered. "I thought I was a goner."

Llywelyn removed his foot from the stirrup so the boy could boost himself onto the horse and sit behind him. "We're not out of this yet," Llywelyn said.

Helping the boy meant that Llywelyn had fallen behind many of his men. He put his head against his horse's neck and spurred him towards the dunes that ran along the rim of the beach, while the boy clutched at his waist and held on for dear life.

Llywelyn checked behind him again. Bile rose in his throat at what he saw, along with real honest-to-God fear that he hadn't felt since that day at Cilmeri when he knew he was going to die. He wasn't ready to die, even if Dafydd was ready to be king. The wind blew the rain into him. His horse struggled to find purchase in the water-logged sand. The men still on the dunes waved and shouted, desperate to help and yet aghast at what was happening to their compatriots.

Llywelyn looked up and saw that the first of his men had reached the grass-covered dune that fronted the fields behind it, Math among them. Math turned, his eyes seeking. Llywelyn knew Math looked for him and opened his mouth to shout—but a wave overtook him before he could.

It lifted the hooves of Llywelyn's horse off the ground and swept Llywelyn and the boy right out of the saddle. Llywelyn tried to hang onto his horse's bridle but the strong current pulled him away and under the churning tide. Jumbled now, unsure which way was up, Llywelyn struggled for air. He knew how to swim, but his clothing had gone from rain-soaked to waterlogged and he couldn't get his limbs to move.

"Jesus Christ, Dad! Don't do this to me!"

Llywelyn's last thought before he lost consciousness was that the voice sounded an awful lot like Dafydd's, though of course it couldn't be, and that when he saw him next, he would speak to him about taking the Lord's name in vain.

26

29 August 1288
Near Caldicot Castle

David

Through the driving rain, David had seen his father misjudge the wave and go under. The boy whom Dad had rescued had kept his head above water and was swimming towards shore. The horse had nearly made it to the beach. But not Dad.

David couldn't see Math from where he sat—couldn't see any of his father's *teulu* who could help. Probably most of them couldn't even swim.

David threw himself off his horse and launched himself into the sea, arms and legs spread, like he'd seen lifeguards do—and he'd played at doing a time or two in a pool--though he'd never had to do it for real himself. He hit the water hard and kept his head above it, more by luck than because he knew what he was doing. Instantly, his boots filled with water and his clothes gained forty pounds in weight. At least his mail armor didn't actually soak up the water.

The force of the current that picked him up the instant he hit the water stunned him. It spun him into a rock that lay inches below the surface but which David couldn't see through the muddy water. With his shoulder and hip aching, David righted himself and swam with long strokes towards where he'd last seen his father. Forty yards from where David had gone in, he finally closed in on him.

David reached out to catch at his father's arm, missed, kicked hard, and surging forward, grasped the collar of his father's shirt. David had seen him go under at least twice. He didn't believe the old tale that you only had three chances, but even so, Dad had surely used up more than he could spare.

David slipped an arm under his father's shoulders and turned towards the shore. The water was more than six feet deep and he couldn't touch. He struggled against the current to keep both his and his father's heads above the boiling surf.

It was raining so torrentially, it was as if David was swimming at the base of a waterfall. The rain threatened to drown him more completely than the sea.

"I've got him, my lord!"

Four hands reached out from above David and grasped his father's arms. David treaded water while two stumpy fishermen hauled Dad into their dingy. Ropes led from iron rings on the boat's rail to the shore, where a line of men held the ends, so the dingy wouldn't float away with the tide.

Dad was the same size as the two fishermen combined and they fell backwards onto the floor of the boat with the king on top of them. David grasped the rail of the dingy and rested his cheek against the smooth planks of the side.

Another wave swamped him and he coughed. "Is he alive?" David could barely hear himself speak above the rush of water all around him.

A retching sound came from inside the boat and David kicked up, hauling himself out of the water with the strength of his arms, to rest his stomach on the rail. His father lay on his side in the center of the boat while the fishermen worked him over, pumping his arms and pressing on his chest, trying to force the water out of him.

David eased forward face first into the boat, shedding water as he did so, and settled in the stern. He didn't know what else he could do for his father than what the men were doing, so he rested, his head on his knees. He prayed silently. And then Dad coughed twice more and the water he had swallowed and breathed in poured out.

Only then did David crawl towards him, careful not to upset the boat which continued to rock violently in the high winds and waves. It had accumulated two inches of water in the bottom thanks to both. David glanced over his shoulder at the shore. Men shouted and gestured at him, and others began to haul the boat in, hand over hand.

His father's forces might not have been prepared for the storm that had overtaken them, but the local men they'd included in their company had kept their heads. Math stood at the front of the line, straining with the effort of pulling in the dingy.

One of the fisherman looked up. "He'll live, my lord."

The bottom of the boat scraped the dune.

"Is he conscious?" Math helped David lift Dad out of the boat.

"He is," Dad said.

David had never been so glad to hear his father's voice. "When I saw you go under the water, Dad—"

"Stupid." Dad coughed. Water mixed with blood dribbled out of the corner of his mouth. Other willing hands reached for him, half-carrying him away from the boat.

The rain continued to drive into them. David glanced at Math, who grasped David's arm to help him out of the dingy, the worry in his eyes ratcheting up again. "I'm glad to see you, brother," Math said. "You arrived just in time."

"Rode like hell to get here," David said. "We left Painscastle as soon as we could after the messenger arrived. It didn't feel like we were in time."

"Painscastle?" Math said. "What were you doing there?"

"Long story," David said. He had quite a few stories to tell Math, in point of fact, some more interesting than others.

"When I saw you jump in," Math said, "and the king go under again ... it occurred to me that it would be better not to return at all than face your mother and Anna if you both had died."

David shook his head. "You would have done what you had to do: protected Cadell and ruled for him until he could claim his birthright." Every time David and his father risked their lives, they threatened the security of Wales. This was a different time than the one in which he'd grown up. You couldn't lead from the rear.

David and Math helped Dad hobble off the dune, all the while surrounded by an honor guard. The rain was so heavy now that when each individual raindrop plopped in the sand at their feet, it created a mini-crater. David had seen similar rain during thunderstorms in the summer in Pennsylvania when he'd visited his aunt's house. It rained a lot in Wales, but the country had few thunderstorms as he knew them. Something about the heat index, or lack thereof.

They reached a cart drawn by two horses, and David sat his father in the back of the bed. With his feet dangling almost to the ground, Dad hung his head as the rain dripped off his nose onto his breeches.

"Let me help you, my lord." Lili swung herself over the side of the cart and crouched beside the king. She threw a blanket around his shoulders and head. He lifted his chin to look at her. She gazed gravely back, her blue eyes turned as gray as the storm.

David stepped towards Lili. Her position on the cart put her head on a level with David's. They'd barely spoken during the long, dark ride from Painscastle, but she'd kept close to him, and stood near him on their few breaks to rest the horses. It was almost as if they didn't need to talk.

Now, without asking permission or thinking too hard about it, lest he lose his nerve, he threaded the fingers of one hand through the hair at the back of her head, leaned in, and kissed her. It was for the first time. She wrapped her arms around his neck, tightening her hold on him as he deepened the kiss. Then Dad cleared his throat.

David put his lips to Lili's forehead, breathing her in, oblivious to the rain and the crowd that had formed around them. Lili patted his chest. "I'll stay with the king, Dafydd. No matter what happens."

David nodded and released her.

"My dear." Dad patted her knee. "Welcome to the family."

"Dad," David said. "I've got to—"

"Go." He put a hand on David's shoulder. "As always, your timing was excellent."

The cart pulled away and Math clapped David on the shoulder, bringing him back to the present. For that single minute, David had forgotten about the English altogether.

David lifted a hand to Lili, who blew him a kiss. Then he turned to Math. "So. How about you and I—and Ieuan if he's around—see what we can do about cleaning up this mess?"

* * * * *

Two days later, the rain still fell. The sun had come out for those few minutes on the morning of the storm, and they hadn't seen it since. All the rivers within fifty miles—and maybe all across Wales—were in flood, making them difficult, if not impossible, to cross. At least the wind no longer blew at hurricane force, rattling the shutters in every window.

David took a deep breath before stepping through the doorway that led from the upstairs bedrooms and into the hall of Caldicot Castle. He, his father, and the Norman lords had talked long into the night. Dad might not be well enough to get out of bed quite yet, but he could always *think*. This war, while unlooked for, was going to give them an unprecedented opportunity to create a stronger Wales, one based on a confederation of mutual respect.

David had no interest in ruling lands beyond his borders, but if an alliance with these Marcher barons could give them some breathing room, and a buffer zone between Wales and England that was of benefit to *Wales* instead of England, David would do everything in his power to make it happen.

As David entered the room, the men at the high table rose as one to their feet: Gilbert de Clare, Humphrey de Bohun, William, Nicholas de Carew, and Math. Math would have ridden north yesterday to look for Anna and Cadell if David hadn't stopped him. David was worried about her too, but Math wasn't going to find her by riding across Wales by himself in the pouring rain.

Ieuan and Tudur, however, had gone back to Chepstow. They would remain on alert, guarding the border, though the threat from England seemed to have abated for now. While Valence had surprised them with the power and force of his assault, they weren't going to be surprised again.

Clare took a step towards David. "How is the king?"

"Improving." David wasn't prepared to say more than that just yet. In his time, his father had survived far worse than a dunking in the Severn Estuary, but he'd been younger then. His mother, who'd arrived at Caldicot Castle before the storm hit (against Dad's direct orders, but that was Mom for you), feared the water in his lungs could lead to infection.

More than anything, Dad was *tired*. He'd slept after the battle, and then through the night and all the next day. He'd insisted on conferring with David and his advisors last night, despite his weakness, and then slept again. David had left his mother by the bedside, holding Dad's hand and urging him to eat some breakfast. So far he'd just nibbled at it, but David felt more comfortable leaving his side than at any time since the battle.

David's attention fell on Carew, who must have arrived very recently since he still wore his travel-stained cloak and boots, with his breeches soaked to mid-thigh. Carew raised a biscuit-filled hand. "My lord! It's a great victory!"

David couldn't blame Carew for his enthusiasm, although David didn't feel the same way himself. He walked towards the table and pulled out the chair at the end. "Of a sort, Carew, and only because we were aided by the weather."

"Who can say that God is against us now?" Carew really was on a high. "The entire English fleet is vanquished."

"What of the dead, Math?" David sat heavily next to his brother-in-law. He hadn't slept more than a few hours since the battle, what with the messages flying back and forth among all the lords of Wales. Rumor had come to his ears an hour ago that Valence had also lost a fleet near Anglesey, but David needed additional confirmation before he could believe it.

"It will be days, still, before a full accounting, my lord," Math said, using David's title as he usually did when others were present. "Roger Bigod, at least, is dead. He commanded one of the boats."

"What about Valence, Mortimer, and this cousin of mine?" David said.

"No word," Math said.

"Cousin, my lord?" Carew said. "What cousin?"

Clare pinched the bridge of his nose and sighed. "Valence has brought forth the son of Owain Goch, King Llywelyn's brother. A man named Hywel."

"My God!" The news choked off Carew's exhilaration.

"Some will say that he should have lands equal to my father's, and be considered an heir in equal in stature to me," David said, "though apparently he was raised in England and speaks no Welsh."

"Valence would have considered that a minor failing, if it was one at all," Humphrey said. "It's not like he would ever have allowed Hywel to actually *rule*."

"Such was my assumption," David said. "And now ..."

"Now that Valence's force is defeated, we all must begin anew, as we discussed," Humphrey said.

David had shaken hands on an agreement last night to create an alliance with these men, even to the point of putting certain Welsh estates back into the custody of Bohun and Clare. The caveat would be that this time, they would tithe to the Welsh crown. It was an offer Carew had accepted in 1284. Now it seemed Bohun and Clare would accept it too. If they abided by the agreement, it gave David and his father powerful Norman allies.

Clare had remained standing. "My lord, if I may speak."

David nodded.

"Lord Bohun and I should ride to Canterbury now," Clare said. "On the other side of Offa's Dyke at Gloucester, I have many men loyal to me. My chief captain may have betrayed me, but I understand that his body has been found with Bigod's. My men thought they were following me when they obeyed him. They will flock to my banner when I call."

David eyed him. "We don't actually want to descend on Canterbury with an army, but with a delegation."

During this exchange, Carew had lifted his head from his breakfast and now gazed at Clare. "I see you have been busy. Is it Archbishop Peckham you plan to see?"

"Yes," Clare said. "The throne of England is in doubt. With the child King Edward dead, and with the conspirators having lost a considerable number of men, we've clipped Valence's wings. But he still has a subtle tongue."

"Every day we allow Valence to court the Archbishop unchallenged is a day too long," Humphrey said.

David met Math's eyes. Last night, they'd discussed the possibility of Math traveling to England with these Norman lords, as it still wasn't safe for either David or his father to leave Wales, even with an escort. Math had agreed to go in their stead.

Math nodded. "My men are ready. Give my love to Anna when you see her."

Carew stood and looked to David. "I would go too, my lord."

"I hoped for it." David gestured with one hand. "You all know my father's position. I trust you to represent it."

The four men bowed. Carew spoke for all of them: "As you say, my l—"

The door to the hall banged open and Bevyn strode across the floor with a man whom David didn't know. Their clothes were as travel-stained and soaked as Carew's, but their eyes were bright.

"Edmund!" Humphrey stepped off the dais to greet his cousin while the rest of the men in the room stared at Bevyn and Edmund in stunned silence.

David got to his feet and went to his old captain. Bevyn bowed low and when David raised him up, clasped his forearm in greeting. "Welcome, Bevyn," David said. "I hope you have good news for me." He eyed Bevyn's companion, who could only be Edmund Mortimer. "Even as you bring a surprise guest."

"An English force tried to take Anglesey and was blown back to the Orme." Bevyn canted his head towards Edmund. "That we were prepared for their attack is thanks in no small part to the assistance of Mortimer, here, who was the one who warned us they were coming. I take no credit for their defeat, though I was among those who retook Aber from the English."

David gaped at Bevyn. That was a lot of information to present so casually in a few sentences.

"It was your sister, Anna, who deserves the most thanks," Edmund said.

"Anna?" David and Math spoke in unison.

"She is well," Bevyn said. "She remains at Aber since I refused to allow her to ride all night and day to get here ... she has quite a story to tell you when you see her next."

"And Cadell?" Math stepped closer.

Bevyn's expression softened. "He is well too. He has a new friend and a new puppy, and is a hero in his own right."

At Math's astonished look, Bevyn laughed. "I told Anna I had to ride south with Mortimer, just so I could see your face when I told you of what she'd done. I am well rewarded."

David clapped Bevyn on the shoulder. "It is good to see you, my friend."

"I have heard something of your ridiculous adventures since you cut me loose," Bevyn said. "You have a lot of explaining to do, young man."

David laughed. "I do. I surely do."

EPILOGUE

November, 1288

Rhuddlan Castle

Lili

"**S**o you're going to go?" Lili sat on a stool, sorting through her arrow shafts, separating the straightest and best from those she would use only for practice.

"*We're* going to go," her husband said. "Anna and Math too, provided Anna feels well enough."

"She's two months further along than I and past the danger point," Lili said. "She won't turn down the opportunity to see England."

Dafydd reached for Lili's hand and pulled her up from her stool. Lili wound her arms around his neck. "It might be dangerous," he said. "More so than when you and I went with William."

"Then it's appropriate that we're going to go *for* William, yet again." Lili's brow furrowed. "I feel sorry for him, actually.

He's all of thirteen and getting married to a girl he barely knows."

"As opposed to you, a woman of eighteen, who is married to a man you adore."

Dafydd said things like this all the time, sometimes in front of others, which embarrassed Lili to no end. Her inner life had always been hers alone, and now she shared it with an entire country. She'd *just* gotten used to the idea of being married to Dafydd at all, and now, only two months later, ten weeks after their victory on the beach at Caldicot, she carried his child.

At least, she had none of the symptoms so far that had plagued her friends. Meg claimed that the nausea worsened with every child. With four royal babies due within seven months of each other (Lili counted Bronwen and Ieuan as part of the royal family, along with their new daughter, born last week), Lili was taking Meg's word for just about everything. Thankfully, King Llywelyn had recovered from his swim in the Estuary and was looking forward to the birth of his third child.

"What is the date of William's wedding again?" Lili said.

"November 20th," Dafydd said. "It's a Friday."

"Why are they moving this quickly?" Lili said. "William is so young."

"Do you feel sorry for him?" Dafydd said.

Lili nodded.

Dafydd shrugged. "I do to, in point of fact. But Humphrey de Bohun wants to take advantage of the disarray among the barons who plotted against him."

"I thought you said Roger Mortimer and that other regent, Vere, were in the Tower of London?" Lili said.

"They are, but Kirby continues as co-regent with Bohun, since Bohun has no evidence linking him to the plot, even if we all believe he knew of it. Even Valence is back at the royal court. He groveled before Peckham, begging forgiveness for his lack of judgment. The stain of his treachery has been laundered clean and we are to behave as if he didn't lose over a thousand men in August trying to invade Wales."

"How is it possible that *anyone* can pretend Valence didn't violate the Treaty?" Lili said.

"Because Valence is powerful and charismatic, and the English court feels the absence of King Edward more strongly now than ever. Without a king—only Edward's surviving daughters—the regents act for the eldest, Eleanor. But how long will that last, especially if her marriage to Alfonso of Aragon comes to pass? And will Humphrey really be able to put his son on the throne through Joan?"

"And what about your cousin, Hywel?" Lili said.

Dafydd barked a laugh that sounded less like amusement and more like disgust. It told Lili that her husband was worried about Hywel, even if he didn't like to admit it.

"Dad invited him to visit Wales, but so far he has refused to come. I assume we will meet him at William's wedding."

The more Dafydd talked, the more interested Lili became in what lay on the other side of the border. She had thought, when they returned to Wales with William, that she might never set foot in England again. "We don't know what's going to happen, do we?"

"No, we don't," Dafydd said. "But that's the fun of it, isn't it? There's always more to the story."

And then her husband bent his head, and kissed Lili again.

The End

Author's Note

The *After Cilmeri* series is a work of fiction (obviously), in that time travel and/or alternate universes have not been shown to exist. At the same time, in writing the series, I have endeavored to remain as true to *real* history as possible, in terms of places, locations, and individuals as characters in the story.

For that reason, I'd like to highlight the events that led up to the Norman conquest of Wales, that David and Anna averted in *Footsteps in Time*, and that I have used as the background for the series.

William the Bastard (also known as William the Conqueror) was a Norman, meaning he hailed from Normandy, in what is now France. The Normans had Viking ancestry (why are we not surprised?), but had settled in France and adopted French customs and language. Even up until the 1300s, the kings and barons of England spoke French, not English, as a primary language.

Upon the death of King Edward the Confessor in 1066, William, a second cousin to Edward, believed he was the rightful heir to the English crown. He was determined to conquer England, even though Harold Godwinson, a Saxon, had claimed the throne and been crowned King of England. William landed at Hastings in October of 1066 and defeated

Godwinson's army. Harold had force-marched his men from Stamford Bridge after defeating a nearly-simultaneous invasion by King Hardrada of Norway.

Harold's forces almost held, but in the end, his discipline did not and he himself died on the battlefield. http://www.middle-ages.org.uk/william-the-conqueror.htm

That was only the beginning of William's military victories. It would be another six years before England was truly conquered. http://www.britannia.com/history/monarchs/mon22.html

Wales, however, took a bit longer to subdue. The Welsh fought what amounted to a guerilla war for over two hundred years against their Norman aggressors. Although the documentation of this war is mostly on the English side, it is interesting reading from the perspective of the Welsh.

In the *Chronicle of the Princes* (from the *Red Book of Hergest*), it becomes clear that there is a form of schizophrenia at work when the authors discuss the coming of William the Bastard in 1066, his claiming of the kingship, and then his subsequent reign. On one hand, the *Chronicle* states:

And William defended the kingdom of England in a great battle, with an invincible hand, and his most noble army. (1066)

And then, the Bastard, prince of the Normans, and king of the Saxons, the Britons, and the Albanians, after a sufficiency of the glory and fame of this transient world, and after glorious victories, and the honour acquired by riches, died; and after him William Rufus, his son reigned. (1085)

In between these entries, the Chronicle states: "the French ravaged Ceredigion and Dyfed" (1071); "a second time the French devastated Ceredigion" (1072) These notes indicate the conquering of south Wales by that same king. Things start to really get bad, however, in the years after William of Normandy's death.

One year and one thousand and ninety was the year of Christ, when Rhys, son of Tewdwr, king South Wales, was killed by the French, who inhabited Brecheiniog; and then fell the kingdom of the Britons ... two months after that, about the calends of July, the French came into Dyved and Ceredigion, which they have still retained, and fortified the castles, and seized upon all the land of the Britons.

Even at this point, in reading these documents, I was wondering 'who were these 'French' who sailed from France to conquer Wales? How did I miss that?' And then I realized that

SARAH WOODBURY

by 'French' the authors meant 'Normans', who'd conquered England—the same group whose king they'd eulogized three pages before.

For in 1095, the Chronicle states:

And then, the second time, William, king of England, assembled innumerable hosts, with immense means and power, against the Britons. And then the Britons avoided their impulse, not confiding in themselves, but placing their hope in God, the Creator of all things, by fasting and praying and giving alms, and undergoing severe bodily penance. For the French dared not penetrate the rocks and the woods, but hovered about the level plains. At length they returned home empty, without having gained anything; and the Britons, happy and unintimidated, defended their country.

Thus begins the long, unhappy saga of the 'French' conquest of Wales. For the purposes of this book, I have not used the term 'French', but rather the more common 'Normans' to refer to the overlords of England and 'English' to refer to the people they conquered (known also as 'Saxons', a people who conquered England after the Roman departure in 410 AD).

Many Welsh today still refer to the 'English' as 'Saxons'.

Acknowledgments

First and foremost, I'd like to thank my lovely readers for encouraging me to continue the *After Cilmeri* series. I have always been passionate about these books, and it's wonderful to be able to share my stories with readers who love them too.

Thank you to my husband, Dan, and my children, Brynne, Carew, Gareth, and Taran, who have been nothing but encouraging, despite the fact that their mother spends half her life in medieval Wales. And to my writing partner, Anna Elliott: As Piglet says, 'it's so much more friendly with two.'

About the Author

With two historian parents, Sarah couldn't help but develop an interest in the past. She went on to get more than enough education herself (in anthropology) and began writing fiction when the stories in her head overflowed and demanded she let them out. Her interest in Wales stems from her own ancestry and the year she lived in England when she fell in love with the country, language, and people. She even convinced her husband to give all four of their children Welsh names.

She makes her home in Oregon.

www.sarahwoodbury.com

18693551R00185

Made in the USA
Lexington, KY
19 November 2012